DEAD AND BACK AGAIN #1.5

VISIONARY INVESTIGATIONS

C. RAE D'ARC

Cover design by 100 Covers

ISBN: 978-1-961733-11-4 (Paperback)
ASIN: B0FKD2KDJC (Kindle eBook)
Library of Congress Control Number: 2025917214

Published by Bursting Box Publishing

www.burstingboxpublishing.com
www.facebook.com/c.rae.darc
www.instagram.com/craedarc/

Praise for the Haunted Romance Trilogy

Don't Date the Haunted

"Certain to have the reader laughing out loud."
– *Readers' Favorite*

"Sitting on my 'Best Books I've Ever Read' shelf."
– *Gee Liz Reads*

Don't Marry the Cursed

"Rating: 10/10 I can't wait for the next one!"
– Leyendo.Lina (Bookstagrammer)

"Don't Pass Up This Series."
– Jim Doran, author of Kingdom series

Don't Dance with Death

"Am I allowed to call this a perfect trilogy?"
– Valerie Evans, author of *Wolves of Worsham* series

"Exciting and engaging from the very beginning."
– *Libromancy Podcast*

Books by C. Rae D'Arc

HAUNTED ROMANCE
Don't Date the Haunted
Don't Marry the Cursed
Don't Dance with Death

* * *

Oz's Haunting Survival Book
From Horror with Love

DEAD AND BACK AGAIN
Specter Inspector
Visionary Investigations

DREAMING PRINCESSES
Dreaming Beauty
Fairest and the Frog
Little Red and the Lumpy Bed
Golden Locks and Riddles

Note from the Author:

This book and series take place in the fictional world of Novel, where *Pride and Prejudice* and *Dracula* are historical accounts in the lands of Romance and Horror. Much of this story takes place in Noir, which is the setting of 1940-50s detective mysteries and retellings. Throughout this book, several lesser-known mystery novels and stories set in Novel are mentioned, including events from *Don't Dance with Death* and *Specter Inspector*. Familiarity with these stories isn't necessary to enjoy *Visionary Investigations*, though awareness may enhance the reader's experience.

Happy reading!

To my siblings and our crazy stories created on The Sims.
I do not kill my Sims… on purpose… anymore.

World of Novel

TOP SECRET

AGENT PROFILE

PERSONAL DETAILS

AGENT NAME:	Truth Locke
ALIAS(ES):	None
D.O.B.	Feb. 26, XXXX
NATIONALITY:	Urban, Fantasy
MARITAL STATUS:	Single
GENDER:	Female

DESCRIPTION / TRAITS

AGE:	45
LATERALITY:	Right/Amb
HEIGHT:	5'3"
WEIGHT:	120 lbs
VISION:	20/40
EYE COLOR:	Brown
HAIR COLOR:	Brown

WEAPONS OF CHOICE

- Browning Hi Power
- Poison

LOCATION

COUNTRY:	Mystery
REGION:	Cozy
DISTRICT:	Recluse
SERVICE AREA:	Noir, Mystery

SPECIALIST FIELDS

- Profiling
- Palm Reading

CLASSIFIED INFORMATION

AGENCY:	Visionary Investigations
DESIGNATION:	Head of Investigations
CLEARANCE:	Yellow

SOLE
SEARCHING

CHAPTER 1

Like most events in Shigaqua, capital of Noir, the event that forever changed my life began with a murder.

In case you're new in town, let me give you a quick tour of Noir, the smallest state in Mystery. As one of my investigating partners once put it, Noir is where the line blurs thickest between mentors and mobsters, victims and villains, and friends and foes. (He likes to pretend he's clever, but I know his sources.) Its capital, Shigaqua, has also been my home for the last two decades.

Stars, that makes me sound old. I'm no spry chick anymore. In fact, I'm a tad older than my working partner's mom. Let's not talk about her, though. Aeron doesn't like it when I bring up his parents, anyway.

As for my own parents, I don't know who brought me into this world of chaos and mystery. All I know is they were peculiar enough to name me Truth Locke when I was born with a magical ability in Urban, Fantasy, then quickly adopted out to a witch in the Mysterious Mountain Range between Fantasy and Mystery. The borders have shifted a few times over the years, meaning that my adopted parents now live in Cozy,

Mystery, despite living in the same house an hour away from Shigaqua.

But I'll get there later. First, let me explain how I got into the mess that led me at age forty-five to drive out to my mama, feeling lost like a runaway.

⋯◇⋯

I'd decided to take my lunch break with a brisk walk along the shores of Shigaqua's bay. My heeled faux-leather boots were quiet in the packed sand, leaving footprints like filled-in question marks. I still clicked and clattered from my colorful beaded necklaces, bangles, and anklets. The chilly breeze caught on the edges of my tan trench coat and my shoulder-length brunette hair beneath my floral headscarf and fedora. In the land of Mystery, my fashion sense was hardly the most curious thing on the streets. That was one reason I liked Noir with its cruising cars and wired operator telephones that refused to update with the rest of the Contemporary states.

Lake Mishi was frigid even in the summer, but that didn't stop teenagers from hanging out at the shoreline parks. Marlowe Park's playground was particularly popular with squealing children, where only mothers could differentiate between joy and pain. The park's large lawns made way for softball catching, and its secluded groves provided shade for picnics or less-than-legal dealings.

Police had always struggled to secure the public park since it was technically owned by the Keys Estate, an old settler's family with their mansion proudly on the hilltop. There was a general consensus to stay away from the house, but the beach, docks, and playgrounds were typically busy with families enjoying the outdoors, ignoring the ominous architecture of the mansion in the background.

Not on this particular autumn day. The whole beachfront was blocked off with yellow tape. Instead of families surrounding a picnic basket on the sand, detectives and cops surrounded a dead body washed up on the rocks.

I approached the caution tape and shouted to the lead detective, "Admit it, you need me."

Detective Montgomery looked up from the body, startled and defensive. In his mid-thirties, the detective was well-rounded in his stomach and nothing more. As if to overcorrect, he had flat eyes, mouth, and a boxy buzz-cut.

"What?" he shouted back. "Is that you, Locke? I don't need you. It looks like an accident, and if it ain't, we found this man standing by the body with her wallet. Case solved."

I analyzed the suspect, cuffed by the police cruiser. He was a beach bum with multiple layers against Shigaqua's autumn chill. He swore up and down about his rights and the tyranny of incompetent police.

"I think you know what I'm going to say about him."

Det. Montgomery glared at me. "And this is exactly why I don't want you here."

I smiled back and repeated, "Admit it."

He rolled his eyes and muttered, "Sure, Locke. I'll let you take a look, but if you accuse Skoller Keys up the hill, I hope you have proof and a darn good lawyer."

"Why would I accuse Keys?"

The detective gestured to the body and our surroundings. "We're right off the edge of his property. I wouldn't put it past the creep to kill one of his servants and make it look accidental by throwing her into the ocean. Just take a look and tell me if this little lady's death was murder or not."

"One look is all I need." I ducked under the caution tape and approached. I held my breath against the scent of decay and stooped lower to analyze the body.

Female, early thirties, 4'11", over-tanned. She was beautiful by society's terms with large eyes, small nose, and thick black hair. Her lean weight and emphasized muscles lay bare with her old-fashioned wool swimsuit that provided extra coverage over her hips and stomach. The back-right side of her head was bloodied and dented with a deadly wound. From a rock? There wasn't enough blood on the nearby rocks to account for her crime scene, and the sand that stuck to her skin said she'd been washed up.

Det. Montgomery cleared his throat. "Our suspect had her wallet on him with the vic's photo ID. Her name's Elizabeth Smith."

I laughed. "For all the work she put into reshaping herself, you'd think she'd have a better fake ID."

"Fake?" He raised an eyebrow.

I knelt over the body again. "Yep. Finding your murder scene might be as difficult as finding your victim's identity."

"What do you mean?"

"This woman went through a great deal to reshape herself. The stretch lines on her arms and legs show signs of surgery, though I couldn't say what kind. She's been tanning naked so that no sign of her true tones would show." I stood to stare Det. Montgomery directly in the eye. "Her ID's fake. She was in the final stages of becoming someone else. You'll need my help to find out who that was, who she was before, what spurred her change, why she was trying to hide, and who found her regardless of her efforts."

Det. Montgomery sighed heavily. "Fine, I'll write you up as a specialist informant on the Case. Do your visionary thing."

I grinned and set to work on a more thorough examination, pulling out my voice recorder. It wasn't a typical tool to keep during midday walks, but my partner's encouragement to "always be prepared" had paid off. I'd thank him later if he ever needed an ego boost. Not likely.

Picking up "Elizabeth Smith's" hand, I did a simple reading of her palm. My basic reading could be easily learned by gypsies to foretell fortunes and futures at carnivals. Most folklore about palm reading was bogus, but I'd learned to sift through legitimate palmographs and charts.

"Her small and spatulated fingertips suggest her cleverness and ambition. She was driven, no matter her circumstances. The length of her middle phalange speaks of her want for power, yet her index says that she was prone to obey." I continued, analyzing every section of her fingers, every line in her palm, and every callus to be found. Go figure, there were crossbars far below her pinky, signifying her violent death. It could also mean that she had a bad temper, but I didn't sense that from the rest of her palm.

For more information, I closed my eyes and *Read* her.

As a Fantasy native, I was one of the lucky few born with an ability. It wasn't magic with spells and potions, but more like a supernatural gift.

I saw things no one else could see. Reading a palm was like reading a book about a person's life, spelled out with wrinkles, chaptered by crisscrossing lines, and themed with calluses. Instead of analyzing patterns of creases, I saw with my hypothetical third eye, seeing rivers of possibilities that broke off hundreds of times with hundreds of choices. The more likely the possibility, the wider the river.

Reading a person also let me experience a "day in their life." I felt what they touched, sensed how they moved, and recognized various muscle memories.

With nearly forty years of practice, I could Read palms with a handshake, but it was slightly more difficult for cadavers due to their withered flesh and soulless bodies. When Reading a living person, I began in the middle of a river of possibilities and could travel upstream to their pasts or downstream to their futures. Reading the dead, however, was all upstream with no more possible break offs.

With Elizabeth's hand in mine, I pulled at my ability and flowed through the rivers of her life. I traveled against her currents, exploring her recent lifestyle of running daily errands to stay hidden and on the run. Her river kinked and wiggled with many new choices and directions, almost as if she was lost without direction.

The bend in the river that signified her choice to start her transformation was recent. Maybe a few weeks ago? Interesting. That meant her change hadn't involved surgery, or there would have been scars instead of faded stretch lines. More importantly, it was a significant river bend. It was a complete U-turn. Before her change, the river was wide but tumultuous. She was steady, obedient, and firm in her ways despite multiple obstacles. Nearly a decade of her life was spent in this straight but troubled river. Reaching her childhood, I found occasional bends when she disobeyed and was severely punished, literally straightening her out. That had been her life.

Even as I flowed upstream through her lifetime, I lived a day in the life of her hands.

On the day of her murder, I sensed everything she touched as she woke up with her hands on the arms of a chair, tightened. Not a bed? Odd. Her palms began to sweat. Her nerves tensed, and she clawed at the armchair for release, but she remained stuck. It seemed like hours passed, sweating, tensing, and shaking until she went limp. After what seemed like a few more hours, she woke again. She gripped the chair arms, tensing with quick bursts, then…the end.

I opened my eyes, dissatisfied. I usually learned more from my Readings.

"I can confirm that her death wasn't an accident," I said, reanalyzing her body. "She was tied to a wooden armchair and tortured before she was killed. It's curious that she doesn't have any obvious cuts, bruises, or burns on her body. It's possible they're hidden by her swimsuit, which would mean the killer changed her clothes before dumping her in the lake. The swimsuit looks like an older style, but it would be newly bought since changing her identity would mean changing her wardrobe. You can use her picture to ask around swimsuit shops, but you'll need variants of her with different hairstyles. She made a lot of choices and changes to herself in the last few weeks."

I stood and faced Det. Montgomery. "P.S. You have the wrong man."

He glared at my smile. "Sure, Locke. Did you officially trademark that phrase?"

"No, it's still in processing. The government can be such a hassle to work with."

The detective's eyes narrowed. "Is that your excuse why you ain't a real detective?"

"I don't need to be a 'real detective' when I'm a real private investigator."

His eyes rolled. "Tell me then, 'real private investigator,' why the man standing over the body with our vic's wallet ain't our guy?"

I didn't answer immediately but stepped further away from the suspect in question. "Did you ask for his alibi?"

"Yes, he—"

"Let me guess." I didn't even need to Read his palm. "He said he was just walking around, looking for cans to recycle when he found our victim. He already wore gloves for his collections, so he thought he'd do his civic duty to investigate a washed-up body when you tramped in and took him into custody. Am I right?"

"That's what he says." Det. Montgomery shuffled uneasily.

"Look at him." I gestured to the man sitting in the back seat of the patrol car. "He's shaking with anger at you guys, not at the woman. He's no more than a homeless beach bum hoping to earn a few pennies from scavenging junk off the beach. Didn't you notice the lack of litter around the area and the fresh bag of trash outside of your crime scene? That bag didn't fill itself. That's his alibi."

"Fine, but we're still taking him downtown. He might be a witness, and he stole her ID card."

"Sure. Do what you have to, but he's not your killer."

The detective huffed. "If he ain't our killer, then we got one on the loose." He groaned. "I swear, sometimes I think your job is just to make mine harder. I ain't got time for Jane Doe goose chases when there's a serial killer on the loose."

"Do you mean the Sole Stealer?" I asked, my eyebrows high. "The one who kills his victims with a dirty cocaine injection and then takes their shoes like trophies?"

He grunted. "You know too much for the average citizen. The man is sick, if you ask me."

I hadn't asked, but found the information intriguing. "Are you asking Visionary Investigations for help?" Heaven knew we needed a good Case to promote our new little agency.

Det. Montgomery gave another grunt. "No. That Case's been priority one for the past month, and trails have gone cold, but we can't have you and your team butting in. We need more than the testimony of a few spirits to nail this guy. But I'll get the department to send you a check for your help here."

I didn't bother hiding my irritation or disappointment. My team could help, and we needed the work. At barely four months old, my little Visionary Investigations Agency needed a big Case to push it into the limelight and boost our credibility. Otherwise, we'd fall behind Noir's overwhelming competition of investigators and crash before we ever really got started.

Returning to the agency office didn't help lighten my mood. Rent was overdue, and it was embarrassing that we couldn't afford that dump. One of my partners, Aeron Spade, had bought a condemned lot near the old part of town, but renovating it into our new office took time and money. He expected construction to pause during the winter, leaving us to find this temporary alternative. At least it was more official for an office than the apartment I shared with our other partner, Nita Incog.

Nita wasn't her real name, but it worked well enough since no one knew her real name, including herself. She was of average height, average bone structure, and medium skin tones with hair that mixed 60% brown, 30% blonde, and 10% red. She was dismissible if not for her finely toned muscles and fascinating eye color that changed every time I tried to define it.

With only three of us in the agency, we made the most of our 169 square-foot office, situated up the stairs of a Western diner that sent taunting smells of meat, bread, and oil up our way all day. It wasn't worth opening our single window for fresh air with its front-row seat to the elevated train and its five-minute interval racket. The faded floral wallpaper was misaligned, and the wooden floor creaked with every step, but it was sufficient for our needs. Aeron brought in a false wall (courtesy of a theater where he solved his first official Case) to separate the space between our office area and meeting area.

I frequently occupied the desk in the "office" with its bookshelf of arcane trinkets and filing cabinet of notes and resources. Rounding the divider, there was a little cabinet with a coffee maker and extra mugs, an armchair (mostly used by our limited clients), and a 6-foot sofa (mostly used by Aeron). As our combat specialist, Nita rarely sat and preferred to stand in the corner with the best viewpoint and quickest hiding spot.

She was out exercising, and Aeron was out on the sofa when I returned from my beach encounter and trouble first called. The heels of women's shoes hesitating on the stairs announced our prospective client before the knock on the door. Aeron woke up with a snort on the sofa. Deciding to test the young investigator, I stayed at my desk, hidden from sight.

The door creaked open, and the ka-clip ka-clop of the heels entered the room.

"Is this the Visionary Investigations Agency?" The client's voice was borderline soprano and youthful. I guessed twenties or early thirties.

"This is," Aeron said. With his peculiar parentage and upbringing, his baritone was a strange mix of a posh Fantasy accent with Mystery's questioning inflections and hints of Horror's hushed tones. He was the very definition of tall, dark, and handsome with blue-green eyes, thick dark-brown hair with youthful highlights, and a smile to charm a grieving widow. I could easily picture his royal and flirtatious posturing before the woman. "What can I do for you?"

"You're an investigator? How old are you?"

"I'll turn twenty-one this winter."

I smirked. In late January. It was barely October and still warm enough to debate over opening the window. "I can assure you, though," he continued, "I'm more than qualified to solve your Case."

I rolled my eyes at his ego. He was supposed to say, "*We're* more than qualified." We were supposed to be a team. Even after four months of building this agency together, he acted like a lone-wolf.

The client hummed, doubtful. "Where's the rest of the agency?"

The floor creaked as Aeron shifted to stand. "You must know a thing or two about who we are, or you would have gone to any of the other investigators on this block. This is Shigaqua, after all. The town's full of PIs ready to swoon before a pretty face like yours. But you came to us because we have a reputation for closing Cases, am I right?"

The floor creaked again with a smaller shift from the client. "I suppose you might know a thing or two. I'll admit, I still have my doubts. Your reputation is less about closing Cases and more about your…unconventional methods. I was told—" she paused to laugh with disbelief "—that one of you is a gypsy, and another is a medium?"

I held back my grumble. How many Cases would we need to close to fix that stigma? Unfortunately, every Case we closed was via "unconventional methods," so both reputations would likely grow together.

Thankfully, Aeron defended us. "Truth and I were both born in Fantasy with abilities."

"You have magic?" the woman asked. "Magic doesn't work in Noir."

"I didn't say magic." I could almost hear his flirty wink. "I said abilities. It's a common misunderstanding. While magics are learned skill sets and basically impossible to use in Noir, abilities are birth-given traits that aren't mutated despite boundaries. As Fantasy natives, Truth can read palms that let her see into people's pasts and futures, and I visit the dead through my dreams."

I shrugged at his most basic descriptions of our abilities. I didn't mind telling people about the strengths and limitations of my ability to Read people, but Aeron had a minor dose of paranoia that liked to keep secrets.

"Is that so?" the woman asked. "Then you might be the only people who can solve this Case. See, the police aren't doing their jobs. My sister was murdered, and they still haven't caught the killer. It makes a defenseless woman like myself nervous to walk around town after dark." Her voice took on a little whine, playing for pity.

"Our third teammate is incredibly skilled with weapons and defensive combat if you need a guard."

"You mean you wouldn't be the one protecting me?"

"I have…" he drifted off for a beat, "other specialties."

Their voices went quiet enough that I needed to strain to hear them.

"I'm sure you do. I could make it worth your while."

"You may try."

"Hmm, be a gentleman and take my coat for me?"

"Of cour—eh, won't you be a little cold without it?"

"Not if you hold me—"

"Get a room," a new voice said, a monotonous alto that I recognized. When had Nita entered?

Our potential client yelped with a jump in her heels while Aeron spoke with agitation, "Nita! I didn't hear you come in."

"Obviously. I bet you didn't know Truth's here, too."

Ah, the game was up. I rounded the divider, sending the client flustering to put on her autumn coat again. She wore a pale red, knee-length dress that hugged her hips and sagged around her shoulders with her low boat neckline. After giving up on her coat, she tugged on her satin gloves and collected her hand purse as if she was only there for business.

Recognizing her failure to act professionally, she blushed. "Um, were you here the whole time?"

"Yep," I said. "I heard everything. While Aeron might accept kisses for payment, Nita and I require cash."

Our potential client tightened her coat around her shoulders. "I can pay. I assume this is the rest of Visionary Investigations, Madams Locke and Incog? I'm Irene Hallman."

Hallman… Where had I heard that name before?

Sifting through the conversation and her name, it clicked. "Hallman. Was your sister Henrietta Hallman? The latest victim of the Sole Stealer?"

CHAPTER 2

s. Hallman filled us in with the limited details she knew of her sister's death, confirming our first step to visit the police station. After a bit of paperwork to officially hire us, I sent Ms. Hallman on her way, and we made our own across town. The city detectives obviously didn't have enough information to solve the Case, but it was currently more than we had.

Since Aeron's roadster only had two seats, Nita opted to take the elevated train, planning to meet up outside of the homicide room on the second floor.

Shigaqua's police station was near the middle of town, only a couple of blocks away from the great lake. It was a sturdy brick building, right across the street from the city's court-house, next to the morgue, and kitty-corner to the massive Hyde Park (another known location of criminal activity after sundown). Mighty convenient.

The interior of the police station gave the overall impres-sion of smoke. The floor was smoky wood, the walls were smoky blue, and much of the police work involved smoke and mirrors; smoking cheap cigarettes and using two-way mirrors for interview rooms and the line-up.

Many of the office rooms had half-walls that let the heat, smoke, and conversations rise to the ceiling and float across the entire floor, making the whole place rather loud and cough-inducing.

Aeron entered the building the same way he entered anywhere; like he owned the place and was there for a surprise inspection. The lands his family owned were nowhere near Shigaqua, but that didn't stop his confident stride to accompany his tall and royal posture. He winked at a passing policewoman, and I could have sworn she swooned a little.

Det. Montgomery worked his jaw with irritation as Aeron smiled his bright eyes at him.

"Guess who was just hired for the Sole Stealer Case?"

"You?" he said, dripping with sarcasm. "I have another Case for you instead. It's called the Case of the Missing Mug. See, someone took my 'I Hate Mondays' mug, and since you want to solve every Case around here, maybe you could solve this one too."

Aeron's smile dampened as the nearby detectives laughed and took notice.

"Ooh-ooh!" Det. Weiss waved his hand as if he had the answer. "I took a nap, and I know who did it! It was—" he leaned in and whispered loudly for effect "—a ghost!"

Others laughed, but Aeron's smile turned cold and calculating. Oh, no. I inwardly groaned, predicting exactly where this conversation would go.

"A simple spirit is an implausible suspect," Aeron said, slipping into the formal diction and accent of his Fantasy royal family. "Even if one tried, most spirits would be incapable of moving your mug as only a select set of spirits have the gift to interact with physical objects. The benevolent kind are usually too restrained to interfere with our realm, meaning the only plausible explanation of a ghost stealing your mug would mean it was the malevolent kind, commonly referred to as poltergeists."

Det. Montgomery shuddered. He'd been the first to bait Aeron down this trail of conversation.

"A polar-what?" Det. Weiss scoffed. "Are you making up words to sound smart?"

Aeron smirked and leaned into his hushed Horror accent as he repeated, "Poltergeist. A demonic spirit with mischievous or evil intentions and has the gift to not simply touch objects or people, but to move, throw, or possess them."

Many of the eyes in the room widened with either fear or disbelief.

The young investigator casually strolled around the room and continued, "They are mostly contained in Horror. However, some of you may have seen my pen and notepad floating without a hand?"

A couple of the detectives nodded with blanched faces. Others jerked around, surprised at the witnesses.

"That would be Neil, my personal assistant—" Aeron grinned "—and poltergeist. Lucky for you, I convinced him to work with me rather than against me. As for you, Det. Montgomery… maybe he stole your mug just for the thrill of the mischief. Let us hope he finds no reason to become angry at you, or you might find your mug as it sails into your shins."

I could have heard a pin drop for the lack of breathing in the room.

Det. Montgomery coughed and slowly lifted his mug from his desk drawer to place it back on its coaster. "Fantasy freak. You know we were just joking, right?"

"Of course." Aeron smiled, but it didn't reach his eyes.

Yep. Exactly as I predicted.

Nita appeared in my periphery. As usual, I had no idea when she entered or how she got so close to me without me noticing. We were fairly certain that she was trained in Special Operations from Thriller, but no one really knew. I'd found her almost two years ago in a hospital when she woke with amnesia after nearly drowning in the lake. I told her about my ability to help people find their identities, and she'd stuck with me ever since.

Her features didn't help narrow down her heritage. It was like she took the most serious eyebrows from Mystery, the most cunning smile from Thriller, the most princess-looking facial structure from Fantasy, and the most otherworldly eyes from Sci-Fi.

She wore her usual slacks, button-down shirt, and blazer jacket—all in her favorite color of black. She wasn't much of an investigator, but she was sneaky, the best with any kind of weapon, and someone you wanted on your side.

I gestured to Det. Montgomery. "We're all here. Can you show us the reports on the Sole Stealer Case?"

He thumbed us toward the copy room. "I'll make a copy for you."

We grabbed our reports and found an empty room to spread out for analysis. Aeron did his usual quick scan over the papers, then grabbed a pillow from the lounge to sit in the corner and take a nap.

Nita and I spent the next two and a half hours reading every line and footnote.

There were six female victims (that we knew of). They'd each received a letter with evidence of someone watching them (a photograph of them sleeping in bed, a recipe taken from one of their personal cookbooks, a transcribed word-for-word private conversation…). After receiving the letter, they'd either boarded up in their own homes or attempted to flee. Regardless, they were each killed by a lethal injection of cocaine and fentanyl.

I studied the report of the deadly compound, curious about the killer's choice of weapon. As an herbalist, I was more than familiar with a few poisons and wondered why the killer chose a deadly mix of cocaine as their modus operandi. Sometimes, finding the reasoning behind a killer's MO was the key to finding the killer, but that trail left me with more questions than answers.

Hoping to piece the puzzle together, I analyzed the other parts of the killer's MO.

Three of the victims had fled their residences, running toward the police station, a church, or a family member's home. The other three women attempted to hide in their homes, but were found sprawled in positions with disheveled pathways that suggested they'd ended up running through their houses. The police had received distress calls from four of the six, though were never fast enough to spot the killer. All the women were found barefoot.

The victims had no other apparent commonalities. No common feature to attract a serial killer, no link through occupations, not even close in proximity, being spread across Shigaqua.

Aeron woke with a quick intake of breath. Nita's attention immediately focused on him.

"What did you learn?" I asked.

"Less than I'd hoped," he said. "The Sole Stealer wears a disguise when he chases his victims. I was only able to meet with one of our known victims, and she said she didn't recognize her attacker. Er, there was something else, but I don't remember… Neil?" He asked the air beside him and set out his notepad and pen.

I pondered the new insight. "If the Sole Stealer wears a mask, it's very possible he has a minor-to-severe case of multiple personality disorder. He could seem like a perfectly normal person every day, but as soon as he puts on the disguise, he chooses to become a new character and plays the part of the murderer. If that's the case, it would be nearly impossible to suspect him from a typical interview."

Nita asked quietly over her pages of reports, "Did they describe his disguise?"

Aeron shrugged. "If I told you, I'd have to kill you."

Nita tilted her head in thought. "Your attempt would be amusing."

I let out a little incredulous laugh while Aeron laughed with a burst of joy.

Nita frowned. "You'll tell us what you know, right?"

"I don't know anything about it," Aeron admitted. "I just thought it would sound cooler to say, 'if I told you, I'd have to kill you.' But no one takes that statement seriously."

"Unless you're Nita." I laughed.

The pen by Aeron's notepad raised itself from the floor. I shuddered at the sight. It wasn't magic. I would have been fine with magic. No, it was held by the poltergeist Neil Martin. It didn't matter if he was bonded to help us by taking notes from the spirit world. The presence of the poltergeist always gave me the creeps.

"Ah," Aeron said, reading Neil's note. "That's apparently the bit I forgot. The Sole Stealer is disguised as an elf… Curses, what kind of elf?"

We all spoke at once.

"Christmas elf," Nita said.

"High elf," I said.

"Wingless fairy," Aeron said. Then he smirked. "See the problem? Neil, could you be a little more specific?"

"Oh, wait," I said, thinking it over. "He takes their shoes. Doesn't your homeland have a history about elves and a shoemaker?"

Aeron scoffed. "You think he's dressed as Margen's helpful kind of elf? That's twisted and unlikely. Those are either invisible or naked because—according to the cobbler—giving them clothes freed them from service. Even the clothed elves or wights are mostly harmless. Their only nefarious deeds are making years pass like days and switching out children for changelings. If we look at the historical account of the <u>Gifts of the Little People</u>, they stole people's hair but thanked them with lumps of coal that turned into gold for those who were worthy."

Nita's brow furrowed. "How does any of that make sense?"

Aeron shrugged. "It works in Fairy." Reading over Neil's newest note, he continued, "It seems that I asked the spirits to follow him if they spot him, then report to me. Good job, me."

I nodded. Catching the killer was sometimes the easy part with Aeron's resources. The hard part came in finding proof. Unfortunately, his testimony of, "The dead victim told me in my dreams," held no weight in court. Still, it was much easier to find proof after finding the killer.

"The problem with asking your spirits to follow him," I said, "is we don't know what he looks like. Your spirits will only recognize him when he's dressed to kill. By the time you go to sleep, they tell you, you wake up, tell us, and then we arrive at the scene, we'll be too late. Your spirits might be able to lead us to him afterwards, but we'll be too late to save his next victim."

Aeron nodded grimly. "We'll need to catch them before that happens."

"How?" Nita asked.

Analyzing the profiles of the victims, I pondered aloud, "The police haven't found anything to link these women, but the Sole Stealer doesn't simply hunt the women. He takes their shoes. Maybe there's a link between their shoes."

"How would we know?" Aeron asked. "We don't know what kinds of shoes they wore since they were stolen. Unless you can read feet as well as hands."

I stared at Aeron. What a gross and intriguing idea.

"I don't know," I said. "I've never tried Reading someone's foot before."

"Why not?" Aeron asked. "They have creases and phalanges like hands."

"Yes," I agreed, "and feet actually say a lot about a person's genetics and habits based on their shape and calluses. In fact, let's try it. Nita, will you take off your boots?"

Our combat specialist seemed only mildly surprised to be chosen as our guinea pig. I couldn't Read myself, and I already knew too much about Aeron (according to him). Nita didn't complain or argue for Aeron to go first. She simply hoisted her pant leg to reveal a layered ring of daggers strapped around the top of her boot. Undoing the laces, she loosened her boot and slowly slipped out her foot to show off long black socks with another strap of vials above her ankle. Her precision and caution while removing the vial strap made me squeamish. Whatever was inside, she didn't want to break open.

"Well…" she paused. "I should probably warn you."

"Of what?" I panicked. Was there something even more dangerous than daggers and mysterious vials under her socks?

She peeled off her sock and let loose a putrid smell. I gagged and covered my nose, afraid of some poisonous gas.

"What is that?" Aeron hacked under his elbow. "Ugh! You could kill cockroaches with that stench."

"I, well, might have athlete's foot," she said, scratching a red sore on the side of her foot.

Aeron made a disgusted sound while I grimaced. This was to be my first foot Reading?

Squeezing my nose closed, I pointed at the door. "Please find the bathroom and wash that foot."

Again, no complaints from Nita, only obedience. She returned with a slightly less malodorous foot, then sat on the floor, extending the offensive appendage toward me.

Holding my breath, I sat before her and picked up her foot. It was common knowledge that no two hands were the same, but only studiers of palmographs understood how those differences could tell you everything you ever wanted to know about a stranger. To strengthen my ability, I'd learned the art of palm reading and the secrets of the best fortune tellers. I understood how to interpret the lines of fate, fortune, head, heart, and life. Each line could define a person's temperament, loyalties, or interests.

After nearly four decades of practice, I could Read someone with a three-second handshake. But, looking at Nita's athlete's foot in front of me, I suddenly felt like a child staring at my first palm. I knew that no two feet were the same, and they had many of the same features as hands, but I remembered nothing regarding specific toe shapes or creases in feet.

When I'd first Read Nita's palms, I instantly felt the cool metal and tough leather of weapons. She had muscle memory to use dozens of weapons I couldn't even identify. She had the deftness of a combat fighter and the steadiness of a hunter. A day in her life was spent exercising, training, and setting traps, all while pretending to be a plain Jane.

The lines in her hand agreed with a dangerous past and a traumatic upbringing, but a future that branched with possibilities. She had every crease to indicate her strong sense of loyalty.

With that knowledge, I'd instantly recruited her.

Taking Nita's foot in my hands, I analyzed the calluses, studied the shapes of her curves, and considered the creases. Unfortunately, I needed a lot longer than a three-second handshake with Nita's athlete's foot. Reading her foot was like my novice days of thirty seconds, but it worked.

I sensed her feet slipping through linen sheets at the beginning of the day. No restlessness. No sleeping in. She stepped lightly across her carpeted bedroom with deep stealth training that let her walk soundlessly. Every step was carefully placed, rolling from the sides or starting on her tiptoes. Socks first, then the strap of vials, next the boots, and finally the strap of daggers. She wore the weapons even as she casually jogged in place in our apartment, bounced on her pads like a boxer, practiced a dozen other exercises, then stretched with her palms touching her toes. Throughout the day, she purposely walked with heavier feet to sound "normal." I sensed her standing at the ready when being addressed, then bouncing impatiently behind my back. At the end of the day, she snuck from room to room of our apartment until confirming all was clear. After more stretches of rolling her ankles, flexing and then relaxing, she climbed back into the linens of her bed.

As for her rivers of possibilities, they were the same as her hands. I'd never met a more vague path. Her infancy had been full of small streams in various directions that gave me no details. She'd chosen one of the least likely possibilities, but it had grown wide and strong with few break-offs. It took a sharp turn—like hitting a wall—as the signifying point of her amnesia. Looking into her indeterminate future, the river hit another obstacle like a large stone. It divided evenly in opposite directions, representing the moment when her amnesia would be cured.

My curious nature needed to know what her diverging paths were and which she would choose.

"It worked," I said, dropping Nita's fungus foot. "Feet don't interact with the world as much as hands do, so I didn't really learn anything new, but…you bounce when I'm not looking?"

Nita's only form of confirmation was to slightly redden her cheeks.

"Alright then!" Aeron laughed, rubbing his hands together. "Let's get you to the morgue for some feet Reading. Then we'll need someone who knows a thing or two about shoes."

I traced the heart line on my palm. "I might know someone to help us with that."

CHAPTER 3

Leaving the Shigaqua Police Station, we crossed the parking lot to the city morgue. I was grateful to escape the smoky building for the clear air. Though Shigaqua's morgue wasn't as sterile as one of Procedural's morgues, at least the technicians knew the dangers of smoking and kept their building clean. The forensic science technician was out for the day, but I was vaguely acquainted with Pathology Assistant Hermann. Enough for access to Henrietta's body after a quick call to Det. Montgomery. We were her sister's client after all.

Nita chose to stay at the doorway as Hermann led us back. He pointed at two body vaults. "We only have the last two of the six victims. The first four have been released to the families for burial."

"Burying evidence," I muttered and shook my head. "Can I see Henrietta first?"

He frowned at me, but opened the doors and rolled out the latest victim.

As I lifted the flimsy covering to reveal Henrietta's feet and ankles, Aeron's eyebrow twitched. "This feels like a backwards Cinderella."

"In what way?"

"Instead of using the shoe to find the damsel's foot, we're using the damsel's foot to find the shoe."

I smirked back. "If the boot fits."

A small tag on her big toe identified the body as Henrietta, our client's sister. Victim number six. Her body had been dead for three weeks, but at least she didn't have athlete's foot. Her toenails were trimmed and cleaned, but that had been part of her autopsy. In Procedural, they found all sorts of information from the dirt found between a person's toes and toenails. The Sole Stealer Case was big enough that Noir might send over samples to have them examined, but that took weeks, sometimes months if they were backed up with their own Cases. The police couldn't rely on that.

Gritting my teeth, I reached for her left foot. Palm reading was typically done on the left hand—the statistically non-dominant hand and closer to the heart, so I made a guess for the similar foot.

I thumbed against the muscles, sliding up the middle, then curving inward with the arch. *Lapides*, it was weird. I was accustomed to working around a thumb and long phalanges. The entire foot was basically an elongated palm but with different creases and flexibility. The most I could guess about her personality was that she hadn't broken any toes, didn't have bunions, and hadn't painted her toenails. A simple woman with a simple life? Why had the Sole Stealer targeted her? Was it possible she was a random target?

If I was going to get anything extra out of her, it would be with my ability. I closed my eyes and opened my mind to sail down her rivers of life.

Similar to Nita's foot Reading, it took much longer than my typical Reading for me to focus on her paths and decipher their meanings.

Henrietta lived a lavish life of silk bedsheets, thick carpets, and polished wooden floors. She didn't wear shoes that simply fit her feet. No, she wore shoes that were made to fit her. Perfectly sized and arched for her unique feet, she walked in heels through the day then fluffy slippers in the evening.

For the day that she died, she'd dressed in luxurious leather shoes, ready to go out for the day. From reading the police reports, I knew Henrietta had received the Sole Stealer's threat in that morning's mail, dropped through her door's letter-slot. I recognized her motions as she walked to her front door, rolled her balance forward onto the balls of her feet to crouch for the mail, then stood still. After a moment of chills, her feet ran. Jumping into her car, she floored the gas pedal.

Based on the report, I knew she'd made it two blocks from her house, going in the direction of her sister's house—our client.

Something forced her to slam on the brakes and flee from her car. She ran again, but not for long. She lost her footing and fell to the ground. Her feet scuffed against the pavement, scrambling back. She kicked wildly through the air until something slammed against her legs and pinned her feet to the ground. Her feet continued to wiggle with feeble attempts for freedom, but faded…then stopped.

My Reading cut off with the end of her life, throwing me back into the present in the morgue with Aeron and the assistant. They both looked at me with anticipation.

I released a heavy breath, slightly overwhelmed from the experience. "Her shoes were custom-made. I have an idea of where we can learn more. First, I'd like to Read her hands, plus the hands and feet of the other available victim. Hermann, could you pull her out? Reading her hand should be quick work."

Indeed, I had Henrietta's hand Read before Hermann could even unlock the vault for the other victim. Her hand revealed fur around laces as she tied her shoes and gave some particulars about her routine as she prepared for the day and the threatening letter she held. The paper had been thin and rough…cheap.

I performed the same Readings on the other Sole Stealer victim in the morgue. The police had found no connection to the victims other than their gender. The other victim had been less well-to-do, living on the poorer side of Shigaqua, but, to my surprise, her last day Read identically to Henrietta's. One particular detail made me open my eyes and grin with eagerness.

"They wore the same shoes! That's how the victims are all connected. That's why the Sole Stealer takes them."

Aeron frowned thoughtfully. "But this victim wasn't rich. She prioritized nice shoes?"

"Wearing custom-made shoes lets a person feel rich even if they're in debt. Hermann, she had a pedicure, didn't she?"

Hermann nodded, giving me a bewildered look. Why was that look so common when I grew excited about my findings?

"Thank you, Hermann. We'll be on our way now."

Aeron and I joined Nita at the front of the morgue and gave her a quick update on our findings.

"Next stop:" I said, "By the Foot shoe store. Let's see if we can identify the missing shoes."

Aeron checked his pocket watch. "Let me know what you find."

"You aren't coming with us?"

"Sorry, I made plans before we were given the Case."

"Another date with Jessica?" I asked.

"Not Jessica," he said with a shrug. "She was a little too serious. But I managed to convince Officer Mendoza to join me during her lunch break. It wouldn't hurt to have a friendly acquaintance within the police department. Maybe I can ask what she knows about the Sole Stealer in case anything was left out of the file."

I held back my cringe, predicting where his "friendly acquaintance" would stand in two weeks. All relationships ended coldly against the most unattainable flirt in Shigaqua.

"Too serious?" Nita repeated with the smallest measure of panic in her eyes. Uh oh. Nita was the most serious person I'd ever met…except when Aeron was involved. She wouldn't admit it, but I knew she admired him. Would she suddenly act less serious in an attempt to please Aeron?

"Anyway," he said, "let me know what you find, and I'll ask my spirit friends to snoop around for anyone collecting those shoes."

"Thanks, Aeron," I said, waving goodbye. Turning to Nita, I asked, "What about you?"

"I'd like to visit the various crime scenes."

I nodded. She wasn't trained as a detective, but she had an instinctual sense for understanding the step-by-step causes and effects of crime scenes.

Her eyes flashed with some self-reflection before her face morphed into a forced tease. "I mean, I don't want to be a third wheel at By the Foot." With another after-thought, she gave me an obvious wink.

By the stars? Nita had never teased me before. Shoot, she really took Aeron's comment to heart about being "too serious?"

We parted ways, and I took a deep breath. Shigaqua had more than its fair share of shoe stores as shoe shopping was a luxury activity in Noir. This would be my first time visiting By the Foot because of one of their employees.

Michael Johnson was a tall and lanky man, like a teenager who never filled out, despite passing his mid-forties. He wore his light-brown hair as if he'd just woken up, and black-rimmed rectangular glasses around his dark-brown eyes.

Eight years ago, we had literally run into each other at a traveling carnival. I'd been barely scraping by as a corporate investigator at Silent Sleuth Services and needed extra cash to afford my own apartment. I'd stepped in last minute to cover for the carnival's sick psychic, running across the park with my box of crystals, incense, and fungi. Michael had just stepped out of the hall of mirrors, dazed and disoriented. Cue: our collision.

"*Sidera et lapides*," I cursed as my box tumbled to the trampled grass, and he said, "Four!"

In unison, we bent over to collect the objects and traded humorously confused looks. "What was that?" he asked while I asked, "Four?"

"I'll go first," I said with my hand up to stop our unison conversation. Yes, I was in a hurry to arrange my tent, but I had time to explain, "It was Latin."

"Latin? Like the language of magic?" His eyes went wide to take in my Fantasy-themed dress and jewelry. He hesitated to return my crystal ball to me. "Did you just curse me like a witch?"

"No, no. Nothing offensive," I explained. "*Sidera et lapides* means 'stars and stones.' But if you want a hex, I know some good ones. I'm actually quite proud of my hexes. The madder I am, the more creative they can be. Now, explain 'four.'"

The man went through multiple expressions of bewilderment (a typical response to my frankness), then humor (a refreshing atypical response). "It's a binary reference."

"Meaning I'm too stupid to get it."

"Naw, it's not that complicated," he said. Adding the last incense stick to my box, he raised his right hand to demonstrate. "See, you can use your fingers to count in binary. Your thumb represents one, and your index is two. So, three is your thumb plus your index finger, and this is 'four.'" He flipped me the bird. "The ring finger is eight, and the pinky by itself is sixteen. With this method, you can count up to thirty-one on one hand."

I coughed and failed to hold back my laughter. I used my next cough to "hide" my comment, "Nerd alert."

He laughed and blushed adorably. "Hey, it's sexy, and my dog knows it."

I joined in his laughter, too embarrassed to admit the truth of his words. "Alright, I need to know more about your dog, but I'll stick to my hexes. My favorite hex is *Quod omnis charta interficiam te.* 'That every paper cut you.'"

"Ouch." He raised his eyebrows. "Does it actually work?"

"Not in Mystery. Even in Fantasy, I don't blow arcane powder in people's faces to activate my hexes unless I'm seriously mad."

The intriguing man nodded thoughtfully. "How would you say… 'May you always step in dog poop?'"

I laughed and considered. "Closest translation might be *Spero pedes tuos semper stercora canina invenire.*"

He took a turn to laugh. "That's way too many syllables. I'll stick to telling people to go count to four."

Sidera, was he honestly someone who could match my quirkiness?

"You're funny." Wait, sometimes people took those words as an insult. I hadn't meant it as an insult.

Thankfully, he smiled and nudged me. "You're the one speaking Latin hexes, and you call me funny?"

The carnival ringmaster spotted me and called me over. We stood to leave, but I couldn't go yet. I hadn't felt this excited to meet someone in a very, very long time. Setting my box back down, I shoved my hand forward. "My name's Truth Locke. Yours?"

"Michael Johnson." Shoot, with a name like that, I'd never find him again. Even his cheap slacks and button-up shirt were ambiguous. I needed to shake his hand!

With his adorable smile and welcoming reach, I grabbed his hand as my temporary employer called my name again with more urgency.

"*Sidera*, it was nice to meet you!" I picked up my box and dashed away, hoping I'd gained enough information.

He waved back with an open palm. "Thirty-one!"

Thirty-one? Oh, all fingers, pinky, and thumb up. What a nerdy way to wave.

I grinned through my whole shift as a mystic, but then the next few weeks were grueling as I worked Case after Case at Silent Sleuth Services. There wasn't a moment to spare for researching the anonymous Michael Johnson, who could use a typewriter like a pianist, research papers like a librarian, and solve math problems like a slide rule. Finally finding a break between Cases, I found Michael's employer and started hanging around the building where he worked. Mystery civilians were accustomed to suspicious people loitering, but after six weeks without seeing him, the security asked for my purpose in the area. Apparently, Michael Johnson had been fired from his desk job.

It took me four months to find him again. The man bounced between jobs like a rubber ball. It seemed suspicious at first, holding me off from contacting him for another few months. Instead, I hovered around his work neighborhoods, hoping to catch a glimpse of him, feeling like a coward for not talking to him, but also excusing my activity as "practice" for investigating. Until one day he caught me. I thanked the heavens for the delectable tea shop nearby as an excuse to be in the area.

We became the kind of best friends who could spend months apart from each other then meet up and act like we saw each other yesterday. My overtime Cases at Noir's biggest agency and his various jobs kept us busy, and the time never seemed right to develop our relationship.

As Head Investigator of my new little agency, I made my way over to By the Foot. I felt like I was about to cross a line in our relationship, but I didn't even know what the line was.

By the Foot was a small shop off of the major road that curved around Lake Mishi. It was the kind of off-market store that cheap people could use and say they "shop local" and "support small businesses." It included new and cheaply manufactured shoes found in pop-up stores or even in the indoor malls of Noir.

A little bell rang as I walked into the shop. Before an employee could welcome me, I was greeted by the lingering scent of cigarettes despite the open window to the brisk autumn air. I bee-lined for the register as the employee emerged from the backroom. Michael wore a white polo shirt uniform with khaki pants. I smirked to see him in such an outfit. Usually, he preferred loose-fit slacks and a baggy shirt held tight by suspenders.

"Welcome to—oh, Truth!" Michael said. He waved with an open hand and greeted me with his usual binary reference, "Thirty-one! What are you doing here?"

"Hey, Micro," I replied with an exaggerated grin. Normally, I hated nicknames and aliases. However, when my dearest friend had one of the most common names of the last few decades, I allowed an exception. "How are you doing?"

"Positive as a proton now that you're here. Did you know I was working, or are you looking for shoes to buy? Is this your first time here?"

"It is. I'm actually working on a Case and looking for shoes worth stealing."

Micro straightened. "Stealing? You're on a Case?"

"Yeah. Could you help me find a type of shoe?"

"Positively." He wound around the counter to slip out a monthly catalogue advertisement. "Do you know their material, style, year, or size?"

"Uhh…real leather and fur? Laces? Probably this year?"

Micro raised an eyebrow high. His dramatic facial expressions made him easy to read. I bet even Det. Montgomery would know what he was thinking.

I shuffled awkwardly. Usually, I had all the answers, but feet were a new and uncomfortable area for me. Recalling the sensations of the feet fitting into the missing shoes, I said, "They cover the toes and ankles, have a low arch, and the heel is thick and sturdy?"

"Boots?" Micro suggested.

"Probably."

He nodded and crouched to rummage for something from underneath the register. He pulled out three fat annual catalogues and dropped them with a smack on the counter.

"If they were made within the last year, you'll find it in one of these."

I stared wide-eyed at the catalogues. "I'm guessing these won't show their inside molding."

Micro popped his lips with the word, "Nope."

"This will probably take some time. Can I borrow these?"

Micro skewed an "unlikely" thinking face. "Eh, they're store copies, and you know how my manager can be."

"Yeah, you've told me about Jo." She was one of those bosses who stuck strictly to the rules while also attempting to be the "fun" manager. I'd never met her, but Micro's descriptions labeled her as certifiably insane and obsessed with Fantasy.

"These magazines are our only copies, so they aren't supposed to leave the store, but Jo would probably understand if you flashed your badge at me."

"No need, as long as you don't mind me crashing on these chairs for a bit."

A customer walked in, and Micro returned to work-mode, allowing me to do exactly as I suggested. I bore into the top catalogue, analyzing shoe after shoe. Not short enough, not round enough, not enough coverage… A half hour later, I slapped down the first catalogue as a dud.

Micro sat down and pulled over the bottom catalogue. "What are you looking for? Four-eyes are better than two." He pointed at his glasses to turn the statement into a tease.

I smiled back, but glanced around. "Won't Jo be mad if you're not helping the customers?"

"Naw, Shirley's here now. And we're slow enough that I can clock out early without Jo knowing."

"Oh, thanks." I shuffled uneasily in my seat. I didn't want to pull Micro into a Case with a serial killer, but this was more research than I could handle alone.

"What am I looking for?" he asked, flipping through the pages.

"Real leather heels," I said, "with velvet tops, and real fur lining bordering its laces."

"So you're looking for a pompous pump." He flipped through the pages.

"With fine craftsmanship. The shape of her feet looked like they spent their lives hiding in a cloud."

Micro looked up. He held up a finger to ask me to wait as he went to a back room and returned with a small black-and-white photo of a pear-shaped woman. She wore ankle boots that matched the notes of my mystery shoes.

"Who is this?" I asked.

"It's my manager, Jo Merivale. She used to wear those boots every day, even though we don't sell them here. They have velveteen upper, houndstooth lining, sheepskin trim, leather foxing, a leather heel, and rubber soles."

"Ummm…" I didn't understand the details, but it looked right.

Micro laughed. "This is a high-end style made by Knees and Toes. Managers must get a hefty pay increase because these boots cost as much as my monthly rent."

My eyes and mouth gaped. "Seriously? Who would ever spend that much on a pair of shoes?"

"Boots," Micro corrected, then shrugged. "They're custom-made."

"Those might be worth stealing," I said. "I need to check with Knees and Toes. Thanks, Micro. I couldn't have done it without you."

He cut off my flattery with a wave. "Yeah, yeah, I know."

I smiled. "Have I ever told you how much I love you?"

"Every day." He smirked and rolled his eyes. Yes, I once blurted out, "I love you" to Micro, and in an effort to hide my true feelings, I softened the phrase into casual love for friends and family. Still, saying it regularly made me hope that one day I could bravely confess it with sincerity. For now, he smiled lightly and gestured to the smoky backroom. "I need to put this back exactly as I found it, or Jo might fire me."

CHAPTER 4

I couldn't leave right away as I had to make a call to the police department. Begrudgingly, I asked for Det. Montgomery, as he was the lead on the Case. He scoffed, "Freak," when I shared Aeron's ghostly insights about the killer dressing like an elf. Despite Aeron's efforts to win over the police, most of them rolled their eyes at any use of resources outside of Noir, including our Fantasy abilities. Still, a killer in an elf costume was easier to spot than a killer in plain clothes.

"Also, we found the connection between the Sole Stealer victims. They all bought and wore the same shoes. I suspect they're a customized boot made and sold at Knees and Toes. I'm heading over there now to confirm. Then, we need them taken off the shelves so no more customers can buy them and become potential victims."

"How do you know that?" Det. Montgomery asked. "Do you have proof?"

"Not yet," I admitted, "but that's where I'm headed next. I'll let you know if I discover anything else, but I expect they'll hesitate to pull their product until the authorities step in."

After an acknowledging grunt from Montgomery, I hung up. Micro emerged from the back room with his lunch bag in hand, and name tag off.

"Are you done with work for the day?" I asked.

"Yeah, Shirley can handle the store on her own. Can I come with you to Knees and Toes? We frequently refer people to the place when they want customized shoes, but I've never been there before."

Spend more time with my handsome best friend? Yes, please.

I smiled. "I could probably use your expertise and research skills. We need a list of buyers of everyone who's bought those shoes."

We took Micro's car for the short trip to Knees and Toes. It was a simple vehicle, nicknamed "Buggy" for its beetle-shape and yellow color. Once parked outside of Knees and Toes, Micro paused me from exiting.

"Truth, I know you don't like secrets, but could you please refrain from mentioning that I work at By the Foot while we're in there? There's bad blood and a restraining order between them and my manager."

I raised my eyebrows. "Your manager who owns a pair of their boots?"

"Yeah, she doesn't wear those boots anymore. So, don't mention my occupation, please?"

He held me captive with his dark brown eyes until I reluctantly agreed.

Unlike By the Foot, this shoe store was well lit and well shopped. Several customers walked through the displays of loafers and saddle shoes, casually browsing the floor models or talking with an employee about a custom fit. There was a group of young women all giving their opinions as one of them debated between colors of a certain heeled shoe.

Seeing us enter, an employee sized up Micro and me, and approached with an unsure expression. He was an older gentleman wearing a full suit and tie with a handkerchief in his breast pocket.

"Welcome to Knees and Toes. My name's Dixon. What kind of shoes are you looking for?"

"Hello," I said. "I'm looking for your ridiculously priced leather and fur-lined boots."

Dixon gave my trench coat and multi-layered, multi-colored dress and jewelry another up-and-down, then plastered on a grin. "Of course. If you'll take a seat, I can size your feet and grab a pair from the back—"

"They aren't for me," I said, flashing my PI badge. For some reason, this made Dixon relax. He was more relieved to answer interrogating questions than to help me buy shoes?

Micro chuckled. "Yeah, finding shoes to match your fun sense of style could make a man sweat." Stepping up, he asked Dixon, "Do you keep records for all of your customers and their transactions?"

Dixon tilted his head like a curious dog. "Of course. We write down their measurements, with their preferred styles and brands, to best serve our returning customers."

"Good," I said. "I need Henrietta Hallman's file."

Dixon repeated her name as if committing it to memory. "The name sounds familiar. One moment, please. And you'd like one of our Lucille boots?"

"Yes," I said, "and your shoemaker, if they're in-house."

Dixon nodded and disappeared into the back room. He returned shortly with a thin file and a small man holding a pair of ankle boots. The group of young women failed to cover their gasps and excited whispers of, "Is that him?"

"That's him!"

"The shoemaker!"

Interesting. It seemed he had a reputation that inspired wide and curious eyes. The shoemaker was handsome but not my type, with thick black hair, narrow eyes, a sharp jawline, and a full head shorter than I was.

"Here is Ms. Hallman's file with her foot measurements and receipts," Dixon said, handing over a slim file. Gesturing to the smaller man, he said, "This is Mr. Schuster, our in-house shoemaker. He personally customizes all of our boots for each buyer. If you'll excuse me, there are customers in need of assistance."

Micro took the file, and I barely acknowledged Dixon's departure as I eagerly reached to shake Mr. Schuster's hand.

"PI Truth Locke," I said as my introduction.

"PI?" he asked in a deep bass with a gravelly texture. "Is something wrong?"

"I'm here to find out," I said, gesturing for him to take my handshake.

His squat fingers and palm clasped mine, and I leaped into a Reading. It only took two seconds of a double-hand-pump to confirm my suspicions.

"You're an elf," I said. Micro did a double take between the little person and me. Mr. Schuster didn't look like the textbook depiction of a Fairy elf because coming to magic-negating Noir had transformed him. On top of that, he'd made additional alterations by cutting his angelic hair and dyeing it black, wearing platform shoes to appear taller, and filing his sharp nails to the nubs.

Schuster's eyes and mouth opened. "I—" He glared at the departing sales clerk and lowered his voice. "Are the salesmen spreading false advertisements again?"

Was that the reason for the whispers about him?

"What false advertisements?"

He waved his hand as if to shoo away the topic. "Nothing. Those commission workers will say anything to hype a sale. How did you know that I was an elf?"

"I recently spoke with a native of Margen about the characteristics of your kind. You have a fetish for well-crafted wearables and have a saintly work ethic despite your rough upbringing. Is that why you came to Noir and cut your hair? Fresh cut, fresh start? Oh, shoot. The police will think you did it. I believe you're innocent, but I'll need to prove it."

His brow furrowed. "Excuse me?"

Oops, did I say that all out loud? Some futures were better left unknown. Besides, it wasn't a sure future, just a high probability.

His uneasy expression cried out for an explanation. I said, "Just because you're an elf working at the shoe store where the victims shopped doesn't mean you killed them."

"Excuse me?" he repeated with a hint of defensive anger.

"Mr. Schuster," Micro asked, lifting a strip of receipt tape from the file, "is this line the receipt code for a Lucille boot sale?"

"Yes," he said, giving me worried glances.

Micro passed Henrietta's receipt over to me and pointed at an item line named Lucille. "Then it's true. Henrietta shopped here and bought those boots. Do the police need to do a search of her home to prove they're missing?"

I shook my head. "Their mere absence wouldn't prove that she was wearing them during her murder. She could have lent them out to someone or simply misplaced them. We'd need the receipts for at least two other victims with those boots to prove the connection."

"Excuse me," Mr. Schuster said again. "Is something the matter?"

"We have reason to suspect," I said, "that a killer's targeting the buyers of those boots. We'll need you to pull them off the shelves until further notice."

"What?" He frowned deeply. "That's preposterous! Knees and Toes shoes are finely crafted but not worth a life. That boot in particular is custom-made for each customer according to their foot length, arch, and width. Anyone robbing those boots would be unable to wear them comfortably."

"I don't know why," I said, considering possibilities. Why did the Sole Stealer target and steal the boots? Despite their expense, they'd be a pain to sell because of their customization. Could the murdering thief want the boots for their materials? "Regardless," I said, "the boot is a connecting factor between two victims. I need to see all of your customer's files and receipts to confirm the rest."

Mr. Schuster barked with a laugh and gestured for us to follow him to the back room. "Our receipts are organized by customer. If you were cops wasting your time and my taxes, I'd wave you away, but since you're PIs, be my guest."

In the back room, there were rows upon rows of shoes in boxes. There was also an entire wall of filing cabinets. Mr. Schuster gestured widely to the collection. "Here you are."

I stared at the wall of filing cabinets with columns of drawers keeping rows of files stuffed with thousands of receipts.

"First things first," I said. "If we can find the receipts of just three of the victims, that should be enough to call suspicion to the boots and pull them from the shelves. It won't keep the Sole Stealer from killing, but it'll confirm the boots as the link between our victims."

"Alright." Micro nodded. "What are their names?"

I listed the names of the six known victims as Micro searched the filing cabinets. Despite it being his first time in the room, he found all six women with folders of receipts like a librarian. Simply finding their files confirmed that all six victims shopped at Knees and Toes. Considering the dozens of shoe stores in Shigaqua, that fact alone was a strong connection. Every employee at Knees and Toes just became a stronger suspect.

Micro and I each picked up a file to scan every receipt line by line for the Lucille boots. One victim had a single receipt in her file with a single item. Lucille.

"Son of a gun," I swore, staring at the six boot receipts of the six victims. "This confirms it. I'll call Detective Montgomery to let him know, and the police can ensure the boot is taken off the market. Hopefully, he'll send us back up."

"Back up?" Micro asked. "For what? Are we in danger?"

"Only of tedious monotony." I gestured to the wall of cabinets. "We need to search every single file to see who else has bought those boots. They could be targets. If we can find them and protect them before the Sole Stealer attacks, we can catch him before he kills again."

I cringed at the sight of our workload while Micro squared his shoulders and went straight to work on the first drawer. Reluctantly, I started at the opposite end. Too bad Aeron had a date and wasn't here. He had a certain spiritual friend who could analyze files like a Procedural computer. Micro was my next best option though, going through three files for every one of mine.

"Your skills are wasted at By the Foot," I said.

Micro grunted. "Jo hasn't fired me yet, so I'm satisfied."

We had this conversation on a regular basis. He would argue that By the Foot paid the bills. I'd argue that working as a statistician or as a computer at some high-end government center would also pay the bills. Then, Micro would doubt his capabilities and say he couldn't compete because he'd been fired from too many jobs. I'd share my theory that he'd been fired because he inevitably rearranged his boss's messy files, finding incriminating evidence or throwing off their precious messy system. Then Micro would shrug like it didn't matter.

After another five minutes of receipt scanning, Micro scoffed. "I'm not sure how we'll find anything in this mess. The files themselves might be alphabetized, but the receipts are shoved in with no timeline. They have receipts up to seven years ago, but if we could narrow our timeline to the last year with the boot's release, it would save us a buttload of time. As it is, it'll take us ages to go through every file and receipt."

I nodded and rubbed my temple from a growing headache. "I'll go make that call to Montgomery and ask for aides. Will you be okay here by yourself for a bit?"

He waved me away. "Thirty-one to you. I don't mind puzzles and paperwork. I'll be positive as a proton until they kick me out at closing."

I smiled gratefully. "You're incredible. Have I told you how much—"

"You love me? Every day. Go on, be amazing."

⚹

After my call to Det. Montgomery from the store's phone, I rejoined Micro until two officers arrived as back up. Promising to catch up on the morrow, I returned to the temporary office of Visionary Investigations to reconsider my new knowledge. Nita was already there, going over the files of the various crime scenes of the Sole Stealer. I shared my findings from By the Foot and Knees and Toes while Nita listened methodically.

"So, it's not a coincidence that they all wore the same shoe?"

"It's highly unlikely," I said, "but why else would the Sole Stealer steal their shoes?"

Nita half shrugged. "Maybe they like that particular shoe. You said it was a heeled boot with velvet lining? Velvet isn't easy to run in. It's a surprise each of the victims made it as far as they did."

I nodded and frowned, joining her side to look over the crime scenes of the various victims. Those shoes weren't the type for wearing casually around the house, but every victim had received their threat and admonition to start running while at home. Had they all been wearing those boots? The killer must have marked them early as targets and watched for the perfect moment as they wore the boots, but before they left the house.

The office door swung open with a squeal as Aeron entered. He called around the little false wall, "Nita? Truth?"

"Here," I said.

His face popped around the corner with his typical charming smile. "Did you learn anything?"

"Yeah—"

"Yes!" Nita said brightly. Oh, *sidera*. Sometimes that kid brought out the worst in her. "Truth confirmed that every victim bought the same boot from Knees and Toes. She has Micro and the police looking for other buyers and possible targets now. How was your lunch date?"

Aeron raised an eyebrow at her change of demeanor, but answered, "It went well. Considering the Case and the serial killer using cocaine and fentanyl as their lethal weapon, I asked Bianca—er, Officer Mendoza if they knew of any local drug dealers who could supply someone with such quantities. She said they've noticed an uptick in drug usage in town with particular concoctions, but haven't found the source."

I hummed in thought, considering Shigaqua's elusive weapons dealer. "It's possible that Sponsor has expanded his dealership from weapons to drugs."

Aeron's lips pinched into a worried line. "That would be concerning, but drug dealers are typically easier to catch than weapon dealers because their clients can be desperate and moody."

Nita cleared her throat. "Versus weapons clients who can be…cocky?"

Oh. My. *Sidera.* Did Nita just make a pun?

Aeron coughed with a laugh. "Takes one to know one. Bianca didn't have any other information for me, but she accepted my invitation for dinner tomorrow. I'm debating whether to take her out for Western or Fantasy foods."

"Why not go for Fantasy?" Nita said, twirling a strand of her hair. When had she loosened it from her usual no-nonsense bun? "That way you can charm her with facts about your homeland."

"Sssure," Aeron slurred. "Did something happen while I was gone? You seem, uh…extra enthusiastic."

"I just thought I should be less serious."

Palm to face. "Nita, maybe I should explain something to you." I beckoned her over to whisper, "When Aeron said he wasn't interested in Jessica because she was too serious, I think he was referring to her being too serious about their relationship, not too serious as a person."

Nita blinked at me as if I'd confided in her that two plus two equaled four. Speaking loudly, she said, "But you don't need to worry about me ever being serious in a relationship. Well, not until I remember my past."

Aeron frowned. "What brought this on?"

"It doesn't matter," I said, "because I forbid you two from dating. For your own good."

Nita gave no reaction while Aeron chuckled and shook his head. "Don't worry, my mom taught me not to have too-attractive girlfriends. The pretty ones always come with crazy exes, and by the looks of you—" he gestured to Nita "—you needed a restraining order."

I ducked my face behind my palm again and wasn't sure whether to groan at his twisted flirt or smirk at the truth of his words. He had no idea the kinds of ex-relationships Nita had. Technically, I didn't either, but I knew there was something about her past that would explode in all of our faces. Her palms said as much.

Unfortunately, his teasing to persuade his disinterest caused Nita's cheeks to redden. For being a little smart aleck, Aeron had no idea what he was doing. If he did, then he had no idea what he was getting himself into with Nita. He was a boy who liked to push buttons.

As if the whole conversation hadn't even fazed him, Aeron continued to grin at Nita. "But on that topic, it's been a while since we've done a getting-to-know-Nita experiment. I heard there's a new roller-skating rink worth visiting on the southern border of Cozy. It would require an hour-and-a-half drive, but we can play more getting-to-know-you games in the car. You can learn a lot about a person during a road trip." He finished by wiggling his eyebrows mischievously.

I narrowed my eyes. "Your car only seats two people, meaning you'd be going by yourselves. You want to plan a day-trip right after your date with another woman?"

He stared at me in surprise. "A day trip isn't a date, especially considering the arguing that usually comes with road trips. Besides, it's only a drive in and out, so we wouldn't need to book a hotel for the classic 'only one bed' problem. Even still, I'm not dating Bianca exclusively. We just met up during her lunch break, and we talked about work. You could hardly call it a date. It's not like we kissed or anything."

"So that makes it alright to flirt with Nita?"

"I'm not flirting," he defended, looking between me and Nita, as if asking Nita to agree. "I'm just being friendly. Who says you can't plan a road trip with a friend?"

"You're not friendly to me in that way."

Nita added, "She has a point."

He squirmed slightly. "You're my boss. Do you want me to—"

"*Sidera*, no," I cursed. "But I don't think Nita wants you to either."

We turned to Nita for her opinion, but she'd returned to her typical silent-with-no-opinion. Shoot, that probably meant that she did want him to flirt with her, but would never admit it.

Aeron shrugged innocently. "I mean no harm in it. I think you're overreacting."

"You're serious?" I balked. "Try treating me the way you treat Nita and tell me it's not awkward."

"Because you're my boss."

"Because you're flirting," I emphasized. "Even if I wasn't your boss, you wouldn't treat me the way you treat Nita because teasing is a way to show your attraction to someone."

He narrowed his eyes at me with a challenging stare, then raised his lips into a smirk.

"Oh, I wouldn't, would I?"

Oh, no.

He took long and slow steps to me like a man with his mark. "I wouldn't smile at you, joke with you, or—dare I say—tease you as a friend as I do with Nita? But the thing is, you're my boss. What would people think if I acted friendly with my boss?" He rubbed his nose at an angle to make it obvious.

"Brown nosing." The gesture was a clear invitation to study his handsome inherited features that reminded me of someone I'd chosen to forget.

Shoot, what had I done? I'd been safe from his noncommittal flirtations. Until now.

He chuckled and nudged me gently with his elbow. "Supernaturals, you look terrified. You need to loosen up. Come on, Truth."

He took my hands in his and then playfully swung my arms back and forth. Blue-green eyes and a royally charming smile grinned at me.

"Theo, stop—"

The name was out before my consciousness caught up with me. Aeron—*Aeron*—blinked wide eyes at me while his mouth wiggled with discomfort. I could guess why. He hated it when I reminded him that I knew his secret. I knew his Fantasy identity—his royal inheritance and heritage, and even his parents.

But with that simple slip, I revealed my own secret. I didn't simply know his dad as Marquis Theodor Fromm. I knew him as Theo. And what had caused me to blurt his name from memories? Aeron's inherited eyes, smile, and *teasing*.

Oh, *lapides*. Did I just reveal my once-upon-a-very-long-time-ago crush on his dad? About the first day I met Theo and shook his hand, I saw his potential and our compatibility. About the time I confessed my attraction, and he denied me like a gentleman because he was waiting for Cupid's arrow. About how I was there when Cupid finally shot Aeron's dad with True Love at First Sight but not his mom. About the moment I kind of sabotaged their first hang out by spoiling Pansy's secrets because I thought Cupid had made a mistake in matching a gentleman with a killer. About my meeting with Mr. Mystery and jumping at the opportunity to transfer to Spyglass University next semester because it was what I wanted, and I'd given up on Theo, who was head-over-heels for his future wife. About the four years it took for me to fully get over him, because it took another eight years until I met the second person who was equally compatible with me.

Aeron released my hands and took an awkward step back as if I'd told him the whole story of my university days with his parents. No, he couldn't know all of that, but it didn't matter. I was past my past feelings.

I tilted my head at Aeron. "Did I prove my point that you are, in fact, flirting with Nita by demonstrating the awkwardness of treating me the same way?"

"Sure," he mumbled bashfully.

"Alright. Can we get back to the murder?"

"Yes, please," Aeron sighed with relief, eager to change to an easier subject.

CHAPTER 5

My team and I theorized about suspects and their possible motives for killing people for shoes until the evening wore late and we each went home. Micro called to report that he'd found one more person by the name of Tracy Cooper who'd bought the boots. I passed the word on to Det. Montgomery, advising that he put a security detail on her right away. Closing my eyes for some much-needed sleep, I hoped Aeron would have productive dreams.

"Nothing?" I asked when we met again in our makeshift office, warming our hands and insides with morning tea.

Aeron shook his head. "My spirit friends are already spread thin between Sponsor and his cronies. This isn't Fantasy or Horror. Most spirits in Mystery move on to the Unknown Beyond unless they want to cry from the dust about their murders. Those who remain are linked to certain people or places and rarely divert. They can't be everywhere following everyone, waiting for someone to put on an elf costume and go on a killing spree."

I groaned and rubbed my temples. Even with Aeron's un-seen army, we hadn't been able to pick up any clues about the Sole Stealer's identity.

It had taken us months to identify Shigaqua's leading mob-ster, commonly referred to as Sponsor. Starting with only a sketch artist's depiction of Sponsor's number one man, we eventually located him then had Aeron's spirits follow him until they caught the number one man accepting orders from a wealthy businessman named Mal Testa. Even knowing Sponsor's identity, the police struggled to prove a just cause to arrest him. Aeron's spirits tailed him night and day, but we couldn't prove Mal Testa's involvement with the local gangs associated with "Sponsor." All we had was a growing list of his partners, associates, and benefactors, ranging from an elderly man named Archie Morris to a little girl named Karen Capone.

Lowering my fingers from my temples, I sighed. "Is there any way we can narrow the field of suspects?"

Aeron shrugged. "I've told the spirits to leave alone anyone who might be an immigrated dwarf. They despise elves. It's possible they might want to frame an elf, but I have a hard time imagining a dwarf stooping as low as to dress like one."

Nita stared at him, slightly bewildered. "Your brain con-fuses me."

Aeron chuckled. "If you knew my parents, you'd be amazed at how normal I am."

"Hah!" I barked with a laugh. "I find that ironically relata-ble. Aeron, your parents are normal compared to mine."

He blinked at me with his wide blue-green eyes. "Oh, curses. I don't even want to know."

"Unless you have time for a full story, no. No, you do not."

Nita frowned slightly. "I thought you were adopted?"

"I was. I'm talking about my adoptive parents. My biological parents might have been normal, but they named me Truth after all."

Aeron laughed. "Point. The worst I got was a gender-neutral version of Aaron because my father hoped I'd be a girl."

I joined in his laughter until I realized who wasn't laughing. Nita. She couldn't join us. I had named her myself because she didn't know her parents or even her birth name.

Following my faltering laugh and gaze, Aeron cleared his throat and nudged Nita.

"Speaking of parents, I asked my mom about your amnesia."

"Pansy?" I asked. "I thought she'd studied to be a paramedic?"

"At university, yes. But in Fantasy, she has researched connections and relations between Fairy's healing magic and her Contemporary medical knowledge. Child mortality rates decreased by thirty percent thanks to her influence."

I tapped down any jealousy of a one-time peer's achievements. I didn't need to save a duchy. Just one individual at a time was good enough for me. "What did she have to say about Nita's amnesia?"

He shrugged. "If it was a magical curse, then only a magical cure would heal her. If not, she may never recover her original memories. It's only a matter of time, but the longer it takes, the less likely it becomes. My mom actually seemed a little irked by how common amnesia is, as if some god wants to make every tenth Adventure include someone with memory loss problems."

Nita pinched her mouth into a thin and thoughtful line. "Considering the fact that I was found on the banks of Lake Mishi, it's safe to say my amnesia wasn't caused by a magical curse. Magic doesn't work here."

"Exactly." Aeron nodded. "Meaning we'll continue to test your memories and personal traits to dig up your past, present, and possible future."

Aeron's flirty smile triggered one too many of my own memories.

I needed to get out of that little office with Aeron's flirting and reminders of his parents. The best way to distract myself would be some pleasant interactions with the person who was equally compatible with me.

I stood with a thought. "Actually, we do have a clue to help you narrow down the field for your ghosts. We know that all the victims wore the same shoe custom-made and purchased from Knees and Toes. If we can complete their list of buyers for that boot, then we can center our research around them."

Aeron frowned thoughtfully. "Except that wouldn't point us toward the killer, only possibilities of his next victims."

Nita gave a half shrug. "Well, it's better than nothing."

"Also," I added, "the Sole Stealer always provided proof of his stalking in his threatening letter to make them start running. If your ghosts notice anyone stalking the possible targets, that could be the killer. Can you ask the ghosts to keep an eye on Tracy Cooper?"

Aeron's smile returned, and he nodded. "Now, that's a plan we can work with. But who else has bought those shoes? Oh, wait," he said with false concern. "It looks like you need to visit the shoe store again. Are you planning to pick up Micro for help? Nita, we have things to do here. Sorry, Truth. Looks like you're going by yourself again."

I scowled at the little stinker. How had he learned about my crush on my best friend? All the more reason I wouldn't want him with me for my second research trip to the shoe stores.

The little bell above the door announced my lone entrance into By the Foot again. No one was at the register up front, but I knew an employee would be along soon from the door-bell. No need to ring the Bell of Most Annoying Customer on the counter. To use Micro's words.

The man himself walked around an aisle, sending my chest into extra rhythms. You'd think I'd be used to it by now, but my eyes couldn't help appreciating his smart looks.

"Welco—oh, thirty-one, Truth. Twice in two days? How's the Case going?"

His curiosity and smile were contagious as I smiled back. "You know I'm not at liberty to discuss the details, but are you available to help me research other buyers of that shoe?"

"Sure! As soon as I finish my shift in an hour," Micro said with extra enthusiasm. Seeing my questioning surprise, he sheepishly shrugged. "What? I'm curious about the Case. I want to help. But my shift doesn't end until after lunch."

I smirked. "Curiosity killed the cat. But it's okay. They have nine lives."

Micro laughed. "You know, according to Schrodinger's thought theory, if you open the box, *your* curiosity killed the cat."

I joined in his laughter. "I always thought it was the cat's curiosity. In that case, if the idiom refers to someone else's curiosity killing cats, then you're safe to join me."

"They have nine lives after all." Micro nudged me with another laugh.

Sidera, why couldn't conversations be this easy with everyone else? Micro not only understood me, but accepted me. I cared about him—maybe a little too much. We'd been casual friends for years and were too old to bother with slow games.

If he liked me, he would have said so by now, right? I'd made my friendship with Theo awkward by explaining our compatibility and confessing my attraction to him after our first meeting. I wouldn't—no, I *couldn't* ruin my friendship with Micro by asking for more.

"Anyways," he said, "I'm glad you stopped by. I did some research after you left yesterday. See, I recognized the names you pulled from the receipts—the names of the buyers of those boots. Also, you name-dropped the Sole Stealer and hinted at that Case. Truth, is that the Case you're working on?"

"*Sidera et lapides*," I cursed as unintended confirmation.

Micro groaned, "Ah, four. You're investigating a serial killer? Those are dangerous Cases, Truth."

"I know," I said. "Which is one reason I have Nita on my team. But she's not with me right now, so I wondered if you'd join me as I visited Knees and Toes to get more information about their boot sales."

He cringed. "I'm a poor substitute for Nita. Also, I'm scheduled to work for another hour. Jo's here and could easily handle the work by herself, but she wouldn't let people off early even if Horror froze over."

I silently pouted about the situation. Micro's eyes said that he wanted to join me, to get away from the minimum-wage occupation and help me solve murders by sticking his nose in a bunch of files.

"Come on," I urged. "Can it hurt to ask? You can blame me, and say I'm hijacking you for a Case."

Micro rolled his jaw as he considered every worst possible scenario, but ended with a tight smile. "I'll ask."

With quivering fists of excitement, I followed Micro through the store. The scent of cigarettes grew with each step toward the back room. He opened the door to spy on his manager sitting at a table of Brannock Devices for measuring feet, smoking coke, and checking off an inventory list.

Micro's manager was a squat woman, shaped more like a pear than a carrot like Micro. She had small beady eyes, a large round nose, and a pointed chin. Of what little I knew about fashion told me that Jo wore the finest for casual business-wear of a pink dress. She wasn't wearing her Lucile boots but another pair with fine fur-lining and leather.

She looked up at Micro with a slightly annoyed, questioning look.

"Hey, Jo. I had a quick question."

"Jo Merivale?" I asked, stepping forward and reaching for a handshake. "I'm PI Truth Locke. Micro's told me all about you."

"All good things, I bet." Jo grinned proudly, but held back her hands. "Michael's told me a bit about you too, doll. You're a real psychic to read people's palms?"

"Not exactly a psychic." Knowing about my ability often made people anxious—either to let me show off or to keep their privacy. It was one of the reasons I preferred working in Noir versus Procedural. In Noir, I didn't need consent to use my ability. Unfortunately, when people refused to shake hands with me, it made me all the more curious. "I could show you if—"

"You don't need to prove anything to me. I already believe in magic. And you can make it work, even in Noir? Even when you're outside of Fantasy?"

"Yeah, but that's because it's not really magic, it's—"

"I knew it! I knew magic was real, even in drab Noir. People think I'm crazy, but your gifts are proof! Michael, you had a question for me?"

I blinked, wondering who was more confused—her or me? I didn't have magic; I had an ability. Yes, they both came from Fantasy, but they worked under different rules.

Before I could try correcting her, Micro said, "Oh, yeah. Truth's working on a Case right now and needs my help."

"Your help?" Jo scoffed. "What help can you offer?"

I stepped up. "Micro's one of the best people I know for organizing and making sense of paperwork. We came to ask if he could leave early because I need his help right away to look over receipts at Knees and Toes—"

Jo's face pinched with suspicion at Micro. "Knees and Toes? You're asking to leave early? To do work at Knees and Toes? Our competitor?"

"Are you actually competitors?" I asked. "You sell completely different styles. Their shoes are customized luxuries made by professional craftsmen, and these shoes are…" How could I describe the cheap production shoes of By the Foot without sounding degrading?

Jo's pinched expression opened with anger. "Are what? Not customized? Not luxuries? Not made by professionals?"

Micro cringed and raised his hands in defense. "That's not what she meant. Truth can be a little callous sometimes, but—"

Jo's eyes flared. "You dare to defend her, you backstabbing traitor?"

Micro groaned and dropped his face into his palm.

With an almost comically red face, Jo pointed at the door. "Get. Out. And leave your nametag."

Micro's face shot back to his manager's. "Wait—no, please, Jo!"

I grinned and whispered loudly to Micro. "Wow. Let's go before she changes her mind." Calling back to Jo, I said, "Also, you might want to burn your Lucille boots from Knees and Toes. They seem to be a target for the Sole Stealer."

Micro kept his face ducked as he removed his nametag. Stepping outside, he slowly slid his hand down his face. When his eyes reappeared, they were frowning at me.

"What?" I asked. "Isn't this a good thing?"

He groaned. "It's hard to stay mad at you when you have no idea what just happened."

"What just happened?"

"I got fired."

Wait…what? Just now? How did I miss that? Was it because he asked to go home early? Or…

"Was it something I said?" I asked. It wouldn't be the first time that telling the truth, the whole truth, and nothing but the truth had caused trouble. It just didn't make sense to me why people lied or talked around their thoughts.

He sighed heavily. "Not like this was my dream job, but…it was something to save me from job hunting and rejection."

"I'm sorry," I said, not sure if I was apologizing or simply sympathizing.

"Meh, whatever." He turned around and shouted at the store, "One-thirty-two!"

"What's that one?"

He raised both middles, saying, "One-twenty-eight plus four."

Despite his anger and frustration, I laughed. His smile cracked, and I knew he'd be alright.

"That's right," I said, slipping my arm around his elbow to direct him away from By the Foot. "Your palms say you're meant for greater things, anyway."

CHAPTER 6

Making our way to Micro's Buggy, a police car sped by, sounding its siren. My subconscious started singing along.

"ooOOO-EEEee-ooOOO—"

I clamped my mouth shut when I noticed Micro restraining his laughter.

"Sorry," I squeaked behind my hands. Old habits die hard. It wasn't even my own habit, really. Singing along with sirens was my mama's thing. A side-effect from her dog days.

He coughed as part of his laugh escaped. "No wonder you're not on the force."

"Hey!" I nudged him playfully but turned my attention as the siren stopped. The colorful lights flashed down a few blocks and around a corner.

"They're close. Do you mind if we go investigate?"

Micro shrugged. "I suddenly find my day open, so why not?"

We took off at a jog to the scene of suspicion, finding a female officer speaking into her car radio, requesting a forensic team. A dead body?

Stepping closer, I recognized Officer Taylors and called out to her.

She cringed when she recognized me. "How did you get here so fast? And who's your partner? That's not the haunted boy."

"I was in the area. This is my friend, Michael. He's a shoe specialist. Speaking of which, what happened to your victim's shoes?"

The officer looked around, but shrugged. "She wasn't wearing any."

"That doesn't make sense." I rounded the body to the woman's bare feet. "She's fully dressed in business attire, including pantyhose. We're in the middle of a commercial district, so it's not like she left her apartment sans shoes for a quick mail grab."

Officer Taylors muttered a curse under her breath. Speaking into her walkie-talkie, "Captain, this is Officer Taylors on 221st Street with the found body. We might have another victim of the Sole Stealer."

The blood drained from my face. We'd been too late to save the next victim. But if we were lucky, maybe Aeron had a trace on them.

Eager to help while the body was fresh, I gestured for permission. "I've been hired onto the Sole Stealer Case. Can I take a closer look at the body?"

The officer grumbled, but waved her permission. She kept a close eye on me as I crouched over the victim.

The woman was large in every direction. For being what I guessed was in her early forties, she had deep lines around her mouth to express her lifetime of emotions. I imagined her as a force to be reckoned with wherever she went. Her dark brown hair was cropped to her chin and covered with a hat that bowled and brimmed below her ears. Despite her pantyhose, I easily noticed the scratches and bruises along her legs in various stages of healing.

Typically, I focused on the hands of victims, but with a possible Sole Stealer victim, I went to her feet. I needed a bare foot to Read, so I switched out my filing blade to carefully cut through the nylon stocking. Thankfully, Officer Taylors only questioned my disturbance of the body with a raised eyebrow.

"She was definitely killed by the Sole Stealer," I said. "She has no calluses and perfectly manicured toes. Her outer toes curve inward, showing this woman wore a lifetime of constraining shoes. But with no calluses, you can bet her shoes were custom made." Rounding up to her hands, I picked up her left one for a quick study. "This woman was married or very recently divorced."

"How can you tell?" Officer Taylors asked. "There's no ring."

"There was a ring worn for a good amount of time, based on the thinness of her finger's base."

"But it's gone now," the officer said. "So, she's recently divorced, or she removed it while having an affair. Or the Sole Stealer took it with the shoes."

"No, it wasn't stolen," I said. "There's no swelling from a forced removal. She took it off herself to keep it from damage. Judging by her expensive business attire, I doubt she works as a maid or pool cleaner. She probably has a business card in her purse."

Officer Taylors rummaged through a mock-brand leather purse until she pulled out a card. "She's a social worker."

"Ah," I said as it all clicked. "She works with underprivileged kids and is overly cautious. Despite her wardrobe, she doesn't want to flash jewelry in front of them, so she takes off her ring. I bet it's quite the rock."

The officer flipped open a notepad and began to transcribe notes. "But she has scars of abuse. My money's on the husband attempting to stage her death to look like the Sole Stealer."

"She wouldn't have called it an abusive relationship," I said.

Officer Taylors scoffed, hovering beside the body. "The abused person hardly ever recognizes the abuse unless it's pointed out by someone else or it's too late."

"No," I said. "Not for this woman. She loved her partner and would have fought to keep him, even though she also worked hard to erase all evidence of him from her clothes. He probably doesn't get all the attention and walks he needs."

"Uh, what?"

"She has a dog," I explained. "Small size, but he's a jumper. The scars on her legs are mostly on her calves from his claws—meaning she doesn't take him on many walks, since pavement naturally files a dog's claws."

"How did you figure that?" Officer Taylors asked. "Did you find a dog hair on her?"

I could have explained my dog knowledge because of my mama, but that explanation tended to raise more questions that weren't important at the moment.

"No," I said instead. "As I mentioned, she tried to hide evidence of him from her clothes, which means she has a lint roller in her purse or vehicle."

Officer Taylors leaned down to finger through the victim's bag. "Alright, she has a lint roller. She also has an ID—Marissa Daw."

I breathed in and internalized her name. We hadn't caught the killer fast enough, and she'd suffered the consequences.

Micro watched from behind the police car as I worked. He seemed to analyze me as much as I analyzed the body. What did he see in me? Did he like what he saw?

I buried my blush and returned to the woman's feet. Picking up her left foot, I Read her. Officer Taylors gave me a funny look again, but I easily ignored her as I became swept into the rivers of Marissa's life.

Marissa had lived a good, quiet life. She worked as a social worker, studying families and placing foster kids in good homes, checking on them regularly, and befriending even some rebellious teenagers. She worked hard, feeling like a chisel against a mountain, but she found satisfaction in what she accomplished. Marissa was the middle child of five, following her older sister's encouragement to attend university and graduate with honors. She met up with her siblings once a month to have dinner with their mom.

As a child, she'd behaved, practiced her violin, and stretched for her ballet classes. She'd bought the furry-heeled boots because they reminded her of walking tall with a fluffy tutu, dancing across a stage and feeling like a princess ballerina. And she'd been killed for it.

I slipped out of the Reading, feeling drained and depressed. I wasn't able to see the rivers of future possibilities in the dead, but based on her past and trajectory, I imagined a bright future of options that could have impacted others for good. But those rivers had been dammed and closed off. All because she bought the wrong shoes.

"Officer Taylors," I called. "I can't stay and wait for Det. Montgomery to arrive as the lead on this Case. Micro and I are headed over to Knees and Toes to make sure their Lucille boot is off the market and to find other buyers who might need protection. We can't let this happen again."

I excused myself from the scene and drove to Knees and Toes with Micro. A different employee—Stephen—greeted us, and Mr. Schuster spared us barely a glance as we entered the back room of his workshop and the cabinets. As Micro went directly to the cabinets to pick up where he'd left off from the night before, I loomed over Mr. Schuster's work. He seemed to be working on a woman's one-inch heel that cut beneath the ankles.

"Mr. Schuster," I asked, "can you think of any reason someone might kill for boots?"

He gave a half shrug as he continued to work. "How would I know? You humans are strange, always saying things you don't mean and doing things that aren't right. I'd hoped to find people of justice in Mystery, but it turns out you're all broken."

I frowned at that, finding it oddly agreeable to my own misunderstandings about people's behavior. "Mr. Schuster," I asked, "as an elf from Fairy, do you have magic?"

He eyed me with a mischievous glint and smile. "Maybe I do, maybe I don't. Not like I'd tell you."

I studied his quick and precise handiwork as he cut the shoe leather. "It's a clever marketing technique, but they don't make posters about their shoemaker embedding magic in their shoes. Is that in case people come looking for magical shoes, become disappointed, and then call out false advertising? Was the magic that's common to your kind lost when you crossed the border?"

He turned back to his workstation with a grunt. Had that been a grunt of denial or affirmation? Maybe a denial in his own mind. Maybe he didn't want to believe that he'd lost his magic.

"You still have your skills," I said. "Like Aeron's and my abilities, you kept the talents you were born with, but magic—a trade you learn and develop over time—becomes muted. You have the skills of an excellent cobbler, but you can't weave magic into the shoes to make the wearer dance or run faster. Isn't that right?"

Mr. Schuster grunted again. "You might know that, but our customers don't. Those salesmen out there love spilling my secret about being a Fairy elf, knowing that the reputation of my kind will sell more shoes. That's why they hired me after their first elf disappeared."

"Disappeared? Like magic?"

He shrugged. "Who knows? I wasn't here yet."

"When was that?"

"About a month ago. Her name was Ms. Stump. She was the one who made all those boots that you recalled."

A month ago? That was about when the Sole Stealer started killing. My eyes wandered to the row of cabinets with receipts. The salesmen couldn't remember all the names of those who'd bought the Lucille boots, but an elf who customized the boots for each buyer would remember every pair of boots sold to every customer.

Pondering his words, I left to join Micro. After his hours of combing through files yesterday, he was only through one filing cabinet among several. He'd found two more buyers of the boots.

I was barely through my first folder when Det. Montgomery burst into the back room.

"Is there a Mr. Schuster in here?"

Disturbed again from his work, the shoemaker sighed with annoyance. "I am he. What is it you want?"

Montgomery slapped down a magazine advertisement for the Lucille boots. "Ain't you the maker of these shoes?"

"Boots."

"What?"

"Those are not shoes. Those are boots."

I smirked at the elf's semantics and loophole wording to deflect from the question. Det. Montgomery rolled his eyes. "Ain't you the maker of these boots?"

"Who wants to know?"

The detective growled. "The families of murdered victims! Your fancy-schmancy boots ain't on the shelves no more because anyone who buys them gets killed by someone who looks like an elf! And guess what I just found out at the personnel records center? You're an elf!"

Lapides. "Montgomery, it's not—"

"Save it, Locke," Det. Montgomery growled. He grabbed Mr. Schuster's wrist and pulled the little craftsman to his feet. "You're under arrest for the murders of the Sole Stealer."

"P.S. Montgomery," I said, glowering at the man. "You have the wrong man. As usual."

He sneered back. "We'll find out at the station. Come on. I know how slippery you creatures can be. You ain't getting away from me."

I followed after the detective and his cuffed victim, shouting what little I knew about the immigrant to prove his innocence. Montgomery listened to none of it. He drove away with the shoemaker in the back of his cab.

I groaned with frustration as I returned to the filing cabinets. The best way to free an innocent suspect was to find the real culprit. I massaged my temples from a growing headache. I didn't want to catch the Sole Stealer as he preyed on another victim. I wanted him off the streets before anyone else was threatened. No more Marissas. No more Henriettas. No more families crying for their lost mother, sister, or daughter.

A hand on my shoulder startled me. Micro stared at me with worried eyes.

"Hey, are you alright?"

"Just tired," I sighed. "And frustrated."

He nodded. "I've got this covered if you want to head home for a lunchtime nap. I'll give you a call as soon as we find anything."

I hesitated, eyeing the folders and files. He didn't need my expertise in this. I could pretend to go home and take a nap, but I knew sleep would evade me. I'd likely end up knitting and rethinking the Case. And maybe that was what I needed to do.

I sighed with relief and a smile. "Thank you. Have I told you how much I love you?"

"Every day."

CHAPTER 7

We hadn't been fast enough to save the next victim. That thought stuttered like a record player in my mind as it screamed with frustration, sorrow, and disappointment. I knew better than to take full responsibility for her death—I hadn't killed her, the Sole Stealer had—but it still hurt to think I hadn't been smart enough to stop him.

After leaving Micro at the shoe store, I couldn't go back to the office. The elevated tracks were too loud, and I knew I'd end up staring at the wall, lost in depressing thoughts.

Instead, I went home. My colorful knitted decor and plethora of plants welcomed me. I warmed the kettle, burned some incense to stimulate my mind, and pulled out my latest knitting project. Nita joked about measuring the difficulty of a Case based on how many granny-squares I knitted in the process.

Rounding my second row, my ears were attacked by two high pitches. I jumped in my seat and nearly stabbed myself as the kettle screamed and the telephone rang. I ran to my kitchen to remove the kettle from the hot burner, then dashed around the corner to my table phone.

"Hello?" I asked, heart pounding. Was it Micro from the store? Had he found receipts of other potential victims?

"Hey, Truth!"

I sighed with disappointment despite the warmth that came from the sound of the older woman's smiling voice. "How are you? Did I catch you at a bad time?"

"Mama," I said, slowing my pulse. "Hey, it's not a bad time. I was just about to have some tea while knitting."

"You're knitting? Is your current Case a doozy?"

I rolled my eyes even though she couldn't see them. "I only just started. Did you need something, or did you just want to chat?" Maybe some brainstorming with my mama could help clear my mind. Shasta Van Pier had been my first teacher to look for solutions outside the box.

She hummed thoughtfully. "I don't mean to take you away from your work, but I wondered when you might stop by again. You usually come to visit for the harvest markets."

Shoot, I'd completely forgotten with the business problems of starting an agency. Pile on the stress of a serial killer, and I'd lost track of time. But I was currently free, waiting for paperwork from Micro to tell Aeron to tell his spirits to shadow possible victims… There wasn't much for me to do at the moment. "Right, I can come down today if it's not too late."

"Not at all! Actually, Truth, could you pick me up on your way to the market?"

I sighed. "Did they revoke your license again?"

"I swear, they have a vendetta against me. You can't do anything to convince these local cops to cut me a little slack, can you?"

"Sorry, Mama," I said. Technically, there were many ways I could heave my weight into their business to make them leave my mama alone, but it wasn't ethical, especially when she deserved it.

My mama was, in a word, peculiar, but who could blame her, considering her upbringing? Like me, my mama was adopted, but unlike me, she wasn't adopted from an orphanage; she was adopted from an animal shelter.

To explain, let me go back another generation. My grand-mama, Sahuie, was a gypsy shunned by Urban. She fled to live as a hermit in the mountains between Mystery and Sword and Sorcery. She was a witch in every sense of the word, an expert with spells, potions, astronomy, and all things arcane. But she was lonely. So, she adopted a dog named Shasta. Then, she turned that dog into a human. Because, "It's magic!"

As if my mama's dog-like instincts didn't make her odd enough, she followed in her mama's footsteps in the arcane studies and married a vampire from a Romance line. Unable to have kids of their own, they'd adopted me.

This was one reason I had connected with Nita when first reading her palms. I related to her sense of lost parentage, felt a motherly instinct to help, and was curious as a cat to know more about her.

The only clues I had about my birth parents was my own name. That was all I cared to know as I considered Shasta and Ricky Van Pier to be my real parents. Sure, they were a little odd, but whose parents weren't?

Putting away my incense and kettle, I wrote a note to Nita explaining my sudden departure, then headed out to the elevated tracks to catch a ride out of town. One hour later, I reached the southern border of Noir where a storage center kept my electric car. I cared too much about the environment to drive a gas-guzzler like Acron's car, but electric cars refused to run within the boundaries of Noir.

Beyond the state line of Cozy, I drove my silver sedan through the forest and inclines of the Mysterious Mountains.

The range was named for more than its border between Mystery and Fantasy. The border shifted and blurred enough that no one really knew what to expect when traveling through. These mountains and forests were the origin lands of night creatures of the paranormal and supernatural before some of them emigrated to Horror and became terrors.

After another half hour of weaving beside cliffs and rivers, I turned off to a little valley of cabins surrounded by plants of the mundane and arcane. Between the pines and firs, crystals sprouted like ferns, and mushrooms grew as large as shrubs. The occasional beanstalk broke the tree line, and griffins soared in the distance.

Crossing a single-lane bridge over a small stream, then passing a healthy herb garden that smelled strongly of garlic, I arrived at a little mound. My parents' house sat on top, crafted from black stones and grey wooden paneling with ashen shingles covering its pointed rooftops. Despite its outward appearance of a weathered haunted house, I smiled with the feeling of coming home.

With my own key, I let myself in through the front door, welcoming myself into a large open room with a grand staircase straight ahead. The black stone floor was marbled with neon red stripes, and a giant chandelier glowed overhead. It had originally been suspended by magic, but with the shifting of borders, a thick chain now secured it to the ceiling.

Needless to say, both of my parents came from old money. But unlike Aeron, I hadn't grown up with servants and high society. My parents were recluses who lived off the land.

"Mama?" I called through the house.

"Truth? Is that you?" a voice barked cheerfully from the basement. "I'll be up in just a minute!"

I smiled, heading down a narrow hallway to stand at the top of the basement stairs. My mama rounded a corner and smiled at me from the bottom. She was a lean woman with thick golden-brown hair that curled in ringlets. She had large brown eyes, a narrow-pointed nose, and a wide mouth. We think she'd been some kind of golden poodle mix before she'd been transformed. She was dressed in her usual thick-rimmed aqua glasses, bulky magical jewelry, a bohemian skirt, and flowing blouse.

"Just in time! We still have an hour before the markets close. Are you ready to go now?"

"Ready," I said.

Being in her mid-sixties, my mama was still spry with plenty of energy. She bounded up the stairs, grabbed her purse, and followed me back out to my car.

Our twenty-minute drive to the market was occupied with my family's typical car conversations.

"Mama," I sighed. "Can you pull your head back from the window?"

"I like the wind in my hair," she said, grinning.

"You're going to swallow a bug if you keep your mouth open like that."

"Not at the speed you're going. Look at all those people passing you!"

"I'm going the speed limit."

"Faster! We need to catch up!"

I grumbled, "And this is why they revoked your license."

Unfortunately, my mama wasn't the only crazy driver in the mountains. A truck swerved over two lanes and cut me off without even bothering to signal.

"*Reveniant libri tui plicatis paginis—*"

"Truth! Language!"

"*—maculis, aculeis fractis!*" I finished my hex, but blushed and ducked my head in shame. "Sorry." Of the few people who actually understood Latin, my mama was among the smaller handful of people to understand the meaning behind my hexes.

Her scolding expression tightened into a suppressed smile until her laugh broke free. "I'll admit, that was a good one. 'Let your books come back with folded pages, stains, and broken spines.' I'll need to remember that for my neighbors who let their cats poop in my yard."

Arriving at the market, we found a parking spot. Mama unbuckled herself and mused, "I miss the days of bottomless hole transportation. We had one installed in the front yard with a direct line to the market and carnival grounds."

I smirked. "Those things were unsafe and unpredictable even before the boundary shift. Did you have a list for shopping or are we just browsing for whatever tickles our fancy?"

"I have a list. And I have some side quests to complete while we're out. Could we stop by the apothecary and pick up some potions on our way home?"

"Sure, what kind?"

"Cough syrup and repellents for ticks, fleas, and worms."

I smiled and took my mama's arm to escort her between the aisles of vendors. My mama purchased a few gemstones and crystals, though her main interest was a vendor selling herbs. The booth was a little disorganized, and the seller was preoccupied with another customer, leaving us to scavenge through trunks of jars for our desired herbs.

"I need some more eye of newt."

I rolled my eyes. "Can't you just call it mustard seed?"

"So long as my recipes use the arcane names, my spices will be labeled likewise. Can you help me find the wool of bat and toe of frog too?"

I sighed with resignation and rummaged through the jars for the mustard seeds, holly leaves, and buttercups. I made a few purchases of my own, for yarrow and roses, to make more of my homemade first-aid supplies. The seller finished her sale and came over to help us, chatting like an old friend with my mama.

"It's the darndest thing, Shasta," she said. "I need someone in Fantasy who's willing to do a little detective work."

"Is it illegal?" my mama asked. "Does it involve cats? If the answer is 'yes,' I might be willing to relocate."

"Mama." I ducked my face behind my hand.

"What? The county is full of witches solving Cases with their cats. I wish it had been this way back in my dog days. I would have loved solving crime with Mama Sahuie."

The seller grinned. "The neighborhood certainly has changed over the years with the boundary shifts."

We continued on, finding another vendor with a variety of cheeses that might or might not have violated health codes. My mama purchased a red cheese that smelled unholy.

Plugging my nose, I asked, "Are you supposed to eat that on crackers or drugs? That's not going in my car."

"That's fine," Mama said. "I'll hang it out the window as you drive."

Probably with her face.

With the market closing and vendors clearing their tents, I urged my mama to say goodbye. It was still another fifteen minutes before we left for the drugstore to pick up the cough syrup and bug repellent. Back at home, my mama glanced out the window as she put away her purchases.

"Oh good, the crows have accepted my offering."

"You tried a new birdseed?"

Mama gave me a knowing smile. "My alliance with the crow queen is strong."

A door opened from the back, and Papa's voice called from the hallway, "Is Truth here? I saw her car in the front."

"Hey, Papa," I called back.

He stepped into the room, smiling at me with his pristine white teeth. Despite his extra pointy canines, one would never know that he was a vampire by looking at him. By most classifications, he wasn't. He didn't have an uncontrollable need for blood, super strength, animal transformations, or endless youth… as long as he didn't sleep on soil from his homeland and he choked down a more-than-healthy dose of garlic on a daily basis.

He'd been bitten by a Romance line of vampires, making him one of the tamer types and a reasonable papa.

"How long are you in town?" he asked, giving me a shoulder hug.

"Just the day," I said. "I'm working on a tricky Case, but I needed a break to clear my mind."

"Can you tell us about it?" he asked, grabbing a carbonated cherry drink from the icebox. "Maybe we can help you sort through it."

"Sorry, Papa. You know I can't talk about ongoing Cases."

He nodded in understanding. "Does it deal with missing people? Or corpses with a significant lack of blood?"

I smirked. "No, I'm not dealing with a vampire."

"Good, because Skoller Keys promised he'd behave."

I nearly dropped my own drink in surprise. Skoller Keys? The man who owned the creepy mansion above Marlowe Park, where we'd found "Elizabeth Smith?"

Aloud, I asked, "Keys is a vampire?"

"You didn't know? That probably means he's behaving then. Let me know if he does otherwise. We can turn him over to the court, and they'll deal with him better than your law enforcement. He comes from an old Fantasy line, so he's still fierce even off his homeland soil. Be careful if you ever run into him."

I put away the rest of the herbs in a daze. Skoller Keys was a vampire. That explained a lot about his seclusion and the general creepy feeling of his mansion. But now I had so many more questions. He wasn't from a Horror line, so he didn't have all the powers and weaknesses of Dracula, but neither was he from a Romance line that could control their urges. Fantasy lines needed magic and potions to reduce their urges, but magic didn't work in Noir. How did he satisfy his need for blood? Was Skoller Keys supporting other vampires in the area? If so, how many?

What other paranormal creatures could be hiding in plain sight in Shigaqua? Could I ask Aeron's ghosts to spy for that detail? Maybe, but they were already spread too thin. I couldn't run with that train of thought while the Sole Stealer and Sponsor/Mal Testa still ran at large.

But my mind drifted back to "Elizabeth Smith" found on the beach of Marlowe Park, below Keys's mansion. She hadn't been drained of blood. She'd been tortured, knocked out, and then dumped in the lake.

I frowned in thought, mentally reviewing her Reading. The killer had gone to the trouble of changing her clothes before dumping her. Why?

Reconsidering Ms. Doe's personality and characteristics, a terrible and terrific idea sprouted.

"Son of a gun," I muttered and abruptly collected my purse and keys.

"Truth?" Mama asked.

"I need to go!" I thanked and cheek-kissed my parents before dashing out the door. I had a foot to Read.

CHAPTER 8

With my Cozy cell phone, I called the landline at Visionary Investigations. It rang and rang. If Nita was present, she would have answered within the first two rings. Even if Aeron had been asleep on the couch, he would have woken up and answered within the first five rings. So, when it rang six times, I hung up and called my apartment. Nita answered during the second ring.

"Hey, Nita. Has Micro called with any findings about purchases of the boots?"

"Yes," she said with no fluff or flair. "He called twenty-four minutes ago to say he'd found two more buyers. I called Detective Montgomery to arrange their protection. Also, Aeron made some interesting connections while talking with his Faenor cousins."

"Good," I said. "Thanks for the update. I'm in Cozy, but I'm heading back now. Grab Aeron, and I'll meet you at the office in two hours."

"Roger that," she said and hung up.

I tested the speed limits of the winding roads on my way back down. I left my cell phone and electric car in my rental storage unit before crossing the border into Noir. Then, during the train ride, I spoke my thoughts and theories into my voice recorder and transcribed my notes.

Running from the elevated trains, I dashed up the stairs to Visionary Investigations Agency, huffing and puffing. I burst into the office to find Nita and Aeron sitting on the floor with their guns dismantled and cleaned, arranged across a towel between them.

"Pack up," I said. "We might have a new lead at the morgue."

They immediately rebuilt their weapons, and I updated them with my recent findings and theories. Nita assembled her Chopped Hi Powers and Remington 51 as easily and naturally as some people tied their shoes. Aeron put together his Colt Detective Special with decent speed, but definitely with more reverence.

"I made a call to my cousins in Faenor," he said. "They reminded me of some older histories about elves. In prehistoric times, elves were known for causing sharp internal pain, sickness, and even mental illness. They also had magic to tell and shape people's futures."

I squirmed a little. As someone who could Read people's futures, I knew how dangerous the power could be in the wrong hands.

Nita pondered aloud, "Sharp internal pains and sickness, like a cocaine overdose? But if the killer had the power to create that, why would they use cocaine?"

Aeron shrugged. "Maybe because they lost their power by coming to Noir."

I nodded thoughtfully. "I'll add it to the list of questions to ask the mortician. To the morgue."

"Field trip!" Aeron said, bouncing with far too much enthusiasm for visiting dead people.

Assistant Hermann was the one to greet us again as I jumped right to the point. "I need to see Elizabeth Smith, who was murdered and found at Marlowe Park yesterday."

"Did you find her real identity?" Hermann asked as he waved us inside and pulled out the unidentified corpse. She looked paler than when I'd first seen her on the beach.

"Not exactly," I said. "May I see her autopsy report?"

Hermann nodded and pointed at the autopsy cuts over her bodice. "I also confirmed your report that she'd been tortured by multiple burns, cuts, and stabbings in places covered by her swimsuit."

Nita studied the aged wounds and scars on the corpse. "Whoever tortured her was a novice. Sure, they avoided damaging her limbs to create a fake illusion of her cause of death, but a couple of these stab wounds could have accidentally ended her life. See these newer burns? That means the torturer learned to be more careful, to inflict more pain without killing."

I gulped, sometimes a little scared by Nita's knowledge.

"Plus," Hermann added, "Miss Smith suffered through multiple doses of drug combinations, particularly fentanyl and cocaine."

Aeron's attention snapped to me. "The same drugs used by the Sole Stealer?"

Yes, but those two drugs were too common to declare a sure connection. We needed more. "I have reason to believe she was from Fantasy."

"As do I," Hermann said. "Her organs all show signs of abnormally quick growth. She used to be smaller, but coming to

Noir made her human-sized. Also, her nails are extra thick, like they were made for drawing in and catching prey."

"Huh," Nita said. "I always wondered how the transformation worked."

Aeron smirked. "Becoming almost human and losing most of their magic is too boring for most Fantasy wights. Can you confirm if she's connected to the other Sole Stealer victims?" he asked me.

I took her left foot in my hands and visually examined it. Considering her in the light of what I'd learned from the other victims, her feet had many of the same features. She took care of her feet, wearing proper shoes and socks for blood flow. Opening my mind for a Reading, I pulled myself into her daily life.

I felt the tightness of sitting forcibly flat-footed as her ankles were tied to the legs of the wooden armchair. She wiggled and twisted in attempts to free herself, then tensed from the torture. Her toes curled and feet arched with pain until unconsciousness relieved her. I sensed her sweating with anxiety again, anticipating her next torture session. Then, she did something I hadn't noticed with her hands. She rotated her feet to scooch her chair slightly to the side. Slowly, she inched her way around the hard floors of her prison. Pausing for a few breaths, she suddenly rose up on her ankles with a powerful push from her toes. She died with her feet dangling from the straps to the chair legs. She'd been wearing a nice pair of shoes.

I usually felt people handle and pull on their shoes in the mornings of my Readings, but this victim had already been tied to the chair for torture when my Reading began. That was why I hadn't noticed her shoes when Reading her hands at the beach.

"Shoot," I swore, opening my eyes back to the morgue.

"What is it?" Nita asked.

"She hadn't been killed by her torturer. She'd committed suicide by tipping her chair back to hit her head on something."

Aeron unclasped and re-clasped his leather bracelet. "But that's good news, isn't it? It means her torturer probably didn't get the information they wanted."

"At least not all of it," I said. "I think she was tortured by the Sole Stealer."

"How do you know?" Nita asked.

"I don't know, but I have a strong hunch. She wasn't wearing any shoes at the beach, but we hadn't questioned it because she washed up wearing a swimsuit. According to my Reading, she'd been wearing real leather and fur-lined shoes when she'd died. Not exactly the same as the Lucille boots, but similar enough to guess that they were made by the same person. So, what happened to her shoes?"

"More importantly," Aeron said, "she's not the Sole Stealer's MO. He shoots his victims with dirty cocaine. He didn't torture anyone else or dress them up and dump them."

"Exactly," I said. "Which makes her different. The Sole Stealer didn't want us to know that he killed her, which means she can probably connect us to him. If we can learn who she is, we might learn who the Sole Stealer is."

"Great," Nita said, "except we don't know who she is." Ironic, coming from a woman with the same problem.

With a curious glance at Nita, Aeron put a thoughtful finger to his temple. "Maybe we're looking at this wrong. Instead of trying to figure out who she is, maybe we should look at who she isn't."

"What do you mean?" Nita asked.

"Truth, you said she changed her appearance drastically. Meaning everything about her current appearance may be reversed to look at who she used to be. How would you describe her now?"

I nodded. He could be onto something. "Tan, thin, and she wore the height of fashion before she was put into that old-fashioned swimsuit."

"In that case," Aeron said, "she used to be pale, heavy-set, and maybe wore simpler fabrics."

"Based on her shoes, I'd disagree about her fashion choices. Tell me, Aeron. What kind of Fantasy immigrant would be short, pale, and picky with their clothes?"

His smile broadened as the clues fell into place. "She's a mythical being from Fairy. Curses, if the Sole Stealer thought we'd be able to find him through her, it's possible they're related."

"Or have some other legal connection." I speed-walked to the exit. "She might have been in hiding, but she wasn't new to Noir. We need to check the personnel records center for immigration files."

Aeron and Nita followed me to City Hall and Shigaqua's Personnel Records Center a block away. Within an old colonial-style building, the records center was like a maze of filing cabinets. As many times as I'd been there over the years, I still needed directions to find anything among those dusty drawers of files and folders.

Nancy Peters was my preferred helper—an older woman who knew the ups and downs, nooks and crannies of that center—but we were greeted by Rosemary Knapp. She was about my mother's age with a cheery pink smile that never seemed to reach her sad brown eyes. She almost always sported a bruise somewhere, leading me to think she was clumsy. Maybe not. I'd Read her only once, before Nancy had warned her about my ability, then she refused to shake hands with me again. Maybe she worried I'd see more of her husband yanking her around. Today's bruise was a purple splotch on her left forearm.

"Hey, Rosemary," I said. "Is Nancy working?"

Rosemary shook her head. "She's enjoying a well-deserved day off. She worked double shifts for me while I went on vacation to St. Mary Mead and met the most wonderful amateur sleuth—"

Aeron stepped up and gently cut her off with a hand on hers. "Romey, dear. We would love more than anything to hear about your adventures, but we're in a bit of a rush with a lot of research ahead of us. Can you point us to the immigration files of people from Fantasy?"

"Oh, sure," she said, "but I just want to tell you one thing—"

"Can we walk while we talk?" he asked with one of his most patient and charming smiles. I thanked the stars for Aeron's charisma. Rosemary was a lovely woman, but her talking could hold people captive for hours.

"Sure, sure." She waved us to follow her around the counter, down the hall, and into a locked room as she prattled on about a Case that she and her new amateur sleuth friend had happened to stumble upon. Those "amateur sleuths" were all walking omens and angels of death, in my personal opinion. There was no natural way the average citizen could be involved in that many murders.

Rosemary gestured to the entirety of a room as large as our office and lined with filing cabinets. "Here you are. Immigrants from Fantasy."

"Thank you, Romey," Aeron said, perfectly hiding his annoyance and intimidation at our workload. "I wonder, could you help us narrow down our research? We're looking specifically for a woman who immigrated to Noir over a month ago, but within…" He glanced at me.

"Ten years."

"Oh, sure," she said again, but her squished eyebrows looked unsure. She checked labels and opened a few of the cabinets to check their contents. This was why I'd asked for Nancy. She knew these filing cabinets inside and out.

A recent memory of Micro fingering through a similar cabinet flashed through my mind. If Nancy had worked extra while Rosemary went out of town, would they be interested in hiring?

I didn't have time to linger on that thought as Rosemary perked up with a discovery. "Ah! These cabinets. From here to here," she said, gesturing at three cabinets of four drawers each.

"Thank you, Romey," Aeron said, then cringed. "And I'm really sorry."

"Sorry? For wha—"

She cut off with a yelp as Aeron pulled an entire drawer from the cabinet and then dumped it across the table in the middle of the room.

"Lestrade," he said to the air, "do your thing."

"What are you doing?" Rosemary shrieked as Aeron opened files upside-down to spill their contents. Nita forcibly removed the personnel records employee from the room as Aeron rearranged every file. Then, he grabbed the next drawer and added it to the pile, repeating the process. Halfway to tipping the third drawer onto the pile, he paused.

"He found her!" Aeron set down the drawer and slipped out a file with its pages blowing in a nonexistent wind.

"Already?" I asked. As much as his spirits unnerved me, they were good at their jobs. "We need Lestrade at the Knees and Toes back room to look over some receipts."

Aeron raised the document, and I read over his shoulder, scanning the information about a female who immigrated from Fairy, Fantasy. She was listed under her fake identification name, but the file also included a page about her name change. She was a former elf.

"Alfreda Stump," Aeron read aloud. "She's from Faenor—the other half of Fairy. I could ask my dad's cousins for their records on her and her family."

"There's no need," I said. "She's the former craftswoman at Knees and Toes."

Nita raised mildly surprised eyebrows. "Did Mr. Schuster kill his predecessor?"

"Maybe," Aeron theorized. "Maybe he found out that she was killing her own clients after they bought her shoes."

"No," I said. "I Read both of them. Everyone has a murderous stream in their river of possibilities, but theirs were barely creeks."

To the side, Nita muttered darkly, "Anyone can kill."

Aeron, however, agreed with me. "Faenor elves believe in punishing the wicked and rewarding the good, but their punishments include money swindling and craftsman trickery. Murder isn't in their nature. Coming to Noir would change their appearances and magical powers, but not their personalities and beliefs. But who else would go out dressed as an elf to murder people with dirty cocaine shots for boots? Why would anyone else kill Alfreda and hide the connection?"

I rubbed my temple. "I don't know," I admitted. "Maybe someone else who's obsessed with boots and magic—" I paused as every clue clicked. "I know who the Sole Stealer—"

A heavy pounding on the door jolted our attention.

"Ms. Locke!" Rosemary shouted from outside. "There's a phone call for you."

Aeron handed over the file, hopeful. "If it's the police, you can share our findings and catch that maniac before he does any more harm."

Rosemary didn't lead me to the phone; as instead she rushed into the room to reorganize the files. I returned to the main room to find the phone off its hook. Raising it to my ear, I asked, "Hello?"

"I know what you know," a falsetto voice squeaked. "But knowledge can be dangerous. Isn't that right, Michael Johnson?"

"Truth! Help! It's—"

A door slammed, muffling his words and smothering my hope. "You have Micro? Let him go! He doesn't—"

"If you want to save him, come to my shoe store by midnight tonight. One minute late, and he's dead. No police, or he's dead. No one else from your little team, or he's dead. Do you understand?"

I gulped. "I understand. I'll be there. Alone."

CHAPTER 9

One hour before midnight, I parted ways with Aeron and Nita to go alone to the By the Foot shoe store. Aeron and Nita kept asking to confirm my plan and their limited involvement.

"Yes," I said. "I can't risk Micro's life to the Sole Stealer."

The front door of By the Foot was locked, but wandering around the building let me find an entrance through the back door. Using a trick I'd learned from Nita, I oiled the hinges before slowly sliding it open. The lights were on, but the dearth of windows made the place feel dark and forbidden. I left the door open with a rock wedge for a quick getaway.

The backroom vaguely compared to the backroom of Knees and Toes. Since Knees and Toes was a high-end customizer with an on-site shoemaker, its organized craft house had made the filing cabinets of receipts feel out of place. By the Foot, however, was stocked with mass-produced styles and rows upon rows of shoeboxes reaching the ceiling. A ladder stood open between two aisles as I made my way slowly down. There was an entire table of metal Brannock Devices for measuring feet. They were heavy enough to use as a bludgeoning weapon. Nita would know how to utilize them. I, instead, carefully drew out my Browning Hi-Power.

A grey haze clouded the ceiling, a visual for the smoky stench that filled my nostrils. A whimper and screechy demand sounded from behind the shelves on my left. I spied through a gap in the shoe boxes an aisle away, spotting Micro tied to a chair and a small woman with pointed ears standing over him.

Bing-bing!

Micro's attention jerked up. Regardless of his disheveled look, he put on the world's greatest smile and said, "Welcome! How can I help you?"

Remembering his situation, he dropped his head and began to sob.

Bing! Bing!

"Stop it! Stop, I'm right here!"

"Tell me!" the raspy screech demanded.

Bing-bing-bing-bing-bing!

"Please! Just stop! What do you want from me?"

Sidera et lapides, she was torturing him with the Bell of Most Annoying Customer.

"The truth!" she screeched. "I know you went through all those receipts! You know who else bought those boots! I need to know their names!"

"So you can kill them?" Micro sobbed.

"One pair of those boots—"

My rock wedge slipped, closing the door behind me with a loud thud. I jumped at the noise as the voices went silent. Micro shouted from around the aisle, "Help! Truth, is that— ow!"

A sharp slap silenced him. My face heated with anger.

"Jo!" I called around the corner.

That squeaky falsetto voice answered. "It's Jolena now. Get over here."

"I'd rather not."

"Come here!" she roared without warning. "If I sense even the slightest hint of trickery, I'll kill this worthless traitor of an employee! Come out where I can see you and lay your weapons on the ground!"

I stepped around the shelving to reveal myself to Jo and slowly laid my gun on the floor. Not that it would have done me much good, anyway. Despite my years of training, I didn't have near-supernatural shooting skills like Aeron or Nita, and Jo crouched behind Micro as her shield. She wore a ridiculous holiday-elf costume and fake pointed ears as she held the tip of a syringe against Micro's neck.

Thick ropes tied Micro to a metal chair. His clothes wrinkled from the tightness, and red bruises rimmed his wrists beneath the ropes. My mind flashed to the other victim of the Sole Stealer with similar injuries. I couldn't let Micro become another victim.

"Let Micro go," I said. "He doesn't own the Lucille boots."

Jo sneered. "But he knows things. You thought I wouldn't connect the dots when you took him away to help you on a Case at Knees and Toes, then you warned me about my boots? I knew you'd found the connection between my enemies. I'll kill anyone who gets in my way."

"Is that why you killed Alfreda Stump?"

"Shoot," Jo cursed, and that was almost as good as a confession. "How did you know about her?"

"She's the former shoemaker at Knees and Toes. She made the Lucille boots. You bought a pair and met Alfreda as she customized them for you. You harassed her until she went into hiding, changing her image, but you found her anyway and tortured her for weeks. You wanted to know who else bought the shoes. One by one, she gave up their names, and you killed them for their shoes. Then, a couple of days ago, she refused and ended her own life rather than give up her customers. You dumped Alfreda's body into the lake and stole her whole outfit. She was wearing a nice pair of shoes when she was your torture toy. I'd wager they're the same shoes you wore when we officially met and you fired Micro."

"That's it?" she screeched with near laughter. "You can't prove anything!"

"Then you used cocaine on the other victims," I continued. "Lots of people smoke in Noir, but based on the scent that follows you, you specifically smoke cocaine. Also, there was your deep love of magic. The Sole Stealer isn't an elf, but they *want* to be an elf with the abilities to create beautiful clothes and sensations of sharp internal pain and mental sickness. You imitated an elf by dressing up and using a deadly blend of cocaine and fentanyl. You're obsessed with proving magic's real and that it works in Noir. What I don't understand is why you killed people for your obsession with Alfreda's shoes."

"It's not an obsession." She sneered. "It's a fact. Magic is real, and Stump could make the Boots of Seven Leagues."

"Since I came alone, I don't have my Fairy expert with me. What are the Boots of Seven Leagues?"

She scoffed. "Don't you know anything? It's obvious, isn't it? The Boots of Seven Leagues are boots that can travel seven leagues in a single stride. Duh."

I frowned. "That seems like a specialized item. Why would she make and sell boots like that in Noir?"

She rolled her eyes dramatically. "How are you so dumb? She had made them once before, so she could do it again. I asked her nicely over and over to make them for me, but the selfish wight refused and filed a restraining order against me! All I wanted was a pair of boots! So, did I let a little paper and security stop me? No! Even after she changed her identity and went into hiding, I found her. And then—" Jo grabbed the torture bell "—I made her—" *bing bing!* "—tell me—" *bing bing!* "—the names—" *bing bing!* "—of every customer—" *bing bing!* "—she'd made those boots for." *Bing-bing-bing-bing-bing!*

Both Micro and I cried for her to stop, but she laughed. "Oh, but Michael, you're so much easier to torture. You'll break before you find a way to kill yourself, won't you? You'll tell me all the names you found, won't you?"

I gulped. He probably would after a week with that bell and Jo's insanity. He'd given the names to the police first, so he'd trust them to keep the buyers safe, but not before he suffered for it. I needed to stop Jo tonight. But I still needed answers.

"Why?" I asked. "We're in Noir. Alfreda couldn't use magic in Noir."

Jo frowned, glaring at me. "Even a person named Truth is a liar? You use magic all the time. According to Michael, it's every time you shake someone's hand."

I cringed to think that I'd somehow helped to feed her twisted misunderstanding of magic. I didn't have magic. I had an ability that functioned under different rules. I started to explain, "I don't have magic—"

"Don't lie to me! I know magic is real. I'm not some commoner who's ignorant of the world around me. I know you're a fortune teller. I knew Stump was an elf, and I knew she could make magical boots!" She nearly screamed with hysteria by the end. She traded the bell for her syringe and eyed Micro with a crazed expression, like a mad scientist who found a willing experiment.

Afraid she was about to do something extra insane, I played for her attention.

"Jo…remember you want Micro alive. You need him for the names."

Jo sneered. "Yes, he loves to talk, doesn't he? He told me all about you and your magic. That's how you found the connection to Alfreda, right? You have a power like the elves, to foretell futures. I need you to shape my future to make sure I possess the Boots of Seven Leagues."

"That's not how my ability works—"

"Don't lie to me!" she shouted and tightened her syringe grip by Micro's neck. "If you don't tell me, I'll kill this man. I can find the names of the buyers another way, but based on how much he talks about you, I'm betting you mean something to each other."

Micro's face paled, though I wasn't sure if it was with fear from her threats or from spilling his secrets.

My mind became a chaotic jumble; terror that she was one stab away from injecting Micro with a lethal combination, curious about Micro's true feelings for me, and panic that I needed to stall her until I could think of an escape from the situation.

She muttered, "I know magic is real. Magic is real, no matter what anyone says. He believed me. He understood."

"Who's 'he?'"

"Magic must be real," she continued to herself. "Because if not…heh, then none of us has a reason to be here. Especially this idiot, who won't tell me anything—"

She stabbed the needle into Micro's neck.

"Jo! Don't—Micro!"

Her thumb squished against the plunger. Micro's expression shifted between pain and shock as the drugs entered his bloodstream. I hated that Jo stood in my way of rushing to his immediate aid or running for the phone to call an ambulance.

I dropped down to reach for my Browning, but Jo beat me to the draw with her own Saturday Night Special. My only relief was that drawing her gun made Jo pause her injection.

She sneered. "Nuh-uh. You're next, you—what was that?" She yelped as her arm jolted outward, yanking out the half-empty syringe. An incorporeal creepy chuckle responded to her question.

"Who's that? Who's there?" she screamed at the air. She shrieked at me, "I told you to come alone!"

Jo aimed her gun at my face.

The room's glass window shattered.

I flinched at the sound, but Jo screamed. She bent over, holding her mangled and bleeding gun-hand.

Yes, I had come alone, but that didn't mean my partners weren't watching out for me. Aeron had sent Neil to push Jo's arm, and Nita had sniped Jo's hand from…somewhere. I rushed for the murderer, grabbing her good hand and slapping it with cuffs. I subconsciously started to Read her, but the horrors of her daily actions repulsed me. I half dragged the insane woman across the storage to secure her to a wall support.

As much as I wanted to rush to Micro's aid, I knew the best way to help him would be with professional medical attention. I ran to the phone at the front of the storage room and dialed for medical and police support. I didn't give them time to question me as I spewed the store address and our needs. The phone may or may not have caught the hook when I finished and dashed back to Micro's side. He trembled with darting eyes, like a spooked rabbit in Horror.

"An ambulance is on its way," I said. Even if he couldn't hear me between his panicking, I needed to say the words for my own comfort.

I wasn't sure whose heart raced more, his or mine. But I could still control mine. I forced myself to breathe deeply, hoping my calm demeanor would influence Micro's.

"Micro, hold on. We'll get through this."

He shivered, but his building sweat suggested it was from the intense chemicals flowing through him. I slipped off my trench coat and carefully draped it around his shoulders. He jumped at my touch and every sound as the elevated train rattled down the block.

"I'm right here. I'm not leaving you, but I need to grab some water for you. We need to regulate your temperature."

"Don't leave me." His teeth chattered. "You'll leave me, won't you? I don't appreciate you enough. Every day, you tell me how much you love me, and I never say it back."

I blinked. True, he never did, but I'd never noticed. It was all in jest, right?

"It's okay, it doesn't—"

"It's not okay! Truth, I might be going crazy and I might not survive this—of course I won't survive, I'm too weak to survive anything—"

"You will survive," I said firmly.

"That's not the point. The point is, I love you, and I need you to know that before I die."

He stunned me into silence for a moment. He loved me? But he said it was a response to the many times I've told him how much I loved him. Was Micro responding with the same level of love or did he mean…

As if relieved of guilt, he lost the will to fight his pain and lost consciousness. He still whimpered with stuttered breaths. I steeled my courage and determination. "You will not die."

CHAPTER 10

A nd that," I said with a heavy exhale to Ms. Hallman in our cramped office the next morning, "is how your sister received justice. You're welcome."

Ms. Hallman blinked at me and then glanced at Aeron and Nita. Why did people never respond to the truth the way I anticipated? Even Mr. Schuster, when I'd gone to the police to verify Jo's imprisonment, wasn't distraught to learn of Alfreda's death. He simply sighed as if he'd expected nothing more, then walked away to return to work.

Aeron cleared his throat. "Truth, I think I'll take it from here. Don't you want to be at the hospital?"

I did. I'd barely slept between my worries for Micro. Besides, Aeron needed practice with the paperwork. "Don't forget to detail the times and locations," I said on my way out. "And, Nita, make sure the client doesn't try to seduce Aeron out of payment. We need that money for rent." Ms. Hallman and Aeron stared, aghast, but Nita gave me a dutiful nod. Good.

I found Micro lying on a gurney, looking pale and in need of a bath. Otherwise, he seemed all right, all things considered.

His expression spoke of troubles but immediately brightened when he noticed me at the doorway.

He barely managed to greet me with, "Thirty-one," before I wrapped my arms around his shoulders.

"How are you doing? What have the doctors said about your condition? Do you hurt anywhere? How long until you can go home?"

"Uhh," he managed to cough out. "That's quite the onslaught of questions. Is this an interrogation? Do you always hug your suspects? If so, then I have my own questions."

I pulled away from him to match his grin. "No, just you. How are you?"

He cringed. "I'm fine. I wish they'd let me go home. Not that I have a job that needs me, but even if I was still working at By the Foot, I don't know how I'll pay for these medical bills."

I offered him a half shrug. "Nita volunteered at the hospital for a few months to pay her bills."

He sighed, despondent. "I suppose I'll have the time."

Squishing my mouth to the side, I pondered aloud, "Or you can stop worrying about rejection and chase your dreams. Between your help with this Case and your natural smarts, I bet you could find a job at Shigaqua's Personnel Records Center."

He rolled his eyes. "I doubt that."

"Shoot that attitude, Micro." I frowned and folded my arms. "When will you stop discrediting yourself? You're as smart as they come, and they'd be lucky to have you. It doesn't hurt to try."

"Maybe," he muttered at his stomach.

I sighed and pulled over a chair to sit beside him. Taking his hand for comfort and encouragement, I whispered, "Why can't you see yourself the way I do? Haven't I told you how much I love you?"

His cheeks shaded pink as he chuckled, "Every day." His voice and expression cut short as his eyes met mine. "Wait, you're serious this time?"

"As the dog." I winced with embarrassment; half for my confession, and half for my tactless pun. I was trying to be serious! Now was not the time for jokes! "I was serious every time, but… When Jo took you… I mean, we're friends, right? So, it's only natural that I care about you, and…"

How could I put into words the agonizing worry that pierced me as I ran to By the Foot, then the immense hope at finding him alive, the boiling hatred I felt for Jo as she tortured him, the helpless terror of watching him suffer through an overdose, then this puddling relief with his recovery? How could I explain what his friendship meant to me? Now, I might have ruined our friendship forever by confessing my feelings for him.

Micro continued to gape at me.

I couldn't face that face. Once again, telling the whole truth and nothing but the truth ruined my possible relationship with an imperfect man who could be perfect for me. I stood, then turned away and muttered, "Never mind. Forget I said anything."

"Wait—no! Don't go."

My eyes snapped back to Micro's. His hand was braced against the bed frame as if he'd jump from the gurney to chase after me. The silly man couldn't have gone anywhere with the IV and monitoring plugged into him. But he would have tried, anyway?

"Please," he whispered. "Don't go." Then, even quieter, "You're positive?"

Oh, *lapides*. Was it possible? Could the man I love possibly love me back?

"As a proton," I said, using his own phrase. I fell back to his bedside, but my nerves stuttered as I considered taking his hands with mine. Was I acting too eager? What was I supposed to do at this point? What exactly was "this point"? He hadn't actually confessed his feelings. Needing confirmation, I asked, "You love me too? Seriously?"

"As the dog," he said, reaching for my hand.

I laughed with the jitters. "That's not how that phrase works."

"Explain it to me then. Slowly. You can take all day. I don't mean to keep you from your work, but...I want you here."

My core warmed with his words. "Good. Because you might have a hard time getting rid of me now."

His gentle smile crinkled with mirth. "All part of the plan."

"Of course, you have a plan. What's the next step then?"

"Uh, normally, I'd kiss you like I've been dreaming about since our first outing. But my dreams never considered this conversation happening with me in a hospital bed."

"Our first outing, huh?" He'd taken me to the carnival as an homage to our first meeting at a traveling circus. He'd impressed me with mathematical equations that explained how the machines worked. Every time he apologized for being "nerdy." Every time, I fell in love with him a little more. I bit my lip and dared to lean over him. "Making me do all the work, huh?"

"I'll make up for it if you decide to keep me."

I bent down and kissed my best friend. His mouth was dry, and the angle was awkwardly uncomfortable, but I didn't care. We could have been in a field of flowers under a starlit sky, because all that mattered in that moment was Micro's acceptance and love for me.

❖

I floated out to the hospital hallway when Aeron and Nita came to visit later that day. I was on cloud nine, and nothing—not even their grave faces—would keep this from being a beautiful day.

Aeron's eyebrow twitched with humor as he glanced at Micro. "He seems to have more blood in his cheeks."

I bit back my beaming smile. "We're doing well—*he's* doing well."

Nita did a better job at suppressing her smile, but a teasing glinted in her eyes. "We're glad to hear that."

"Unfortunately," Aeron said, "we can't say the same for Jo. Guards found her dead in her cell this afternoon."

Oh. Shoot. That was a downer. "How?"

"She overdosed," Nita said. "The guards suspect she kept a stash of her own poison."

"We, on the other hand," Aeron said, indicating himself and Nita, "suspect foul play. We were allowed to observe her interrogation this morning as she started to spill the beans on her cocaine and fentanyl supplier."

"Sponsor?" I asked. Had Mal Testa spread his business of weapons into drugs?

"Skoller Keys," Nita answered. My eyebrows went high. Then the vampire was involved with the underworld after all. If he dealt with addictive drugs, what other dangerous materials did he possibly deal?

Aeron explained, "Jo had dumped Alfreda's body around his property, hoping he'd take the blame."

I smirked. If Keys was to kill anyone, it wouldn't be with blunt force trauma to the head and then dumping in the lake.

Nita gave a tiny shrug of disappointment. "With her death, we lost our main witness to his crimes. It'll be hard to prove his involvement with the Sole Stealer now."

I allowed my good mood to show with a sly smile. "I'm not worried about that. Between the three of us, I think we have enough resources to shine a light on the truth."

VISIONARY
PRIVATE DETECTIVE
VI
INVESTIGATIONS
AGENCY

Aeron! Stop writing on my files!

But they need to be accurate.

AGENT PROFILE

PERSONAL DETAILS
Agent Name: ~~Earl Aeron Fromm of Margen~~
Alias(es): Aeron Spade, the Haunted, Ace of Spades, Duke of the Dead, Digger (from Det. Ross)

You have too many names, kid!

D.O.B. Jan. 25, XXXX
Nationality: Fairy, Fantasy
Status: Single *and loving it!*
Gender: Male

DESCRIPTION / TRAITS
Age: 21
Laterality: Right
Height: 5'11"
Weight: 170 lbs.
Vision: 20/20
Eye Color: Blue-Green
Hair Color: Dark Brown

WEAPONS OF CHOICE
- Colt Det. Special
- Parrying Daggers

LOCATION
Country: Fantasy
Region: Fairy
District: Margen
Service Area: Noir, Mystery

SPECIALIST FIELDS
- Link to Spirits
- Wealth

Hey! Is that all I'm good for?

CLASSIFIED INFORMATION
Agency: Visionary Investigations
Designation: PERC
Clearance: White *Good luck keeping secrets from me!*

DEATH IN THE FAMILY

CHAPTER 1

ometimes life is too good. Too good to be true. Too good that it's scary. Because everyone says, "Life is hard," so if all's going well and smoothly, something must be wrong, right?

That was how it felt during my first summer of being in love and equally loved by Michael (Micro) Johnson. I felt like a giddy schoolgirl, a generation younger, back at university, excited to learn, and eager to dive into new experiences.

My fear of everything going too well was amplified by my work situation. I was head of the private Visionary Investigations Agency. We were about to hit our one-year anniversary and hadn't yet run ourselves to the ground with debt. Instead, we were more likely to run ourselves into the ground from being overworked. Our reputation for closing impossible Cases had spread, bringing in new clients and earning trust with Shigaqua's police department.

So, I wasn't terribly surprised when it all threatened to collapse like a sandcastle in a tsunami.

The day to best begin this story started like many others; with Nita, Aeron, and me sitting in our little agency, working on tedious marketing.

We'd finally settled into our new and official office, but that meant updating all of our advertisements and fliers with our new address. Aeron technically owned the place, having purchased the condemned lot and overseen the new construction. According to the desires of some spirit who resided in the area, he blueprinted the bottom level for a commercial bakery, the second floor as our agency, and the top two floors for residential rentals. Suffering from the updraft of the bakery's dough, butter, and sugar was much more pleasant than our former office above a Western diner, but my waistline was starting to show just how pleasant it was. I didn't have the same youthful metabolism as my partners.

Our little agency consisted of two rooms and a half-bath that could easily be converted into a one-bedroom apartment with a full bath. The front room lobby had a worn couch that was long enough for Aeron to take his naps, plus an armchair and a tea cabinet. We had replaced our fake wall with a real one and a door to separate the lobby from the office. As the official head of our little agency, I spent most of my time in the office area with its shelves and a desk with a corded phone, typewriter, and cabinets of files.

We currently sat together on the lobby floor with food and flyers arranged around us.

To bolster our motivation for the monotonous editing work, we'd bought breakfast sandwiches from a new fast-food joint. They claimed to use real eggs and sausage patties, but I was fairly certain they were "real" powdered eggs and "real" mutton sausages. To wash it down, we'd ordered two citrus teas and a black coffee for Nita. Since this was Mystery, sometimes citrus meant orange, and sometimes it meant grapefruit. Today, citrus meant lime.

We ate together, passing around the fliers for edits, and sharing fries, family style. Unfortunately, the sides weren't the only meal attribute that we shared like a family.

"Truth," Nita said, her voice on the edge of a complaint. "He's doing it again."

"Doing what?" Aeron grinned innocently.

Nita glared at him. "You know exactly what you're doing."

"I'm doing a lot of things: breathing, eating, talking… If you say my breathing or eating is offensive, I'd think you wanted me dead."

"Tempting."

With a heavy sigh, I rubbed my temple. "Why do you two make me feel like a mama with twins?"

Nita wasn't one to complain, argue, or talk back, but this was Aeron's unique effect on her.

Turning to me, she said, "He keeps winking at me."

"What?" Aeron defended. "I'm not allowed to have an eye twitch?"

"Not with that smile of yours. What does a wink even mean?" Nita asked, halfway to baffled.

"Aeron," I chided, "get a girlfriend and leave Nita alone."

He rocked back with an expression that mixed defensiveness and amusement. "As if I haven't tried? I'm fairly certain I've already asked every policewoman in Shigaqua."

Nita faked a concerned smile. "And none of them stuck around longer than a month? Hmm, I wonder why?"

"Nita," I scolded. "Aeron, when was your last date?"

He squirmed a little. "A few weeks ago… Maybe a month or two."

Or three or four if my memory served me correctly.

"Again," Nita mused, "I wonder why."

He stuck his tongue out at her.

"Ah," she said, pointing at his face. "That must be the reason. You're secretly a child."

"I know you are, but what am I?"

The phone rang, saving me from the conversation. I stood with aching joints and headed for the office, hoping for a long conversation with a tricky new Case to keep us all occupied.

"Visionary Investigations. How can I help you?"

"Thirty-one, Truth," Micro's voice called through the phone with his typical nerdy greeting. It wasn't a tricky new Case, but I was relieved regardless. Weird how even the sound of my boyfriend's voice could make me smile.

"Hey, Micro. Are we still on for tonight at Rosemary's?"

"I was just calling about that. Would you be willing to bring something to share? I said I'd bring an appetizer, but I won't have time to prepare anything after work."

"Sure, no problem," I said. "Were you thinking of fruits or vegetables?"

"How about vegetables? Those stuffed mushrooms you make are a real party pleaser."

I mentally reviewed the contents of my refrigerator before saying, "Yeah, I should be able to make those in time. I think I'm out of paprika, but I can substitute."

"Thank you, hon. You're my brightest star. I can buy you more paprika as thanks. Can I pick you up at twenty till?"

"That should work," I said. "I'll see you then."

"See you then. I love you."

My insides warmed, unfailingly amazed by his affections. "I love you, too," I said before hanging up.

Fortunately, Aeron and Nita had stopped bickering, but unfortunately, Aeron heard my departing phrase. His grin was the only warning before his tease, "If you love him so much, then why don't you marry him?"

Sometimes, the best way to combat teasing was to go along with it. At least, that was my mind's excuse as my mouth said, "You know what? I just might."

Combat successful, Aeron's teasing halted with surprise. "Wait…will you?"

"Nita, how go the fliers?" Shoot my foot and then shove it in my mouth. I couldn't afford to linger on that thought. What I had with Micro was good, almost too good to be true. I could ruin it by acting greedy and asking for more.

CHAPTER 2

While my co-workers and I were on friendly terms, Micro's co-workers at Shigaqua's Personnel Records Center (or PRC) were another breed of "close." Nancy Peters and Rosemary Knapp were empty nesters with grandchildren, and they'd taken in Micro like one of their own children—probably pitying him for being a "lonely bachelor." Of course, when they found out that Micro and I were dating, they'd been all too eager to include me in their monthly dinners. I recognized their expressions of tested tolerance for me when I made requests of them at the PRC, but I also recognized the youthful lights in their eyes as I talked about solved Cases or my relationship with Micro.

They wanted me for the gossip. I didn't mind since they fed me with free, well-prepared food and juicy gossip in return. The archivists knew things about Shigaqua and its people that Aeron's ghosts could only dream about. They were the kind of people I wanted on my side, and there was no better way to get to know someone than eating with them in their homes.

Micro showed up at my apartment twenty minutes before our dinner appointment, still wearing his work clothes of a white long-sleeve button-up restrained in a plaid bowtie, and tucked into waist-high dress slacks with suspenders. I greeted him with a little kiss and waved him inside.

"I'm almost done with the appetizers. How was work today?"

"The food smells good," Micro said, following me to the kitchen with a pleasant nod. "Work was fine. I've been working at the PRC for over seven months, but I realized something today."

"Oh?"

"I can relate to the archive. It's a lot like my mind. It's both quiet and secluded but still hectic with overtime. There are always ten projects left undone with four cabinets left open, a few jammed shut, and no matter which drawer you open, you'll find random facts galore."

I laughed and settled my dish of stuffed mushrooms into a wicker basket for transportation. "I'm glad you're enjoying work. There. We're ready."

Micro helped with the doors as I carried the basket of food to his yellow Buggy. He drove us to an older side of town where the lots were wider, and the houses on them were built with character, lacking any sense of uniformity. As we neared our destination, several of the lawns were decorated with weeds, far too many pink flamingos, cheap wind chimes, and other trinkets.

Micro had once pointed to each of the crowded houses and counted, "They're from Procedural. They frequently visit family in Romance. It's either this house or the next that has a family of ten kids." To my questioning eyebrow, he'd shrugged. "We see all sorts of documents at the PRC, and Romey likes to stalk-then-talk about her neighbors."

"Remind me never to live near her."

Unlike her neighbors, Rosemary Knapp's lot was trimmed with green grass, free of broken gutters, and sparse on decorations. A single rocking chair with a side table furnished the porch, but only solicitors used their front door. We took the familiar path up the driveway to the side entrance with its screechy screen door.

Nancy greeted us and gestured for us to come inside. The Knapp home interior was similar to the exterior; tidy but built with character. Before entering the house proper, there was a set of narrow and steep concrete stairs going to the basement. Like many buildings in Noir, the construction would have violated a dozen housing codes if built in the technologically advanced (and paperwork heavy) Procedural State. We stepped into the family room with teal carpet and wood-paneled walls. Beneath the smell of a honey-glazed ham, the house had a permanent scent of wet wood and dust despite the cleanliness.

"Micro!" Rosemary called from the adjacent dining room. "Nancy was just telling me about the project you've started— to re-categorize the immigrants' folders. Quite the endeavor! How've you been?"

"Positive as a proton," he said, taking off his shoes. I set down my basket of mushrooms on a bench to remove my own shoes.

"Oh, Truth," Nancy said with wide eyes on my mushrooms. "Before I agree to eating this food, I might need to see some terms and conditions."

Micro laughed. "It's not poisonous. Don't worry. I've had it before, and I managed to keep it down. At least for an hour."

I elbowed him lightly. "You didn't vomit at all. Right?"

"No, I kept it down entirely, but saying I kept it down for an hour wasn't a lie."

He laughed, and Nancy joined him. "I suppose I'll give it a try. Don't mind if I make notes during my experience. For research, of course. I'm always on the hunt for new recipes."

"Of course," I said, following her to the dining table where Rosemary's husband, Brody, sat with the newspaper wide open.

With everyone present, Rosemary brought the ham over to the table. She wore an abnormally excessive amount of make-up, especially around her left eye. A failed attempt to hide a bruise.

"Rosemary?" I asked, then gestured to my own eye. "What happened?"

"Oh." She blushed with a quick glance at her husband and then toward her basement staircase. "I fell down those awful stairs."

"Again?" Nancy pointed. "I keep telling you. You need a new railing down those tripping hazards. And some kind of carpeting."

Rosemary's blush remained as she glanced again at her husband. "Brody's been busy with his new job lately and has other projects around the house that take priority."

While Nancy seemed ready to debate what should take priority, Micro asked, "Where's your new job again?"

"I'm a driver for Open and Shut."

Of course, he dropped the highly recognizable and reputable courier brand with a puffed chest. I asked, "They regularly deliver between government buildings, right?"

"And hospitals." He nodded with pride.

Rosemary beamed at him and picked up the carving knives. Her eyes bounced between the ham, the knives, and her husband for a good five seconds. Her hands quivered before she cleared her throat with a little cough. "Brody? Would you do the honor of slicing the ham?"

With a grunted sigh, he set aside the newspaper and grabbed the knives.

I took a turn to squirm. "You're not going to wash your hands between handling the newspaper and the food?"

Brody openly glared at me. "You're going to tell me how to serve food in my own home?"

When it concerned health safety, yeah. His fingers were blackened from the newspaper ink.

Nancy laughed. "That's one way to claim the whole ham for yourself. Be a good host and go wash your hands before touching the food." Despite her tease, her eyes spoke with a reprimand.

With a grumble, Brody set down the knives and went to wash his hands at the kitchen sink. Nancy winked at me, mouthing, "I got your back." One day…I'd have the magical authority of an elderly lady to boss people around like that.

Rosemary asked if we had any updates about catching the elusive Sponsor—Mal Testa, the head of most weapon deals and cause of most gun crimes in Shigaqua. Unfortunately, the only curiosity that my team and I gathered (via Aeron's ghosts) was that the man seemed oddly concerned about the disappearance of a young schoolgirl named Karen Capone.

Brody returned and sliced into the ham, releasing a divine aroma. We dug into the food to excuse the silence with pleasurable munching until Rosemary broke it.

"Oh, Truth? Have you heard of any developments in the art forgery vandalisms?"

"What's that?" I asked.

Micro's eyebrows raised. "You haven't heard of it? Maybe because it's not a physically endangering Case. It's just some nutcase slashing forgeries in people's homes."

"Some people," Nancy said, "think that the art vandal's cause is noble. They only cut up forgeries as a way to protest mass production of art. Art should be unique. That's what Sherie says."

"Sherie?" Micro raised an eyebrow. "Your crazy cat-lady neighbor?"

"She's not a crazy cat-lady," Nancy said. "She only has nine cats, and I'm fairly certain you need to be in the double digits to earn that title."

Micro scoffed. "You said none of those cats are neutered or spayed. You can bet her count will triple by next season. Truth, you're a dog person. Why don't you go over and talk some sense into her?"

I gave him a small smirk, but asked, "How do you know about the incidents? Have people filed burglary reports or insurance claims for their lost art pieces?"

"They've tried," Rosemary said. "Without the proper documentation of their pieces, there's little they can claim from insurance. It makes me slightly worried about our own art." She gestured to the oversized painting on their dining room wall. It featured dogs playing billiards like men after a long day of work. "The original hangs in the Museum of Modern Art. Seeing how much Brody liked it, I paid an art student to—"

"You didn't pay her," Brody growled. "She couldn't claim any copyright of the piece."

"Right, right," Rosemary hurried to correct herself. "I gave her a hefty donation after she gifted me with her imitation of the painting."

Brody's face drew into a deep frown, and I could have sworn he grumbled.

"In short," I said, "no, I haven't heard any developments, as you obviously know more about it than I do."

"Oh, bother," Rosemary said lightly. "I'd really hoped to dig into another Case. You know I used to solve one a season, right? Back when I lived in Cozy." Rosemary's eyes became glazed with pleasant dreams.

Nancy's, however, rolled. "Yes, yes. We all know you were a super Mystery solver in Cozy, solving crimes with your pet rat and pies."

"Don't forget me," Brody grunted. "Without my help, you'd've had no authority to arrest those criminals."

"Yes, of course, dear," Rosemary said. "Oh, to be young and carefree again."

Brody grunted.

I eyed them carefully, hoping to catch nuances to confirm or deny the gossip about their marriage situation. Last month, Micro said that he and Nancy had held a "work meeting" intervention to urge Rosemary to leave Brody, but she denied his abuse and even became offended by their accusations.

I prided myself on withholding personal judgement before drawing my own conclusions, but was there a hint of sadness in Rosemary's eyes and wistful smile? Was there a sense of regret in Brody's grunt? Maybe they once worked as a team of a small-town cop and cozy sleuth, but those days were gone. Without Cases to excite them, they'd lost the thrill for life… and love.

Rosemary abruptly stood. "Is it time for dessert? Truth, will you help me in the kitchen?"

I blinked, surprised to be called upon with my cup to my face. Swallowing, I said, "Sure."

I followed Rosemary to the next room, a tidy kitchen with frilly curtains and pictures of roosters in more places than visually pleasing. With a pie server, she sliced into a round cake and carefully placed evenly sized pieces onto dessert plates. I took the initiative of carrying the first two plates to the dining room. After a second trip, I returned to find the last pieces of cake served and ready, but Rosemary stood braced against the stove, eyes down and frowning.

"Truth?" she asked.

"Yeah?"

She opened and closed her mouth a few times, gripping the oven handle.

I prodded, "Rosemary?"

With a deep breath, she asked, "What kind of investigations do you do?"

The simple answer was "All of them," but I got the feeling that she was looking for a specific answer. Maybe Micro would have been able to guess, but I was better at Reading palms than people.

"We help a lot of lawyers of convicts when they think the police haven't done their jobs right. The most common purpose of hiring private investigators is to find missing persons or to follow spouses who are suspected of being unfaithful." Did she think Brody was cheating on her? "But our prices and specific set of skills tend to bring in the more…desperate or crazy types. Why do you ask?"

She gripped the stove again, then shook her head. "Never mind. Forget I asked."

"Rosemary?"

"Romey!" her husband shouted from the dining room. "What's taking so long?"

"Coming!" she called back and transferred her nervous energy into flustering over the last two dessert plates. I reached to hold her back, but she flinched away and shook her head at me with wide eyes.

She wouldn't say more. Not for the moment at least. I had to be satisfied with the thought that she had my phone number and could call me when she was ready to ask for help.

CHAPTER 3

Whe continued to chat around the dinner table even after clearing the food. In our casual conversation about upcoming activities, I mentioned my agency's first anniversary, which, apparently, was an invitation to host a party for everyone to join. Odd. No one ever cared to come to my parties growing up. Nancy and Rosemary even volunteered to bring appetizers and drinks as long as it started on Friday at 5:00 PM and finished before the city lights turned on. Something about driving in the dark made the elderly ladies uncomfortable.

While I'd been happy to celebrate quietly with a glass of wine and quiet knitting, Rosemary beamed with anticipation. "Any excuse to have a party."

My partners and I had little experience in hosting, but Aeron had plenty of experience attending parties. He took over the decorations to theme the party like a one-year-old birthday party with dinosaur toys and wall hangings. We turned one-year-old, and suddenly we were surrounded by extinction? That seemed like an ill omen.

As the hour neared, I busied myself with arranging my desk like a table of appetizers while Aeron used the dinosaur toys to interact, tease, and flirt with Nita. Unfortunately, Micro had the last shift at the records center and wouldn't be able to help set up, but he'd promised to help put it away.

To my annoyance, Brody was the first guest to arrive, five minutes before the hour. I frowned as he walked in alone.

"Welcome. Is Rosemary coming?"

"She's not here already?" he asked. "She said she'd come separately because I had to come directly from work."

I shrugged, hoping she came quickly to give her grumpy husband a legitimate reason for his presence. He overloaded a dessert plate with appetizers, then plopped in the middle of our three-person couch as if to claim the whole thing.

My nerves grew as the official starting time came and went with no more attendees. I didn't need to Read a palm to foresee how awkward our party would be with just Aeron, Nita, Brody, and me. Micro was never late. Where was he?

Abandoning my preparations, I went to call him. No answer. Did that mean he was already in his car and on his way or… I shuddered as worst-case-scenarios filled my mind.

Micro walked into our office ten minutes after the hour. He graced me with a quick kiss and an apology. "Sorry for being late. Traffic was unbelievable."

Indeed, I found it hard to believe it took him half an hour to get here from the personnel records center.

Micro's attention briefly frowned at Brody's presence then smirked at Aeron and Nita. Ghost Boy was trying to break Lost Girl's shell again with his shameless flirting. His current game involved balancing a stegosaurus on her shoulder and a brachiosaurus on her head.

Micro muttered to me, "Are those two together yet?"

"Not to their knowledge."

"What's that mean? They're in denial?"

That too. I explained, "They're destined to drive each other crazy, though it's unknown whether it's to love or madness."

"Is there a difference?"

I smirked at Micro's tease, though my words were somber. Hoping to look less conspicuous as we gossiped, I busied my hands with cutting pieces of cake onto plates. "Nita has two opposing paths ahead of her. Neither is easy, and either way, they're star-crossed."

"Did their palms say that?" Micro asked, adding a fork to each cake plate.

"Yes and no," I said. "Aeron's heart line crisscrosses with many options and lovers, while Nita's is one solid crease that forks between her family and occupational lines. Then, their very natures contradict. Aeron is the heir to a duchy, bound to marry for status and power. Nita is a literal nobody with a destiny to choose between the life she once lived or the one she has now."

Micro frowned. "She can't have both? You don't think she was a bodyguard of sorts before her amnesia? She has all the skills for it."

"Those skills," I said, "can have many purposes."

Micro's frown turned toward the young couple. "Yeah, a prince dating a mercenary wouldn't go over well."

"Like I said; star-crossed." I released a slow breath and let myself watch the two of them as Aeron balanced a third dino, and Nita's smile cracked. "I invited Aeron to partner with us because he breaks Nita out of her shell. She's stoic like a rock around everyone except him. They're good for each other as friends, but I don't know if Aeron knows how to be 'just friends.' For now, his flirting's still harmless. They haven't kissed or confessed feelings for each other, as far as I know. They both deny their affection…even though they're both lying."

Micro raised an eyebrow at me. "You think they've fallen for each other?"

I teeter-tottered my shoulders. "Possibly. Aeron's in denial, dating other women as if to prove it to himself. And I don't think Nita recognizes what she feels. With her amnesia, it's like her first time falling, and she doesn't have a clue what to do about it."

Micro nudged me. "Then you could help them figure it out. Didn't you encourage their first date? Encourage a second. For Nita's sake, right? Help her figure out who she is—what her passions are, and what kind of life she'll want to live—regardless of the past she discovers about herself."

I slowly thought it over and then nodded. "I guess a second date might help them recognize their friendship compatibility versus their romantic compatibility. Thanks, Micro. I knew you could help me make sense of it."

The door squeaked with Nancy's entrance. She loudly greeted each person as she made her way to the desk/buffet table and set down her soda bottles.

"Has anyone seen Romey?" she asked. "Brody's here."

Suddenly, I realized what that nagging worry had been about. The Knapps didn't have two vehicles. If Brody came straight from work, how was Rosemary supposed to come?

Hearing his name, Rosemary's husband looked our way. "Micro? I thought you were supposed to pick up Romey on your way here."

Micro's eyes bulged and his face reddened. "Oh, four! You're right! I can't believe I completely forgot. Truth, want to go with me to pick her up?"

Brody growled. "If anyone should join, it should be me."

Nancy glanced at Aeron and Nita then whispered to Micro, "Can I come too? I don't want to be left as a third wheel with those two."

"Is everyone going?" Nita asked.

Aeron caught onto the conversation and grinned. "Road trip!"

I rolled my eyes. "We'll be right back. We don't all need to go to pick up Rosemary."

"Apparently," Brody grunted, "we do. You all better hurry, because I'm not waiting."

Micro groaned. "I can't believe I forgot." I frowned. I couldn't either. Had there been something else on his mind?

Nancy, however, giggled. "Why don't we all go to show her how much we missed her?"

Nita and I didn't have cars, and Aeron's roadster only had two seats, so we piled into Micro's Buggy with Nancy sitting in the front.

"There was more room in Brody's car," I said.

"Hah," Nancy laughed without mirth. "No way was I riding alone with that jerk."

I couldn't argue with that since I'd also chosen to ride in the crowded vehicle.

The lights were off when we arrived at the Knapp home. Brody had left before us, but arrived as we all walked up to the side entrance. Nancy suggested we do a friendly surprise shout when Rosemary answered the door, but she hadn't answered by the time Brody walked up with his set of keys.

Before he even walked through the door, Brody paused on the threshold.

"Something's wrong," he muttered. I frowned. How could he tell? Everything looked fine and in order, but it wasn't my house to know exact details.

Unlocking and opening the door, Brody stepped inside carefully. "Hello? Romey?"

Micro asked, "Could she be in the baseme—?"

"The picture!" Brody gasped and ran to the dinette. From the doorway, I could see to the dinette wall, but we followed. As if a closer look would explain why we ended up staring at a blank wall.

The fake painting was gone.

Brody sputtered and spun around in a frantic search. "Wha—how did—where did…"

Unfortunately, I found a bigger problem on the floor by the kitchen door. "That's a blood stain."

And a big one. Big enough that I started looking for a body, not a first aid kit.

Nita stepped over to analyze it closer. "Someone tried to clean it, but it puddled here long enough to seep into the wood. Hours at least."

Nancy called into the house, "Romey! Should we call an ambulance?"

Or the cops. The size of that blood stain filled me with dread. Looking into the kitchen, I noticed a carrot on a cutting board, but no knife. Reaching into my pocket, I subtly turned on my voice recorder.

Nancy's breathing quickened, and Aeron helped her into a dining chair. Settling on the cushion, her eyes met his. "Should we call the police? What if Romey's been badly hurt? I have a bad feeling that something has happened to her."

"Where's the phone?" he asked. Brody pointed him to the kitchen phone, and I lightly eavesdropped as he called his best (and only) friend among Shigaqua's police detectives: Kenneth Ross.

Micro opened the basement door to shout, "Romey? Are you down there? Hey, Truth, is that more blood?"

I joined him at the doorway to analyze the threshold. Yes, there was dried blood in the cracks of the transition between floor types. The blood had been cleaned before it could stain there, but the cleaner had missed the crevices.

Their unfinished basement was mostly for storage and laundry, with washing machines, gardening tools, a workbench for various metal projects, and an entire wall covered by shelves with canned food and an icebox. A quick look confirmed that Rosemary wasn't down there, but something about the room didn't sit right with me.

Brody's footsteps thundered down the stairs until he stood behind me.

"Mr. Knapp," I asked, "does anything look amiss here?"

He frowned and started to walk around. "No. Everything down here is—" He paused at his trash bin, then walked on with an agonized huff.

I hurried over to peek in the bin. Inside was a glass frame of their wedding picture. Shattered.

I stared at Brody. The evidence pointed to domestic abuse gone horribly wrong. There was a reason for the phrase considering murders, that "It's always the spouse." It was a statistical probability. However, the shock on Brody's face was real.

Nita had joined us in the basement. Unlike Brody, I hadn't even noticed her until she waved me over, crouching by the icebox. "The cleaner missed a few more drops of blood over here."

Sidera et lapides. That icebox was padlocked and large enough to hide a body.

"Mr. Knapp. I need you to open your icebox."

"Why, it's not—why is there a lock on it? We've never locked it before."

I eyed him. Was he honestly clueless? Grabbing a pair of garden cutters, I handed them to Brody with the command to "Open it."

He broke the padlock with a grunt of effort, then opened the icebox to confirm my suspicions. Rosemary lay inside with a cleaned kitchen knife. She, however, was covered in blood. Dead.

CHAPTER 4

"N̲o!" Brody cried. "This isn't right! How did this happen? Who did this?"

I analyzed his facial cues and unconscious nerves. He didn't seem terribly grieved by the death of his wife, but maybe it hadn't hit him yet. Either he was secretly a talented actor, or he was truly suffering from the first stage of grief: denial.

I easily imagined the scenario: Brody came home early from work, fought with Rosemary, broke their couple's photo, lost control of his abusive nature, and killed her. He must have let her lie on the dining room floor for a long time for that stain to grow. Maybe he struggled to decide what to do; call for an ambulance or hide the murder. Ultimately, he'd decided to hide the murder by dragging her down to the icebox. He had time to clean the blood, but not enough time to dump the body elsewhere.

The facts didn't match. I wouldn't expect a former cop to be so sloppy when attempting to hide a murder. The blood stain upstairs looked like it had settled in for hours before any attempts to clean it, and Brody typically worked until four-thirty. That was why he'd come to the party directly after work. We'd need to check his work schedule and alibi.

Also, what had happened to the painting?

"Truth," Nita asked, "what happened?"

Nita also seemed unfazed about finding a violently murdered corpse. How had she grown such a mental callus?

"I have a theory," I said, "but it's almost too obvious." I knelt by the icebox to reach for Rosemary's hand. Then, I Read her.

This wasn't my first time Reading Rosemary. I'd Read her once, when she first started working at Shigaqua's Personnel Records Center six years ago. Then, she learned about my ability and kept to herself. Still, I'd frequently interacted with Rosemary as I visited the center for Cases over the years, and she was a talker. I knew she grew up in Cozy, child to a grandma amateur sleuth who spoiled Rosemary as a child with culinary masterpieces. Despite her personality as a wonder seeker, she'd lived a fairly tame childhood. She became her own amateur sleuth while studying for her Associates Degree at their local community college, meeting Officer Brody.

Unlike other victims I'd Read, I already knew her personality and life choices. I'd known her.

I couldn't think about that. Forcing my mind to be objective, I focused on her last day's activities.

Her morning began with a quick jolt within satin sheets. Her hands were sweaty and shaky as she'd woken from a nightmare. As her day off from work, she took her time to calm her heart rate before leaving the bed and dressing for the day in a simple cotton house-gown that she tugged into place around her comfortable figure. She picked up a basket that required both hands and some careful balancing to open doors. Grabbing a variety of wrinkled clothes, she tossed handful after handful. Laundry? That meant she'd come down to the basement. Without using the stairway railing. For someone who claimed to have fallen down those stairs multiple times, she hadn't seemed afraid of falling.

She merely patted the wooden stair railing on her way back up to the kitchen, where she turned a few knobs, set out a pan, cracked an egg, sprinkled spices, and toasted some bread. She paused several times and slowly wiped the counter with an old washcloth as if she was distracted. Her entire meal preparation, consumption, and clean up took a surprising amount of time with her distracted focus. When she washed her dishes and turned one knob back the other direction, it clicked in my mind. She'd been listening to the radio.

Her hand slid down the stair railing as she returned to the basement to grab various wooden and metal handles, then a bucket handle. A summer morning chill brushed her skin as she stepped outside. She dropped the bucket and then enveloped her hands in rough gloves. Time passed with the repetitive and strenuous activity of gardening, but the way she clapped her hands together afterward seemed to share my satisfaction with the cultivation. Putting away the tools, she returned to the laundry, pulling the load from the washer to go back outside, pinning every piece across tight strings in their backyard.

I recognized a few of her other cleaning activities as she pulled laundry from the lines and scrubbed at a particular linen shirt in the kitchen sink. Setting that aside to dry, she started meal preparations by scrubbing a carrot, then set it on a cutting board with a heavy knife.

Her hands flexed with surprise. Was this the moment she noticed someone was in her house? She held onto the knife and went through stages of anxiety, hesitated relief, then back to anxiety. She became tense and emotional with her hand gestures. They talked? Her hands became sweat dispensers as she raised her knife to defend herself. Someone grabbed at her, making the knife slip from her hands. She tried to grab back, but twitched from the painful impact. Her hands slammed onto the wooden dining room floor as she fell. My Reading ended painfully slowly as she bled out.

I opened my teary eyes and turned to Nita. I felt like I'd lived a whole day, but not even three seconds had passed.

"She definitely died while trying to defend herself. She was murdered."

Brody frowned and stared eagerly. "Can you tell who did it?"

I shook my head. "Not exact details." I frowned in confusion. The Reading and arrangement of the crime scene pointed to a murder of domestic violence. But a closer inspection said the crime scene was all wrong.

"Someone staged the crime scene."

Brody gaped. "Well, yeah! But why? Who?"

"Good questions. Maybe if we start with the when, where, and how, we'll find answers."

"Obviously," Brody scoffed, "it was in the dinette sometime during working hours."

"Agreed," I said, "meaning the crime began upstairs."

I moved to shut the icebox and preserve the evidence, but hesitated. I'd never again get to hear Rosemary's extended and enthusiastic stories, or help her with the Case she almost brought to me.

With a heavy sigh, I closed the box and led Brody and Nita back up to the dinette. Aeron sat with a comforting hand on Nancy's shoulder as she cried on the living room sofa. Seeing our return, Aeron asked Nita for the update and informed us that the cops were on the way.

From my Reading, I could confirm that Rosemary had been awake for a few hours and preparing her second meal of the day before the attack, but, "What time did she typically wake up?"

Brody frowned as if my question made no sense. "She usually sleeps extra during her days off. She's always asleep in bed when I leave for work in the morning."

"But not too late," Nancy added. "The Golden Age Talk Radio broadcasts at seven, and Romey never missed a morning."

Ah, while she ate breakfast. Considering her other activities, that put her murder sometime in the early afternoon. Except her body didn't seem frozen enough for that timeline.

Sirens approached from a distance, and I consciously restrained myself from singing along. When lights flashed through the front windows, the sirens reached their maximum and then shut off. Det. Ross exited his car as the forensics team arrived.

The lean detective was in his mid-thirties with a rounded eyes, nose, and mouth. I was perhaps the only one who knew about the scar and bald spot he always kept hidden beneath a fedora. I knew because every time I Read him, he touched it obsessively in the privacy of his home.

I met him at the door, and he greeted me back with an eyebrow raise.

"You did your thing?"

"I Read her, if that's what you mean."

He nodded. "How about you tell me about it?"

I did. I also added my theory about the staging of the scene, pointing out the arrangements and cleaned blood.

He frowned. "You think the murderer wanted us to think it was the husband?"

I shrugged. "It has all the signs of domestic violence. Cleaning the blood. The broken family picture tossed in the trash. Hiding the body on the lot for later disposal. Her co-workers suspected Mr. Knapp of abusing her. But it feels off. Mr. Knapp was genuinely surprised by each of those pieces of evidence and didn't try to keep us from finding his wife in the icebox, like he honestly didn't know she'd be in there. Also, why is the dining room painting missing?"

He nodded and wrote down a few notes. "I'll look into it. Mr. Knapp," he called to Brody, "is there a room where we can talk privately?"

No doubt to pester him about his alibi. The two disappeared into a side room, and I joined Micro, Nancy, and my partners around the living room sofa.

Nancy sobbed. "At least he can't hurt her anymore."

"Was Brody physically abusing her?" I asked. "Can you say for sure?"

Micro frowned. "You couldn't tell from your Reading?"

"I only Read back to this morning, and Brody was already gone for work by the time she woke. But I can confirm that she had no problem with her hazardous basement stairs."

Nancy shook her head. "She always denied it, but I knew. I told her again and again, 'Romey, you need to get yourself away from him.' I even gave her the numbers of a few good divorce attorneys and helped her make some calls, but she always chickened out before setting a meeting."

"We knew," Micro confirmed. "She claimed to fall down the stairs or drop pans on herself, but she wasn't clumsy. In all the times I've worked with Romey and seen her work in her kitchen, she never had an incident."

"Other than the occupational hazard of papercuts," Nancy muttered. "I should have tried harder to get her away from him."

I shook my head. "It looks like Brody was framed, though. I'm as stumped as you, but Kenneth Ross is a good detective. I'm sure he'll—"

Nancy shook her head. "He doesn't know Romey like you do." Pointing at Aeron, she demanded, "You owe me one, remember?"

"Ah, what?" he sputtered. I raised an eyebrow at him. Being from Fairy, I thought he was wise enough not to leave an I owe you. But Nancy was too serious to be making up demands.

"Last year, I expedited files for you all the way from Paranormal. You said it yourself. You'd owe me a 'big one.' This is me calling it in. Solve Romey's murder."

Aeron looked at me with wide eyes. Was he asking me to give him an excuse out of it, or was he asking for permission?

I shrugged. "Rosemary was like family to Micro, which makes her like family to me. I planned to stick my nose into her murder, anyway."

Aeron's shoulders slumped. Apparently, he'd been looking for an excuse. Too bad. I wanted to catch this monster. Thankfully, Aeron seemed to catch my drift as he jumped on board with a determined nod.

"We'll take the Case, Mrs. Peters."

Brody emerged from the private room only to grab a beer and hide in another room. Det. Ross pulled Nancy next for her alibi. Aeron pinched my elbow and steered me away from Micro and Nita.

In low tones, he said, "We can't take on this Case. Or any Cases right now."

"Why not?"

Fiddling with his leather bracelet, he confessed, "The spirits aren't talking to me right now."

I frowned and repeated, "Why not?"

"They're mad at me. I don't remember exactly what happened. Neil won't tell me—as I said, they aren't talking to me—but we had an argument."

132

"About what?" I asked.

He fiddled with his bracelet more. "I don't know their side of the story, and I don't remember the lead-up, but I vividly remember my exact words before they turned their backs on me, so I can make a guess."

"What did you say?" I asked through gritted teeth. "They're our greatest resource, and you insulted them?"

"Not exactly insulted, but yeah, they were offended. I think they wanted me to spend more quality time with them, such as hanging out without asking them for help or using them as resources. I'm not sure. All I remember is saying, 'some of us still need to work for a living.' Emphasis on 'living.'"

I cringed. "I mean, you're not wrong, but you need to say sorry and make amends."

"You think I haven't tried?" he hissed back. "No one is more stubborn than the dead, and they have all the time in the world to stew in their bitterness."

Worry bubbled in my stomach as I asked, "Aeron, how long has this been going on?"

Fiddle, fiddle. "Six days."

"Six days?" I whisper-shouted. If we'd been in the privacy of our office, there would have been no whispering. "Six days ago? They haven't been working with you since our last Case?"

"I've been trying to hide it by doing my own work in my sleep."

That explained why I hadn't noticed Neil's hovering pen, leaving notes recently.

He made a visible effort to stop fiddling by shoving his hands into his pants' pockets. "Now you know why we can't take this Case. I want to help, but I can't. I'll have to find another way to pay back Mrs. Peters."

I frowned. "We can still do this without your ghosts. You graduated from Spyglass University, didn't you? You passed the licensing exam, right? You're a decent investigator even without their help. Now's your chance to prove it."

He blinked at me and straightened his back a little. "Right. Yes, alright. Let's do this."

CHAPTER 5

Detective Ross simply nodded with met expectations when I told him that Nancy hired us to solve Rosemary's murder.

"How about I send you a copy of my own interviews if you do some probing among the neighbors?" He gestured to the front yard, where a crowd of curious neighbors gathered behind the flashing police cruiser.

Unlike Det. Montgomery, I trusted Det. Ross to be thorough in his interrogations and agreed to trade interviews. Aeron, Nita, and I stepped outside and were immediately targeted by the gossipers.

"What's happening?"

"Are the Knapps all right?"

"Are they in any trouble?"

I took note of the vocal onlookers and the quiet observers. Those who spoke out were likely the easiest folks to glean information from, but it was always the quiet ones who knew the most important details. I pointed Aeron toward the talkers since he was better at steering conversations and I was faster at perceiving secrets. Nita lingered back to watch for any suspicious behavior.

I shook hands with a Misty Russ to discover her secret fascination with death and psychology. She was a shut-in who did far too much research on corpses and past Cases, but once I found out that she was a writer, it all made sense. Unfortunately, her attention had been too focused on her latest manuscript to look down the street for any disturbances at the Knapp residence. She mentioned hearing a gunshot around noon, which would normally be helpful information, except Rosemary hadn't been shot. Misty asked far too many probing questions about the ongoing Case, but I'd learned the hard way not to share confidential details with the public.

Next, I met a former PI by the name of Luis Forrester.

"Was she shot?" he asked first. "I thought I heard a gunshot after lunch."

I sighed. One of the problems of living in a Case-riddled country was there were often multiple Cases going on at once.

I answered, "I didn't notice any gunshot wounds. Did you hear or see anything else in the neighborhood that seemed suspicious?"

Mr. Forrester shrugged. "Good fences make good neighbors. I didn't see anything, but their screechy side door makes my pet bird squawk. I remember hearing it open a couple of times in the middle of the day, again during my mid-afternoon nap, then again while listening to *The Adventures of Sherlock Holmes* broadcast. That was around 17:20."

I took note of the times, scratching off the last one as it fit with the time we arrived as a group.

From there, Mr. Forrester became less interested in helping me with the Knapps than in sharing his theories of the Case of the Art Vandal. He refused to accept my attempts to redirect our conversation. *Lapides*, Aeron should have interviewed this man.

"It's possible," he said, "that the art vandal is one of my neighbors. We have a lot of artists in the area who gather for biweekly paint nights. I've been keeping track of the vehicle models and license plates that regularly attend. I even went undercover and attended once. I wrote down names, and Ms. Clay made some passionate comments about imitation art."

I wasn't in on the details of that Case to confirm the accuracy of his information. It was possible he knew only about the incidents near his own home.

I shook hands and interviewed two more quiet neighbors, quickly determining their lack of knowledge about the Knapps. It was a sad fact that most people didn't know their neighbors in Noir. Everyone was always suspicious of each other being secret investigators or spies from another state.

Despite Aeron's charismatic skills in steering conversations, he lingered in an interview with a young woman. When he made some joke and she responded with a teasing push of his arm, I realized that Aeron was in fact still leading the conversation…just in unhelpful directions.

I rolled my eyes and snapped my fingers for his attention. "Aeron. Wrap it up."

He frowned at me and then apologized to the woman. He had the gall to exchange phone numbers, "In case you think of anything else." Yeah, right.

As soon as he and Nita joined me back inside, I asked, "Did she have anything important to say?"

"Perhaps. Jean said that her grandparents were among the first to build in this neighborhood, so she knows a lot about the history of the area."

To my surprise, it was Nita who called out his lost attention. "I have a hard time seeing how that will help us with Romey's Case. It's possible she knows something, but she distracted you with other topics. I don't trust her."

"Because she was nice to me?"

"And other reasons," Nita said. "We aren't in Cozy. Noir suspects don't flirt with their inspectors unless they're trying to get away with something."

Aeron scoffed. "She's less of a suspect than a curious by-stander. Is it ridiculous to hope she's simply grateful we met and wants to know me more as mutually good-doing people?"

"Yes."

"You're hopeless."

"I disagree," Nita said. "I'm full of hope. I hope I'll remember my past, and I hope we'll catch this killer."

"Hope is a feeling," he said with a point. "You've said it yourself that it's better to live without feeling."

"Well, in most aspects, sure. Even if I was hopeless, you're the one who's *helpless* against women. You can't help but to flirt with them, even in an interrogation."

"Ouch!" he said, but with a laugh. "Good job, though. Your insults have definitely improved lately."

"What can I say? You bring out the worst in me."

I wished that wasn't true, but Aeron was right. With each passing month, Nita's stoic façade chipped to reveal a budding personality.

His return smirk lasted only a second before it soured. "Am I really a helpless flirt? It's not like it's working. My last date was months ago, and I cannot say why."

I snorted at the irony. For an investigator, he could be clueless sometimes. "Other than the fact that you're secretly an earl? You visit the dead in your sleep. You talk to ghosts, who gather information for you. That's why they call you the Haunted, right?"

He squirmed and glanced around to make sure no one overheard. "I asked you not to drop my titles—"

"Everyone knows you're the Haunted," Nita said, her impatience leaking. "Well, all the detectives do. What you do is unnatural. You know what they say in the lounges and break rooms? 'Don't date the Haunted.' I thought it was a phrase not to be stupid, but, well, they're talking about you, aren't they?"

He gaped in disbelief. Yep, that explained his lack of dating recently. Still gaping, Aeron asked, "Why? I'm the perfect gentleman on my dates."

I rolled my eyes. "You're not just a gentleman, Aeron. You're the Earl of M—"

"Shhh!" Aeron hissed with a finger to his lips.

"Oh, come on. No one else is around. And it doesn't matter if you keep your royal status a secret, because your natural mannerisms and supernatural ability are enough to intimidate any common person of Mystery."

"Anyway," he said loudly, "I think it's obvious we won't learn anything more about Romey's death until the forensics and autopsy reports are due. I don't know about you guys, but I could use a break to think."

"Right," I said. "Go take a nap and make up with your spirits."

Nita frowned. "What's wrong with the spirits?"

Aeron grumbled and left without another word. He probably expected me to fill her in, so I did that as we took public transportation back to the office. We debated whether the party food was salvageable and were too drained to bother taking down the decorations. I wanted my own rocking chair, tea flavors, and knitting supplies to stimulate my mind while considering everyone's alibis.

Stepping over our apartment threshold, Nita said, "If Aeron's spirits aren't talking with him, that might explain his sour mood the past week, but he's been a little downcast for at least a month. There must be something else bothering him that made him lash out at his spirit friends."

For someone who didn't interact much with people, she was surprisingly intuitive. And she was right. What else could be troubling Aeron?

Considering the timeline, the process of emotions, and my limited facts, I groaned with a realization. Maybe I was wrong, but if I was right, it was a simple fix.

I sighed. "He's pent up and distracted with hormones. Nita, he needs to go on a date, and you're our best option."

"Me?" she started. I raised an eyebrow back. She rarely questioned my directives.

"Yes, you. It can't be me. Even if I wasn't his boss to make it awkward, I'm a whole generation older than he is and happily in love with Micro. So, yes, you." Besides, based on Aeron's constant flirting with Nita, it wouldn't surprise me if he held off pursuing other women because he was falling for Nita. Pushing them into a date was a terrible idea that would surely cause problems later, but I could let Future Truth deal with them. We needed a solution today.

Besides, this temporary fix with future problems was likely to happen, anyway. After Reading Aeron and Nita's palms, I knew the probabilities of their possible futures. I knew they were a good match as friends but would clash as lovers. Hopefully, a date would help them realize that.

Nita cringed. "I don't know if I can go on a date with Aeron. I can work with sharks, but being with Aeron is like dumping me in a dolphin tank. I don't know how to handle him. He puts me completely out of my element."

"It's just a date. You don't need to make him flip or do tricks, just survive in the tank for an hour or two."

"'Just a date,'" Nita scoffed. "As far as I can recall, I've only been on one before, and it was with him last year at your insistence. That makes this a second date. I'm not dipping my toes in the water, you're pushing me in, telling me to dive. 'Just a date' with the master of flirts."

I smirked. "You handle him better than most women."

She didn't retort, but a quiet grumble sounded from her throat. I raised my eyebrows again at her emotional leaks. Muttering something about needing to exercise, she escaped to her bedroom.

I frowned at the phone in the living room. She wasn't going to call him? Maybe it was better this way. She'd been the one to initiate their first date. Again, at my insistence, to fix Aeron's mentality. I knew this would work because I'd done it before.

I picked up our phone and dialed. He answered on the third ring. "PI Spade, here."

"Aeron?"

"Oh, hey, Truth. Did you find a break in the Case already?"

"No. We're taking a break. You're going on a date with Nita tonight."

"I-what? I am? Since when?"

"Since the moment you ask her," I said, enjoying the play between past and future tense. "I'm going to hang up, then you call back to ask her out. It'll be good for her to have the experience of someone asking her out where she actually says yes. And she'll say yes. Good luck."

"Wait—what—?"

I set down the phone to hang up. The boy took a full minute to gather the gumption to call back. I had settled into my rocking chair with a knitting project and the kettle on the warmer before the phone rang again.

"Nita," I called toward her room. "Could you get the phone?"

Nita emerged slightly sweaty from her bedroom and slipped over to answer the phone. "Hello? Oh, hey, Aeron."

I kept one eye and ear on their conversation. Maybe that was why Nita picked up the phone and stretched the cord to talk around the corner. My eyebrows went high with teenage memories in older Contemporary, stretching the curls of the corded phone down the hall to my bedroom to talk in private. Nita wanted to keep me out of her conversation with Aeron? Why? Because she was embarrassed? Because she was plotting something? Technically, they were plotting a date.

Maybe Nita simply acted on her natural instinct to keep secrets. Maybe. But when she came back around the corner, her cheeks were tinted red.

"You said yes?" I asked.

"He's picking me up at 20:00. Shoot," she muttered. "What will I wear?"

I suppressed my smirk and continued my knitting project as Nita disappeared into her bedroom again. It wasn't long before I heard her heavy exercise breathing. I smirked to myself. While I knitted to think, Nita exercised.

Det. Ross called next to share his reports from the interviews he took of Brody, Micro, and Nancy. Since we'd found the body together, I hadn't expected anything other than "work" alibis. I shared my interviews from the neighbors, but neither of us felt strong suspicions about anyone in particular as we ended the call.

I mentally reviewed each of the interviews. Who could be lying, and if so, how would I catch them in their lie? If everyone had been telling the truth, who else was suspect?

The more I sat and pondered everyone's arrival times, the more I worried over Micro's alibi. His shift had ended half an hour before the party started. Forty minutes was more than enough time to stop by Rosemary's and then arrive ten minutes late to the party. I knew Micro couldn't have killed her, but his alibi didn't sit well with me.

Our plumbing squealed as the shower turned on. Unable to settle my mind, I set down my knitting to call Micro. He answered on the third ring.

"Hey, Micro. Would you like to come over for dinner?"

"Oh, sure. I can save my canned soup for another night. How's it going with Romey's Case?"

I gave him a glancing overview of our recent findings and then carefully steered the conversation into other topics that kept us busy until a shout broke behind Nita's door.

"Son of a gun! What the crapshoot do I wear?"

I nearly dropped the phone in surprise and blinked at her door, wondering if I should intrude. I'd never heard Nita shout at herself before, meaning she'd wanted me to hear and to help her? "Uh, Micro, I need to go. I'll see you soon." I was still hanging up the phone when Nita's door flew open to reveal her wearing her bath towel and an anguished expression.

"Truth," she moaned. "Help me."

I pinched back my surprise and laughter at her distress. I'd never seen her distressed. Ever. To think, choosing an outfit for a date would be the trigger to push her over the edge?

Joining Nita in her room, we stared together at her problematic wardrobe. Everything in there was business fashion and utilitarian. Most of it was black.

Tapping my chin, I asked, "Do you know what you're doing tonight?"

"'Dinner and a show,' is what he said."

"Then you want sit-down material. Don't you have a skirt in here somewhere?"

She rummaged through her small selection of options and brought out a skirt that looked more suited for a school uniform than a date. We went through a few more options until I shook my head. "What happened to that pink skirt? Remember the one you wore for that undercover job?"

"I donated it. Clothes can be recognizable, and since I wore it for an undercover job, well, I couldn't risk wearing it again for someone to recognize me."

I groaned and searched through her blouses. With our time dwindling, we eventually settled on a light purple blouse with her black dress slacks. Instead of putting her hair up in a bun as usual, I convinced her to do a half-up. I helped her add a Fantasy-style braid on one side, and she pinned it in place with a long needle that could easily double as a weapon.

Nita refused to let me do her make-up until I proved that I did, in fact, have subtle colors (I just never used them). Studying the results of her highlighted eyes and blushed cheeks, she bit her darkened bottom lip.

"What if," she started, but nerves made her pause and begin again, "What if he tries to kiss me?"

"What do you mean?"

"What else could I mean? What if he tries to kiss me? What do I do?"

I eyed Nita carefully. She had a natural beauty to her, but her hairdo and makeup could push her into the "irresistible" territory. Aeron claimed that he only kissed women he wanted to date exclusively and seriously. Nita worried that Aeron wanted that with her? It was definitely a possibility. While I hoped this date would be enough for them to realize their incompatibility, I recognized the moment to drop some hints about their possible futures.

"That depends," I said. "Do you want him to kiss you?"

"No."

"Then don't let him, you liar."

Nita gave me a slight scowl. After a moment's thought, she relented. "I don't know."

"Good," I said. "Then that's your mission."

"My mission?" She perked up with interest. She could handle a mission.

"Yes. During this date, you have a mission: to have fun and gather intel until you can answer this question; do you or do you not want Aeron to kiss you? That way, when he tries, you'll know whether or not to let him."

"Wait, *when?* You think—"

The doorbell rang, cutting her short.

"Don't forget the other part of your mission—to have fun!" I pushed her out of the bathroom and then walked past her to open the door. Aeron stood in the entryway looking like he always did; dashing and too young for my tastes. I kicked Nita out with a final warning to both of them to "Behave!"

CHAPTER 6

Even as I told Nita and Aeron to behave on their date, I considered how I'd behave while they were gone and Micro came to visit. I'd invited him over for dinner, but my real plans were to interrogate him more about his alibi. Was that considered bad behavior? Maybe I could make it better by making Micro's favorite dinner of blueberry pancakes.

I slapped a few strips of bacon in a pan as I began on the pancake mix. Micro knocked on the door as I scooped the batter into a second pan.

I welcomed him with my attempt at a normal smile. Thankfully, he didn't seem to notice as he stepped inside and sniffed the air.

"Bacon?" He grinned. "To think, I almost had canned soup for dinner instead."

My smile became a little more genuine with his gratitude. Knowing I wouldn't be able to keep it up for long, I returned to the stove to pretend the food needed more attention.

"And pancakes?" Micro added, following me into the kitchen. He stepped behind me and wrapped his arms around my waist. "You really know how to spoil a guy. How did you manage to stay single for all those years?"

I snorted my guffaw. "You're one of a kind, Micro."

"As are you," he said, tightening his embrace and kissing my temple.

Oh, *sidera*, I could see us growing old like that. I leaned into him, absorbing his warmth and wishing this dinner had no ulterior motives. Pulling out the sizzling bacon, I asked, "Did you want eggs?"

"Depends," he said, releasing me to work freely in my kitchen. "Is there dessert?"

"Whether there is or isn't, there's always room for it."

"Fact. Two eggs, please."

"Coming right up," I said. He pulled out plates and silverware to set the table, and a few minutes later, I served our first batch of pancakes.

With his first bite, he closed his eyes and moaned with pleasure. "I needed this. Proof that there's still good in the murder capital of the world."

"We don't need to be in Mystery to have pancakes."

"I know, but...tonight was a mess. We were supposed to have a fun party, but Romey was killed. She didn't deserve to die like that. It doesn't feel right to celebrate anything with her gone."

"Yet she'd been the one to say, 'Any excuse to have a party.'"

We sat in silence for a moment, stuck in our memories of the kindly woman. I dished out his eggs before he spoke again.

"I feel like there's a literal hole in my mind. Especially with the thought of covering for her at work until we hire someone new at the PRC. No one can replace Romey, but the world keeps going and work needs to be done. Nancy was closer to her, so I'll try to take more shifts to let her...cope. I had all these plans to spend time with you, but...everything was ruined."

I reached over to take his hand for comfort and attempted to distract his grief with another topic. "Plans?"

His cheeks reddened, and he became suddenly invested in his eggs. "These are really good."

"Micro," I urged. "What are you not telling me? I believe you're a good man, but your alibi doesn't add up. Your work-shift ended at four-thirty, and you had half an hour before the party to pick up Rosemary and drive over. But you forgot to pick up Rosemary and arrived late. You don't forget things like that, and you're always on time. I know sometimes you get off later because there's someone lingering in the center or they left a mess of papers for you to put away, but you didn't give that excuse. You said 'traffic.' What really happened that distracted you so much?"

He squirmed a little and scooped his food around his plate. "I, uh, was…"

"Micro," I said softly. "You know you can tell me anything, right? Please don't lie to me."

He coughed to clear his throat and then took a swallow of milk. I waited. Setting down his drink, he sighed and glanced around as if to check for eavesdroppers.

"I had plans for the party and actually closed up the center early because we were empty, but then…I didn't forget to pick up Romey."

"You finished work early then went to her house?"

He nodded and cringed. "I walked up to their side door and found it ajar. I worried there'd been a break-in, so I went inside to check."

Lapides. This couldn't end well. If Micro finished early from work, that gave him extra time before arriving late to the party…

He flustered. "I know what you're thinking, but it's not what it looks like."

"You know what I'm thinking? When did you learn telepathy?"

"I know you well enough." He smirked uneasily before he continued, "It looked like there'd been a break-in. I didn't see Romey at first, but noticed something wrong with their billiards painting. It had slashes across the canvas. Going closer to check it, I found…Romey was dead on the floor. It looked like a burglary gone wrong, like she'd caught the art vandal in the act and they'd stabbed her after slashing the painting. There was…so much blood, but I'd hoped she was still alive, so I rolled back her sleeve to check her pulse." His twisted grimace turned angry. "She was covered in bruises. We all knew Brody hurt her. I thought…if Romey's death could serve any justice, it would put that awful husband of hers in jail."

I struggled to keep my face neutral as I realized what was coming. "You staged the crime scene to frame Brody." That explained why the blood stain was deeper where she'd lain for hours before Micro came and attempted to clean it and his tracks as he moved her down to the icebox. It explained why her time of death didn't match with her time in the freezer.

Micro gave me a wide-eyed "oops," grimace. "I'm not proud of it, especially since you figured it out so quickly, but that man deserves jail time for abusing Romey."

"Micro," I moaned. "Whoever killed Rosemary deserves jail time for killing her. You tampered with evidence. I know you acted with good intentions, but you can't break laws for justice." Just because Noir PIs did it all the time didn't mean I'd stoop to their level.

His lips pinched together with worry. "Are you going to turn me in?"

I rubbed my temple and groaned. I had no reason to doubt him, but if what he said was true… "You were the first to find the body, the first on the scene of the crime. You have information pivotal to solving Romey's murder. The cops need that information, meaning you must tell Det. Ross everything you just told me. If you go willingly and confess your involvement, he should be more lenient."

He cringed. "I don't know if I can."

"If you don't, I will," I threatened, then offered him a small smile. "But I believe you can do it. You came clean to me. The first confession is always the hardest, but you're stronger than you think, Micro. It's one reason I love you. Have I told you how much I love you?"

"Every day. I love you, too."

He reached across the table for my hand, and I took it to give him a squeeze. "You can finish dinner first."

He smiled and took another bite, then exhaled loud and slow through his nose as he chewed, like releasing a heavy burden.

We continued to eat and procrastinate the inevitable trip to the police department by slowly finishing our meal and then baking some of my frozen cookie-dough balls. While the distraction was nice, my mind kept circling around Micro's words about how he'd found the crime scene. A burglary gone wrong pointed us in a completely new direction.

We were well into the graveyard shift when I finally convinced Micro to leave the table and head to the police. Walking together down the apartment complex hallway, we ran into Nita. A simple blink signified her surprise at Micro's presence.

"Hey, Micro. Are you heading home?"

"Um, not yet."

"Oh," she said, slightly disappointed. "I hoped to talk with Truth alone."

I shared a look with Micro. "Can you talk to the police without me?"

He faltered as if to say, "No," but I gave him a reassuring smile.

"I know you're a good man. I believe you're strong enough."

His face settled into a clenched grim smile with a nod. We shared a quick kiss before he stepped into the elevator, then Nita and I went back to our apartment.

As soon as the door closed behind us, Nita said, "I completed my mission."

"What mission?" I asked, still thinking about Micro's confession and what it meant to Rosemary's Case.

"I decided whether or not I want Aeron to kiss me."

"Oh?" I asked, redirecting my attention. "Did he try?"

Nita hesitated. "No?"

I made myself comfortable in my rocking chair, expecting a long talk. "That sounds like it comes with a story. Come on, spill."

She released a breathy laugh. "He might have—a few times—if I'd given him the invitation. He took me to a magic show, which I found ironic since he's from Fantasy. For someone who has a magical ability, he knew next to nothing about street magic. After the show, we ate dinner at DaVinci's, and I explained the arts of misdirection and sleight of hand."

DaVinci's, huh? Fancy dinner for a last-minute date.

Nita continued, "I demonstrated a few tricks to swipe his wallet, pocket watch, and even his necktie. The tricks involved a lot of…close proximity and desensitizing with touching." Her face shaded with a blush. "I sensed that he would have kissed me if I had asked for it."

"But you didn't ask for it. Then that's the verdict? You don't want him to kiss you and go exclusive?" I prayed she'd say, "Yes."

She pinched her lips into a tight line. The slight reddening of her cheeks answered for her. Ah, shoot.

"During the date," she said, "I gathered intel as you suggested. I acknowledged the feelings I have when I'm around Aeron, considered the type of man he is—including his inheritance, current occupation, and the way he acts toward others. I weighed the possible meanings behind lip-locking and the pros and cons of starting a romantic relationship with Aeron. My conclusion…is that I would very much like Aeron Spade to kiss Nita Incog and start a meaningful and exclusive relationship."

My expression twitched with confusion. "That's a funny way of stating it."

"That's because," she continued, "he's not simply Aeron Spade, and I'm not simply Nita Incog. He isn't simply a private investigator of Mystery, and I'm not simply a combat specialist. He's Aeron Fromm, an Earl of Fantasy, and I'm…someone still waiting in the lost and found."

I smiled like a proud parent. As hard as it was not to tell people about their possible lifelines, it gave me deep pleasure to see them figure out their paths on their own.

"I need to learn who I am first. For all I know, I have a family waiting for me. I can't afford to fall in love if I already have."

I bit my cheek to stop myself from saying more about her lifeline possibilities. She'd figure it out on her own. Eventually. Besides, if I told her what little I knew of her past, she'd likely let herself fall in love with Aeron, and that for sure was a conflicting interest.

I asked her for the smaller details of their date as we started for bed. I was in my sleeping gown with my teeth brushed when the phone rang. The wall clock ticked at nearly midnight. Who could be calling this late?

"Hello?" I answered.

"Truth!" Micro's voice breathed with relief. "I don't have a lot of time, and I only get this one call. I need your help! They're arresting me!"

CHAPTER 7

I burst into Micro's interrogation room at the Shigaqua Police Station. Unfortunately, it wasn't Det. Ross babysitting my boyfriend.

"Celso Montgomery! You've got the wrong man!"

The detective stared at me wide-eyed and sluggish. Apparently, he didn't do well on the night shift. Blinking into awareness, he asked, "Isn't there usually a 'PS' in there somewhere?"

"This is serious! You've got the wrong man! It can't be Micro! He liked Rosemary and hates violence! When other kids played Cops and Robbers, he played Lost Books and Librarians!"

"Sure, Locke," Montgomery said sarcastically, standing to face me. "Look, if you don't separate yourself from this Case, I'll force you off it."

"Micro, don't say a word! Lawyer up!"

"I don't have a lawyer," he returned.

"You will! Don't let anyone goad you into talking."

Montgomery barked with a laugh. "Too late for that. He already confessed to everything but the murder. But since you're bent on working against me, I'll need to have you removed."

He grabbed my arm and started to steer me out of the room. I struggled for a good two seconds before another cop entered to secure my other arm, forcing me away from Micro.

Lapides! Noir didn't have laws against excessive force and police brutality like Procedural. They could rough up Micro and me as much as they wanted.

"*Spero digitos tuos excidere,*" I cursed, angry enough to wish my hexes worked. Maybe if their fingers fell off, they wouldn't pinch me so much as they threw me out of the interrogation room. As much as I wanted to scream and punch the door until they let me in, I knew that throwing a tantrum wouldn't help Micro. It would only get me thrown out of the station or locked in my own holding cell. Instead, I fumed silently while pacing down the hallway. What could I do to help him?

I blamed the late hour as my brain came up empty for ideas. Maybe this wasn't something I could fix by myself.

With a coin in the station's public phone, I called my own apartment. Nita answered on the second ring and listened quietly as I ranted about the situation.

"I don't know what to do, Nita. I can't do anything! They kicked me out of the room, so I can't even talk to him or hold his hand for support! I don't know what I can do to help him. He's all alone without backup, and—and…gagh!"

Nita said nothing, absorbing the information that I spewed everywhere. When I finally finished my rant, the young woman took a deep breath.

"Maybe you can't help him with what you can do, but with who you know."

"What do you mean? Is there something you can do? Unfortunately, breaking him out or doing something illegal would only make matters worse for him." No doubt, Nita had the skills and means to break Micro free, but I was really trying to set a good example for the malleable amnesiac.

"I have an idea," she said. "I'm going to hang up and make another call, then meet you at the station in half an hour."

After meeting with Nita outside, I marched back into Shigaqua's Police Station, confident and spiteful.

"Locke?" Celso Montgomery blinked from his desk of papers. "I thought you were removed from the building?"

I simply smiled and gestured back to my companions.

"Aeron Spade," Aeron said, flashing his ID as if he wasn't buddies with nearly everyone in the department. "I'm here to represent Michael Johnson. I need to speak with my client. Truth's here as his counselor."

Montgomery gaped. "You can't be serious."

"As the dog," I snapped back with an extra cheesy grin. With Montgomery unable to stop us, we made our way back to Micro's interrogation room. Nita delivered an icy glare that dared anyone to question us. As soon as we walked in, Micro tried to stand.

"Tru—ow!" He stumbled as the handcuffs held him down to the desk.

I ran to his side. The bags under his eyes spoke of his restless worries, and the redness of his wrists told of his uncomfortable bonds. "Are you okay? Did they hurt you?"

"I'm fine. What are you doing here?"

Aeron set a briefcase on the table and removed some recording equipment and legal paper. "We're going to get you out of here."

"You're busting me out?"

"In the most legal way possible." I took Micro's hand in mine and began working a soothing lotion around his sore wrists. "Aeron's going to represent you."

Micro's eyes and mouth widened. "I don't have the money to pay for a lawyer."

Aeron shrugged. "I can do this pro bono since I technically don't have the right credentials in Noir. Just fill out the necessary paperwork and pay your taxes, and that's enough for me. Nita, can you make sure this room is secure? Then we can get started." With a nod from Nita, Aeron turned on his recorder. "Michael Johnson, what did you do yesterday, starting from the time you woke up?"

Aeron prodded him for as many details as possible about his alibi. Despite the recording and Aeron's studious note taking, I listened for any detail to help Micro as he shared his side of the story.

He drove to the Knapp home directly after work to pick up Rosemary for the party. He entered the house around 4:30 PM, found her body in the dining room with the painting slashed like a vandalism-gone-wrong. He set everything back in order and placed the misleading evidence.

"You tampered with every piece of evidence?" I groaned and landed my head in my hands.

"I can remember everything exactly as it was," Micro said. "It looked like a break-in and accidental killing as Romey caught the art vandal."

"Do you know what happened to the painting?" Aeron asked and paused his recorder.

"Positively. It's in their neighbor's outside dumpster. I could show you."

"That's not going to happen," I scoffed. "You're a suspect who has already tampered with evidence. Can someone else do it? I bet Nita could recover it."

Micro nodded. "I could tell you exactly where it is."

Aeron grunted. "Except we aren't allowed to do it. If Micro gives them the details, they can easily suspect that he slashed the painting himself before hiding it. We need Det. Ross to find the painting, so he should be the one to retrieve it."

"How do we make that happen?"

Aeron smirked in a dangerous kind of way that might have appalled his mom. "I can be the master of subliminal messaging when I want to be."

Micro stared wide-eyed between the two of us. "Is this one of those moments where I don't want to know what's happening?"

Aeron chuckled. "Perhaps. Plausible deniability and all that. Just walk us through your steps so we can retrieve the painting."

With some extra specific questions for exact details, Micro explained where he'd disposed of the painting. As soon as he finished, Aeron packed the notepad into his briefcase. "Fantastic. I'll get some sleep and take care of this. You'll be free before dinner tomorrow. Or I guess today, since it's well past midnight."

"Get some sleep?" Micro echoed. Whispering to me, he asked, "Are you sure he knows what he's doing?"

I smiled back. "I'd take care of you myself, but the Haunted Fromm's not a bad backup. He's as good as his word."

Micro snorted. "You can't say that about most lawyers." He began to reach his hand across the table to me, but the chains kept him back. Instead, he clasped his hands together, suddenly embarrassed.

"Thanks," he mumbled.

"Of course," I said. "I know you didn't do this. We'll find the real villain of Rosemary's murder."

"Are you sure?"

"I'm positive," I said, hoping to cheer him with his usual quote. "As a proton."

"It sounds like," Nita said from her quiet corner, "we need to find and apprehend the art vandal."

I nodded. "They're our number one suspect right now."

Aeron clasped his hands together thoughtfully. "I can do some research as a spirit. With Ross leading Romey's murder, I may have more influence on the Case. He trusts my spirits and the leads they reveal."

I frowned. "I thought the spirits weren't helping you right now."

"They aren't," he said, then added with a wink, "but the police don't know that."

A little laugh escaped me.

Det. Montgomery came in to move Micro into a holding cell.

"What'll it take," I asked, "to let me stay with him?"

The detective raised a confused eyebrow. "You wanna be locked up too? Fine by me, but I'll need you to remove all personal items."

Despite Micro's protests, I immediately began taking off my bracelets, beaded necklaces, and earrings. Det. Montgomery led us both to a cell and locked us in with a scoff under his breath, "Fantastic freak."

I frowned. Why was it that whenever I did something people didn't understand, they automatically attributed it to my ethnicity? I didn't want to stay with Micro because I was a Fantastic, but because I loved him.

Micro gave me a sad smile. "I didn't mean for you to join me in here."

"I know," I said, "but there's little else for us to do during the sleeping hours. Aeron will do his work, but it takes time."

Micro's smile dampened more as he surveyed our accommodations. "We're in a holding cell. There isn't even a bed. How do you expect to solve Cases without proper sleep?"

He had a point. We sat on a concrete slab of a bench, and I knew my middle-aged bones would hate me in the morning.

Still, "Worrying about you would keep me up anyway." I took his hand and rested my head on his shoulder. He tucked me in by leaning his head against mine. We were a perfect fit. I sent a wish to the stars that we could spend every night together like that.

CHAPTER 8

Sometimes, I hated when my predictions came true. As expected, Micro and I didn't sleep well in our cushionless holding cell. We tried various positions of cuddling but ended up stretching for a good ten minutes after finally giving up on sleep. I could have used a massage too.

Det. Ross came to our rescue early in the morning, holding a sliced painting of dogs playing billiards.

"You found Rosemary's painting?" I asked.

He grunted. "Digger's spirits found it. I'm taking it to the evidence room for analysis."

A little laugh escaped me before I could hold it back. Master of subliminal messaging, indeed.

"Can I see the painting?" I asked, stepping up to the bars.

He shrugged. "As long as your parents taught you that you see with your eyes, not your hands. Celso says you volunteered to be locked up, which means you can volunteer to come out."

I thanked him and parted from Micro with a comforting hug while Det. Ross unlocked the gate. I bent low to examine the painting. There was blood on the edges of the cut.

Then they'd killed Rosemary before slicing the picture. They were so passionate about forgeries that they wouldn't let a murder shake them from their cause?

"Interesting," I said. "This is my first time seeing the handiwork of the art vandal. Are they all like this?"

Det. Ross scratched his head. "Basically. Large cuts right through the middle. Did you want to see the others?"

"Please," I said.

The detective led me down the hallway to the basement for the evidence storage. He gave me a brief rundown of the Case and the four (now five) targeted paintings. Up until Rosemary's murder, the only victims of the Art Vandal Case had been the paintings.

Passing through the inspection gate, Det. Ross pulled out the other four paintings. One was a small portrait of a nurse sitting in a hospital chair and looking blandly at the painter. Another was a collection of sailboats in cubist style. The third one was a still-life of a flower vase, and the last was a speckled cityscape.

"According to our art expert," Det. Ross explained, "these are all forgeries of historical paintings." He shrugged as if he couldn't tell the difference.

I studied each of the ruined paintings. They all had one long slice that reached from the top left corner to the bottom right. Each of their cuts was clean and flat, except the slice through Rosemary's canvas, which curled around the hole. Was that an effect of the storage environment or because the vandal was flustered from being caught?

"Have you released details of the vandalism to the public?" I asked.

Det. Ross shrugged. "Only to warn people to lock their doors and buy from legitimate sellers. We left out details of victims or methods of the break-ins and vandalism."

Good, so it would be fairly easy to catch a copycat. Looking over the paperwork of the evidence, I found notes indicating detailed insurance claims for the damaged art filed and sent through the personnel records center. That meant the employees at the center had more information than the average citizen about the art vandal, explaining Rosemary's dinner gossip and worries for her own painting.

Thanking Det. Ross, I returned upstairs to find Nita and Aeron waiting for me.

"Can Micro be bailed out?" I asked Aeron.

"Technically, but I suggest he stays in the cell until we solve the Case. Being locked up with supervision gives him a convenient alibi if anything else goes wrong. Also, I expect we'll wrap this up soon enough. I visited Romey's neighbors as a spirit and had a strong impression that we need to interview Jean Clay again."

Nita did a full eye-roll. "Right. This has nothing to do with you wanting to flirt with her?"

"Hey, just because I don't remember the exact reason doesn't mean it wasn't a legitimate one."

"Jean's last name is Clay?" I asked. "Someone I interviewed mentioned a 'passionate' Ms. Clay among the people who attended the painting nights. Maybe she can tell us more about the paintings and forgeries involved in the Case."

Nita relented with my reasoning, but still murmured something threatening to Aeron as I started toward the police station exit. One night in a cell was enough to make me glad to leave that building.

Jogging up to me, Aeron said in a low voice, "Thanks for pushing Nita into going out with me."

"Who says I did anything of the sort?" I asked innocently. "I simply told you to ask her out."

He answered with a doubtful eyebrow. "Regardless of your influence in the matter, the spirits found the event entertaining and teased me relentlessly. They haven't accepted my apologies or requests for help, but at least they're talking to me again."

"Sounds like progress," I said.

Thanks to Aeron's exchange of numbers with Jean Clay, we had her address and arrived within the next half hour. She opened the door wide for Aeron, then stuttered at the sight of Nita and me.

"You brought friends?" she asked.

Had he implied that he was coming alone? I suppressed my impulse to smack the back of the boy's head. Instead, I rushed forward to introduce myself. "Hello. My name is Truth Locke. I didn't have the privilege of meeting you the other day."

"Jean Clay," she said, taking my offered handshake.

I immediately jumped into a Reading. Swimming against the currents of her past, I became aware of her ambition and pride. She was a charmer, like Aeron, but more interested in the arts. I saw her passion for paintings, her knowledge of original pieces and expertise in spotting forgeries. I sensed her hands heat with anger each time she saw one.

"You're the art vandal," I said.

She snapped away from me. "Excuse me?"

"You studied art history and have done extensive research on art techniques for particular artists. You can spot forgeries, and they infuriate you. Someone close to you was a renowned artist who had their works copied and sold to undercut them. A sibling? Parent?"

Jean swallowed. "My grandpa. He was a genius. Dozens of copycats tried to imitate his masterpieces, but none came close.

Still, those imitations sold with their cheap quality and cheap prices, nearly putting my grandpa in the poorhouse. Art is meant to be an expression of self. Forgers don't care about art. They care about money, and I hate them."

"Enough to slash their products even when people pay for them?"

"Those who pay for the forgeries are enabling the fakers while the true artists suffer!"

"And that excuses you for murder?"

"Murder?" She jolted back again. "What are you talking about? I never—"

"Rosemary Knapp," I accused. "She caught you in the act of your vandalism, and you killed her."

"Killed her?" she balked. "What? No! I never hurt anybody. You mean the lovely lady with the grouchy husband? No, she was nice and didn't own any forgeries."

I raised an eyebrow. "She commissioned an artist to copy a painting from the Museum of Modern Art."

Jean frowned. "Which one? Wait—you mean the one with the dogs playing billiards? Huh. It's been a while since I've been to the MMA. See, I specialize in historical art. I've learned how to spot forgeries of the classics, but anything modern..." She finished with a confused shrug. "Besides, I wouldn't kill anybody over a forgery. The whole point is they're worthless—definitely not worth a life. If someone ever caught me, I wouldn't resort to violence. First, I'd try sneaking away, but if that didn't work, then, um, I have other excuses to convince people why I'm sneaking around their houses." She ended with a wink as if I was supposed to know or assume what those excuses were.

"Look." She stood and grabbed a pair of heavy-duty scissors from a drawer. "These are my forgery slicers. Have them tested for blood. I swear they're clean."

I frowned as I retrieved a handkerchief from my purse. We already had murder weapon, but… "You use scissors to cut the paintings?"

"Of course," she said. "What else would I use?"

A knife, obviously.

I accepted her scissors by folding them into my handkerchief, but already doubted we'd find any evidence on them. Maybe Jean used Rosemary's knife to kill her and then slice the painting, but why would she change weapons when she already had the scissors in hand?

I could force it to make sense, but my Reading made me inclined to believe Jean's innocence. Unfortunately, that left me without a suspect…other than Micro.

Did that mean Rosemary's death hadn't been a vandalism gone wrong as Micro supposed? Had the real murderer staged the house to mimic the art vandal before Micro re-staged it? Who?

I sighed and rubbed my temples. I needed some tea and my knitting needles.

With her plausible innocence, I didn't glare at Jean as she casually flirted with Aeron. If Nita was fazed by their interactions, she gave no indication. Still, my own gag reflexes could only take so much.

"Come on," I said to my teammates. "You already have her number, and Micro's still wrongfully accused of—"

A gunshot echoed through the neighborhood.

Before any of us could react with more than a twitch toward our guns, the sound was followed by a low gurgling rumble of a vehicle. The source of the noise was an Open and Shut delivery truck as it drove up to the Knapp house.

I frowned, recalling multiple neighbors mentioning a gunshot during our interviews.

I ran to the truck as it stopped, and I flagged down the delivery man.

"Excuse me," I asked, "do you work with Brody Knapp?"

"Sure, you know him?" the driver asked. He was a burly blond who I expected lifted more drinks than weights. "I have a message for him and can't seem to reach him. I heard something about his wife being murdered?"

"Yeah, just yesterday," I said. "Quick question; do you always drive this truck?"

"No," he said, scratching his head. "We don't have any designated trucks, but there's a sign-in list at the lot."

"Thanks," I said, making a paper note of the license plate and to call the lot's office.

The delivery man tapped an envelope against his palm. "Anyways, it looks like Brody ain't home now?"

"He's temporarily relocated while the Case is still open."

"Rotten luck," he said, as the understatement of the year. "Do you know where he's staying? I need to get this message to him. It's from someone on his route. Since he didn't finish yesterday and is out today, I picked it up for him."

"We can deliver it," I said, accepting the letter. It was a simple envelope labeled for Mr. Knapp and "URGENT."

An urgent letter from someone on his route? Also, was it normal for Brody to not complete his route?

As soon as the delivery driver drove off, I slipped the letter into my coat pocket. Ideas circled through my mind without conclusions. I needed evidence. "Considering the crime scene had been rearranged—possibly twice, I'd like to take another look at it."

Aeron and Nita agreed and followed me to the Knapp home. We entered through the side entrance, which made its usual screech, even with Nita opening it carefully.

Aeron cringed at the sound. "You know, one of the neighbors I interviewed mentioned hearing the door screech around the time of the murder."

"One of my own interviews can confirm that," I said, retrieving my notes. "Mr. Forrester. He said he heard the side door open around mid-day—probably the killer, then mid-afternoon—probably Micro, then when we arrived as a group."

Nita made a quick examination of the house. "This house has a front door, side door, and back door. It doesn't make sense that a sneaking vandal or killer would use the side door that alerts the whole neighborhood."

"Good point," I said. "That probably means our killer hadn't entered with the intention of sneaking or killing. Also, anyone who knew the Knapps used their side door. Rosemary knew her killer, and this wasn't their first time coming into her home."

In all honesty, I didn't expect to find anything new from the crime scene, but I was in the mood for a cup of tea. Careful not to disturb the crime scene further, I placed a kettle on the stove to warm. Nita gave a slight head tilt at my behavior.

"Does tea actually help you think better?" she asked.

"In a way," I said, pulling out the URGENT letter for Brody. Pouring the hot water into a cup, I held the envelope over the steam for a few seconds. This wasn't allowed in Procedural, but in Noir…

"Nita," I said, offering her the letter. "The adhesive should be loosened now. Do you think you can open it without damaging it?"

She gave me a half-smile that accepted my challenge. Flipping out a kunai from who knows where, she carefully slipped open the envelope. The letter inside was brief.

Mr. Knapp,

While delivering your fifteen packages of 'oh so negative' contents to your key customer, I suggest checking the grounds for outside entries to basement cellars.

It was signed by M. Testa. Sponsor. The man allegedly behind most of the weaponized crimes in Shigaqua.

Brody was in correspondence with Sponsor? Was he doing more than deliveries? Why was Shigaqua's leading mobster asking Brody to look for cellars?

CHAPTER 9

I held Micro's hand as Aeron set up his sound recorder and notes again. We sat in the hard and cold holding cell with Aeron acting as Micro's lawyer and me as his counselor.

Knowing Brody wasn't home to fulfill the delivery from Sponsor, I'd turned it over to Det. Ross (after making my own copy, of course). He'd know where the widower was staying these days to pick him up and bring him in for questioning.

"Unfortunately," I said to my boyfriend, "with Jean Clay's explanation, that puts you back on the top of the suspect list, especially since you work at the PRC, where you had access to insurance claims about the damaged paintings. Tell us about the crime scene again. Any and every detail you can remember of how it looked, sounded, and even smelled before you rearranged it can help us find the real killer."

"I'm sorry," he muttered. "I deserve a negative one."

"Yeah, I don't know if one thumbs-down is enough," I agreed. "But you can make up for it by helping us solve this. Micro, I'm going to Read your palm from the last twenty-four hours, okay?"

Nita frowned. "You haven't already?"

"I ask for permission as a sign of love and respect."

Aeron scoffed. "This is the first time I've heard you ask for permission."

Micro's eyes bounced between speakers in the conversation, but landed on mine. "Yeah. You already know I didn't do it, but...could you only Read about my time in the Knapp house? I, uh, got a paper cut at work, and don't want you to feel that."

I raised an eyebrow as I saw no evidence of a paper cut. Was he still hiding something from me? What and why?

With forced restraint, I jumped into Reading Micro's palm, focused on the time after he left work and before arriving at the party. I felt his grip on Buggy's steering wheel, making the turn into Rosemary's neighborhood. He parked the car and walked up to the door like a gentleman to pick up Rosemary. His movements slowed as he approached the door. A light knock on his knuckles nudged the door, and a gentle push opened it wide. I sensed his hesitation and building nerves as he stepped inside. I felt everything as he did, then pulled out of the Reading.

"I can confirm that the door was left unlocked," I said.

"I couldn't believe she was dead," Micro said. "I was also terrified, thinking the killer might still be in the house."

I picked up the narrative to say, "You checked all the rooms on the main floor—"

"—by yourself?" Aeron asked, incredulous. Right, that probably went against one of his family rules about how to survive in Horror. I shushed him and urged Micro to continue.

"Then I went down to the basement—" Aeron groaned and hid his cringing face behind his hand "—and, I remember feeling relieved to find no one in the house."

I nodded, recognizing the change of tension in his hands. "But then you started staging the house to frame Brody." I frowned as a thought occurred to me. Speaking of frames… "You never touched the photo."

"What photo?" Micro asked. "You mean the dog picture that I pulled from the wall and—"

"No, the family photo of Rosemary and Brody that was in the trash. I never sensed you picking it up or smashing it."

"Because I didn't," he said. "There was a family photo in the trash?"

"Truly?" Aeron asked me and Micro. "You're sure you didn't touch the photo?"

"Positive. Like my blood type."

"What?" I asked.

Micro chuckled with a goofy grin. "I'm just trying to follow my blood type's instructions to *be positive*."

I groaned and slipped my palm over my eyes. "That was terri—" Wait a minute. B+? I pulled out Sponsor's note to Brody. "Micro, that was terrific!"

"Really? You usually despise my puns."

"Oh, I still do, but you might have helped crack this Case! Have I told you how much I love you?"

Despite his confusion, he chuckled again. "I love you, too."

With my excitement, Aeron and Nita leaned over my shoulder to see what I saw in the note.

"Ah." Nita got it. "The 'oh so negative' contents are O-blood."

Aeron frowned. "What could anyone want with fifteen packages of blood?"

O Negative was the universal donor for red blood cells. But Aeron's question hung open and unsolved. Why would someone need that much blood?

My own blood chilled as I remembered who had sent the letter. Was Mal Testa dealing in more than weapons? Was he in fact colluding with Skoller Keys, the city's secret vampire?

The note had said the delivery was for a "key" customer. But if Brody hadn't finished his deliveries from yesterday and hadn't picked up this letter from Sponsor, that meant he also hadn't dropped off his "negative" packages. If he truly was supplying blood to a vampire, that seemed like a dangerous delivery to miss.

"Where's Detective Ross?" I asked. "He needs to confirm some details for us."

Nancy Peters and Brody Knapp arrived at the Shigaqua Police Station a few hours later. With my team plus Micro present, Det. Ross had everyone involved with the scene of the crime. I let the detective take the lead as he addressed the room.

"You're all here?" Det. Ross confirmed more than asked.

Brody muttered, "Not like we had much of a choice. You said you had a message for me?"

"Yes," Det. Ross said and then handed over the letter. "This had been dropped off by one of your fellow drivers. Luckily, Visionary Investigations was in the area and noticed the urgency of the note. They brought it to me to contact you."

Brody snatched the letter, but didn't open it. At that, the detective raised an eyebrow.

"Aren't you going to read it? Doesn't it say it's urgent?"

With an annoyed sigh, Brody slipped out the letter and scanned it with widening eyes.

"I need to go—"

"Stay right there," Det. Ross said, "Care to explain what the letter means?"

"No."

The detective sighed. "Fine. But if you can provide us with proof or information against Mal Testa, the police could make things easier for you to return to your own house sooner."

Brody frowned. "I don't work for Mal Testa. I can't even say this letter's from him. It just says 'M. Testa.'"

I leaned forward. "You work for Skoller Keys then, right?"

His frown grew annoyed. "No, I work for Open and Shut, like my uniform says."

I wanted to press the specifics, but Det. Ross moved on.

"Yes, you work for Open and Shut. You told me that you left for work that morning and didn't return home until you arrived with PI Locke and her team, right?"

"That's right."

"When you all arrived together at the crime scene, the clues indicated a fight between a husband and wife and attempts to hide the evidence."

Brody growled. "But even that Fantasy woman could tell the crime scene was tampered with. Someone framed me!" I did my best not to bristle at his disgusted tone when he said, "Fantasy woman."

"Speaking of frames," I said instead, "when seeing the broken picture frame of you and Rosemary in the trash, you didn't ask who broke it or how it got there. You ignored it because you knew who had broken it. Either you or Rosemary during your fight."

"I…" He blinked, confused. "I don't remember exactly what I did or said in the moment. I was in shock of it all. Besides, I couldn't have killed her. I was at work."

I shook my head. "Det. Ross?"

The detective pursed his lips. "You might have been clocked in, but I checked with your manager at Open and Shut. He said you took a truck that's known for backfiring and didn't finish your regular route. As that note indicates, you

174

missed an important pick-up and drop-off. While Skoller Keys and Mal Testa deny any knowledge of your deliveries or their contents, the fact remains; you took an extra-long lunch break yesterday. You have no alibi."

He swallowed. "So, I was a little slow with my work yesterday. That doesn't mean I killed my wife. It couldn't have been me—it was the art vandal, wasn't it?"

I frowned. "How did you know the art vandal was suspected?"

He flustered. "It's obvious, isn't it? The painting was gone! It must have been sliced up by the art vandal, then tossed by the son of a gun who tried to frame me!"

"Sliced?" I asked. "With what?"

"What? With a knife, of course."

"First of all," I said, "the art vandal only targeted historical forgeries, not like the modern piece hanging in your dining room. Second, the vandal used scissors to cut the paintings, not a knife that was used on your piece. That explains the different cuts in your painting. The others had been clean cuts with no curling of the canvas, but yours had been sliced with a knife, stretching the canvas and causing it to curl and fray after. And finally, why would she use a knife from the owner's house to kill someone who snuck up on her when she already had scissors in hand?"

Micro glared at the abusive husband. "Give it up, Brody. We know you killed Romey."

Sweat beaded on his forehead. "I…I'd been at work…"

Det. Ross smacked his fist against the table. "That's not good enough. We have witnesses placing your truck at the crime scene, Mr. Knapp."

"Also," I added, "the killer used the family-and-friends side door to enter. I Read Rosemary's hands. She hadn't let them inside, but there was no sign of breaking and entering. That meant the killer had a key."

The man choked on his emotions and then ducked his face to hide his tears. "I'd been at work…when I saw a delivery for Romey… It was a packet from a divorce attorney. Romey had never said anything to me, so…I went home to confront her about it… I don't know how it happened, I just…lost control. How dare she leave me? After all this time? After all that I'd done for her?"

I sneered. "All you'd done was abuse her. Killing Rosemary only proved the fact that you didn't deserve her."

Det. Ross cleared his throat. "Now, there's no way you'll get out of going to jail for murder, but as I said before, if you can provide us with proof or information against Mal Testa, the police could make things easier for you to return to your own house sooner."

Brody shook his head. "I already told you. I don't work for Mal Testa."

"Or Skoller Keys?" I pressed.

Brody hesitated. "I…make deliveries to Skoller Keys… And lately, I've gotten requests from Testa to poke around the Keys lot while I'm there… I think he's looking for someone. But if I rat them out, I won't be in jail as long?"

Micro muttered, "He deserves jail time."

Nancy was too busy weeping angrily into her handkerchief to agree, so I supported Micro with a silent nod. Regardless of the juice he spilled on Skoller Keys and Mal Testa, I hoped Brody Knapp would see the full treatment of justice.

CHAPTER 10

s soon as he was officially released from custody, Aeron drove Micro home, saying he had "lawyer business" to discuss. Nita disappeared soon after, to…somewhere. I was fairly certain they just wanted an excuse to get out of the paperwork I needed to file as a Shigaqua police consultant and then hired investigating services with Nancy.

I hadn't yet finished Nancy's paperwork when she suddenly complained, "I'm starving and need to get out of this stuffy building. Can we finish this at your office and order take-out?"

I glanced around the police station. Sure, we technically had no reason to be there any longer, and I missed my own desk.

We took the elevated train and reminisced with tender memories of Rosemary. Knowing the full truth of her death put me in a somber mood, wishing I could have done more to help her before it had been too late. My mood took a U-turn as I walked through the main door of Visionary Investigations.

"Happy anniversary!" Aeron, Nita, and Micro shouted, popping a champagne bottle and paper streamers. Apparently, they'd lied about going home.

My eyebrows went high. "You want to hold a party? After losing Rosemary?"

Nancy smiled with a hint of a sad memory. "Any excuse to have a party."

Pouring drinks for everyone, Aeron said, "Exactly. It's what Romey would have wanted. We need more reasons to party. I'll make a toast unless our head agent wants the honors." He gestured to me while handing me a glass.

Put on the spot, I wasn't sure what to say.

"Actually," Micro stepped in, "can I say something?"

I made way to let him take the spotlight. He raised his glass. "To a year of success and many more to come."

"Hear, hear!" Aeron said, and we all raised our drinks to clink in the middle.

Before we could swallow, the phone rang.

"Ah, let it ring," Aeron complained. "If it's important enough, they'll call again."

I gave him a downward stare. "Sometimes I wonder how we have any clients at all."

Micro's expression looked slightly torn, like he wanted to agree with Aeron—as if he'd lost an opportunity—as I walked to the desk phone and answered. Hopefully, the call would be quick.

"Visionary Investigations. How can I help you?"

"Hello, Miss Locke," a scratchy voice said. "It's my understanding that you intercepted the letter I sent to Mr. Knapp?"

I did more than hang up. I slammed down the receiver. Then, I lifted the phone off the hook to keep it busy from any further calls.

"Who was that?" Aeron asked.

"Mal Testa," I said, hoping to return to the party mood as fast as possible.

"Sponsor?" Aeron gaped. "He called us? What did he want?"

"Don't know, don't care."

Nita frowned. "What if he slipped with information we could use against him?"

"It wouldn't be recorded," I said. "He asked about the letter he sent to Mr. Knapp, meaning he knows I read it. I bet every star in the heavens he was about to tell me how I looked pretty in this dress or something else creepy and unnerving, because he lost his mole on Keys. He wanted me to play his game, but—" I shrugged "—I can't play if I don't know the rules, so I hung up. He'll have to find some other entertainment tonight, because we're going to celebrate another Case closed and forget about him. At least for tonight."

"At least for tonight," Aeron said, raising his glass again.

Micro tipped his drink forward as well. "I'll drink to that." Downing the rest of his drink, he set his glass down and flexed his hands nervously. "Actually, since Aeron was kind enough to set up this party, I wonder if I could get something off my chest. See, when I was put in jail, I had a lot of time to think, and I realized that if my life were to suddenly change, I didn't want to have any regrets."

I tried to follow his words and guess where he was going. I became all the more confused when he reached for me and took my hands. "Truth, you know I love you, right?"

"Yes," I said. "I love you too."

He smiled nervously. "Yes, I know. I never would have asked you to prove your love to me, but you did when you believed in my innocence and did everything you could to release me. But there comes a time in every relationship where we either move forward or..." He cringed awkwardly.

By the stars, was he breaking up with me? Now? In front of Aeron, Nita, and Nancy? Did he finally realize what a crazy nut I was and how much better he'd do without me?

Biting his lip and staring at our clasped hands, he continued, "Truth, can't you see how much I need you? I've thought about asking you this for a while, so, here I go." He dropped to one knee and finally met my gaze. "Will you marry me?"

He pulled out a ring box and flipped it open. A little solitaire sparkled at me, but I was already captivated by Micro's plea.

My eyes widened, and my mouth blurted, "Are you serious?"

"As the dog." He smirked nervously, stealing my usual line.

I couldn't help but laugh a little. Not that I was incredulous that he'd ask me such a thing, but I was incredulous to realize how well he knew me. I knew a lot about a lot of people, but conversely, the more people knew about me, the more they tried to avoid me. Micro didn't. He knew my family situation (bizarre as it was) and wanted to become a part of it? He knew my past, my present, and he wanted to be a part of my future? Yeah, he had to be crazy to want someone as crazy as me, but he was the right kind of crazy.

"Michael Johnson," I said, surprising him with his full name. "I thought you'd never ask."

He gaped, disbelieving. "Are you positive?"

I grinned back. "As a proton and your blood type."

Micro stood and pulled me into a joyous kiss.

"Thank the Supernaturals," Aeron cursed under his breath.

I pulled away from Micro, laughing and giving Aeron a questionable look. He shrugged. "I'm just glad you said 'yes,' for Micro's and my sakes."

"What's he talking about?" I asked Micro.

Aeron answered, "I can't Read people like you do. I can't predict what people will do, but Micro was sure enough about your answer to ask me about renting the upstairs apartment."

I gaped at Micro. "We'll live here? Upstairs?"

"We'll both save time on our commutes to work," Micro said, grinning.

"Micro! Yes! It'll be perfect! Thank you—" I cut myself off by smashing my lips to his again. He tightened his hold around me, and if Aeron or Nita complained about our affections, I didn't notice or care.

When I managed to tear myself away, I smiled at Aeron. "Thank you. I recognize that was a business risk to end your contract with the current residents up there."

"Actually," he said, pinching back a smug smile, "now that I have confirmation of your upcoming nuptials, I can sign the papers over. You won't be renting from me. You'll be living free of charge without a mortgage."

Micro joined my disbelief this time. "You're…hold on, you're gifting us the apartment?"

"It'll be more like a condo since you'll own it, but yes. Consider it your wedding present."

"That's too much," I said, still gaping.

Aeron shrugged. "You're a friend of my parents too, so we can say they contributed."

I laughed, filled with elation. I hopped over and kissed his cheek, making him turn a shade of red. Before Micro could pretend to be jealous, I dashed back to my fiancé and took his hands. "You realize what this means, right? No getting cold feet now. We'll have our own home."

He grinned and brushed his nose against mine. "I'd have to be a real dimwit to second-guess my love for you. However, if you wake up one day and realize the trap you're walking into, I know the perfect shoe store to warm any cold feet."

I can't wait to reprint this with some answers...

TOP SECRET

AGENT PROFILE

PERSONAL DETAILS

Agent Name:	???
Alias(es):	Nita Incog
D.O.B.	???
Nationality:	???
Marital Status:	Single? *Hopefully...*
Gender:	Female

DESCRIPTION / TRAITS

Age:	20s?
Laterality:	Ambidextrous
Height:	5'5"
Weight:	125 lbs.
Vision:	20/20
Eye Color:	Variable
Hair Color:	Red-ish Brown

WEAPONS OF CHOICE

- Browning Hi Power
- Remington 51 *If it's a weapon,*
- ~~Welrod~~ *she can use it*

LOCATION

Country:	???
Region:	???
District:	???
Service Area:	Noir, Mystery

SPECIALIST FIELDS

- Melee Combat
- Guns
- Stealth
- *Obeying orders, unlike someone...*

You're not talking about me, are you?

Aeron, how many times have I asked you to not write in my files!?

CLASSIFIED INFORMATION

Agency:	Visionary Investigations
Designation:	Combat Specialist
Clearance:	White

UNDEAD MURDER

CHAPTER 1

Most people wouldn't expect to open a door to an investigations agency and find a cold-hearted special operative in an intimate position with a foreign earl. However, this was Visionary Investigations Agency, and the earl and operative were my partners. After two years of working together, some things no longer surprised me.

I walked in with new cups and tea herbs to resupply our office stash and caught Aeron and Nita in the act…of dancing. Aeron had slipped Nita into a low lover's dip, his face mere centimeters from hers, tempting her for a kiss. They had moved our interviewing chair into the office to make more room in our 13x13 lobby, furnished with a full couch, armchair, a bookshelf, and a floor cabinet for our tea maker. I thanked the stars for the extra office room with my desk, another bookshelf, and three filing cabinets since the lobby felt "cozy" even when we weren't dancing.

As usual, Nita noticed my entrance first. She scrambled to stand at attention and look presentable while Aeron remained lost in the moment a second longer.

As expected, Nita didn't try to make excuses. Her guilt was subtle, but it was there. Almost three years after her amnesia onset, she still had patterns and behaviors ingrained from her unknown past. At least her expressions leaked through her stoic façade more with each passing year. Nita looked ready to accept whatever punishment her higher-ups deemed worthy.

Where had she learned such abusive discipline?

Aeron, however, accepted no guilt, as if their actions had been completely innocent. Casual as jeans, he explained, "I was testing her muscle memory. It seems that Nita has learned to dance in multiple forms."

Aeron claimed to be a bad liar—and he was when he knew it was a lie—but he lied to himself so often (that he could be an investigator instead of a duke, that he wasn't in love with Nita, and that he could convince Nita to give in to her own feelings about him) that this lie about his dancing intentions came naturally.

"So it seems," I said with doubt inflecting my voice. I unloaded my groceries to their proper storage places, wondering if I'd use any before leaving for my parents'. They needed my help more often with my mama's recent diagnosis of aggressive lymphoma.

I reversed the train of those depressing thoughts to return to Aeron and Nita's dancing. "Were you practicing for the party tonight?"

"Yes," Nita said. Dressed for the party, she wore a blood-red dress with sleeves that hung off her shoulders, crisscrossed around her chest, down her core, and hugged her hips with a low knotted ribbon. She accessorized with a black shawl and handbag, though I was willing to bet there were at least five weapons on her somewhere. To my surprise, she had asked to borrow my golden ruby necklace and diamond bracelet. Was she trying to impress someone? They were as fake as Sherlock's

186

disguises, but I doubted that she'd let anyone come close enough to notice. Except Aeron.

He was dressed in a dark-blue double-breasted military coat and a three-piece pin-stripe suit with a pale blue scarf-tie and golden pocket watch. He even wore a matching top hat and carried a dueling cane-sword. Leave it to a royal to dress to the nines.

Aeron smirked below complaining eyes. "Do we have to go? How about this; we skip and have our own party here?"

Finishing my tea duties, I faced Aeron with raised eyebrows. "I had to pull strings to get invitations, and you want to reject attending a powerful and dangerous man's highly exclusive party of the city's most influential people?"

"When you put it that way," Aeron scoffed, "it sounds like every party I avoided as an earl in Fantasy. If we have our own party here with just the three of us plus Micro, I'm pretty sure that's more exclusive."

I rolled my eyes. "Fine, Earl Fromm, the Haunted." Aeron winced as I dropped his real name. "Micro and I are going to Skoller Keys' party, and I'm taking Nita to help sneak around and unlock doors. You stay here, alone, and shudder to think about what the rich and influential host might do to someone who rejected his invitation to his personal home and prestigious event." I wasn't sure whether telling Aeron the true nature of Skoller Keys would persuade or dissuade him more. On one hand, he'd recognize the true dangers of angering the Fantasy vampire. On the other hand, Aeron's half-Horror instincts might tell him to stay as far away from Keys as possible.

Aeron grunted. "Wouldn't be the first noble I've disappointed."

"I think that would be a bad idea," Nita said, stating the obvious.

"I'm with Aeron on this one," a voice said from behind me. Micro had finished work at Shigaqua's Personnel Records Center and joined us to ride together up to the Keys Mansion. He wore his fanciest suit, which included a suit jacket and pants that actually matched, a white button-up shirt, and a black tie with a single knot. I ogled openly at my husband of seven months as he ogled right back.

I wore a sunflower-yellow dress with a deep V-neck and only lace covering my shoulders. A golden ribbon tied around my empire waist above layers of more golden lace that draped loosely over my skirts. My accessories included a simple golden necklace with a large pendant and a little faux-leather handbag with everything I hoped not to need.

When Micro's eyes eventually managed to rip themselves from me, he grimaced at Aeron and Nita. "Maaan. Now I feel underdressed."

I gave my husband a reassuring smile and a kiss on the cheek. "You're fine. Aeron just doesn't know how to dress normally."

Micro graced me with a small smile despite his annoyed eyes. "I can't believe we're going to this pompous jerk's party. We know he's working with Sponsor and deals drugs. If we'd been able to prove his cocaine supply to the Sole Stealer or his suspicious dealings with Brody, any party he'd be hosting would be in jail."

"I know," I sympathized, "but if we search his house during the party, we might finally gain the evidence we need to put him away for good." Therein lay our real agenda for seeking an invitation to Keys' party. I needed proof that he was involved in the kidnappings around town.

Youth disappearing without notes wasn't anything new in a city like Shigaqua, but we'd been hired by a mother of a missing child. Mary Argall was twelve years old and had been missing for a whole month. My intuition sensed that her disappearance was somehow linked to several others over the past year, but I couldn't pin down the connection. The students ranged in every grade, going to different schools with different backgrounds. But the variety itself almost seemed like a connection. As if the kidnapper wanted one of each, like a collector.

"Hey," Micro nudged me, pulling me from my thoughts. "Are we going to the stupid party then?"

"We're going," I said. "Aeron's ghosts have verified that Keys is dirty, and this party will give us the perfect opportunity to sneak around for clues and proof."

CHAPTER 2

Since the elevated train stopped across the street from the front gates (an entire half-mile away from the mansion), and Aeron's car only seated two people, we took a taxi to save us from the rain. Just shy of six feet tall, Aeron was easily the largest among us, letting him sit in the front by the driver while Micro, Nita, and I squished in the backseat. We piled in and directed our driver to Marlowe Park on the southeast end of Shigaqua, right up against the shores of Lake Mishi.

The gates were already closed for the night, but a show of our invitations let us through. Not like that ever stopped the gangs from regularly sneaking into the park. The size of Marlowe Park always amazed me considering its proximity to the lake and city center. We crossed a large pond via a wooden bridge and climbed the hill toward the main house.

Aeron leaned over to check our driver's speed.

"Fantastic. At these speeds, the party might be over by the time we arrive."

Our driver grumbled, "I ain't goin' any faster on this road. This park's full of animals and wild things that might jump you outta nowhere."

Not to mention the gangs with their various illegal activities. With the beachfront on one side and the public Marlowe Park on the other, the lax security of Keys' large private property woods was an open invitation for crooked meetings and hangouts. The darkening night and rain clouds added a foreboding mood to our drive.

Our vehicle slowed as we reached the lights of the Keys Mansion with its wide and circular motor court. Arriving later than the official start time, we passed a long garage and several parked vehicles before a valet met us at the front entrance. I hoped we weren't the only group to arrive in a taxi as the parked cars let me estimate fifteen to thirty guests. It might be harder to casually sneak through a mansion with fewer people to hide between.

The outside walls of the three-story mansion were built entirely of stone, with sculpted columns and castle-like architecture. Its tall windows were dark with curtains, but bright lights greeted us inside. We stepped into an atrium with beautiful marbled flooring and a vaulted ceiling. We brought in the smell of rain to mix with the mansion's scent of dust and cleaning products.

The by-invitation-only party was already in full swing with the limited guests spread through the house. Voices echoed through the atrium with its upstairs balcony, mixing casual chatter into dissonant murmurs. A boisterous laugh broke from the room to our right while smooth jazz serenaded the room to our left. A butler offered to take our coats to an open walk-in closet near the door.

True to character, Nita's eyes quickly scanned the area for exits and possible threats.

"How does anyone live in such a house? This place is huge."

Aeron chuckled. "For Shigaqua, yeah, it's pretty big. Compared to the castle where I grew up, though…" He finished with a small shrug and another chuckle.

I could only imagine the castle of a palace he'd been raised in. While my parents' house in Cozy was considered large for Shigaqua's standards, it wasn't used for gatherings like this mansion. My parents needed to rearrange some rooms lately to accommodate Micro and me staying over more often.

Our host, Skoller Keys, stood near the back, talking adamantly with a young woman in a dress that mixed business and feminine wiles. Her knee-length pencil skirt matched her blouse with a sweetheart neckline and short-sleeved suit-cut. She held a pen and notepad in hand to studiously take notes.

A reporter? Maybe this party wasn't as prestigious as I expected.

My expectations were confirmed as a large man in a crisp pin-striped suit walked around a pillar. Mal Testa, commonly known as Sponsor.

I stepped up to meet him, debating whether to offer a handshake. On one hand, I really didn't want to experience a day in the life of his hands, but on the other, I could learn something about him that could condemn him. We'd come to find dirt on Keys, but I was open to options.

I stuck out my hand. "Mal Testa? I don't think we've officially met."

"Nothin' official," he said with narrowed eyes on my face. "PI Locke, right? What's a gumshoe doin' here?"

"I have connections," I said, still offering my hand.

He glanced at Aeron and then smirked. "I bet you got some pull. Beggin' your pardon." He stepped around me, leaving my hand hanging. Maybe it was for the best as I spotted deformities in his nails as if they'd been bashed and split from his childhood.

He locked eyes with our host and nodded toward us before calling to the reporter. "Ms. Lanner, when you got a sec, I got a matter to rap with you."

Before I could follow the man responsible for most weaponized crimes in Shigaqua, a loud voice called across the entryway. Detective Montgomery. How did he manage an invitation? The prestigiousness of the party dropped two more levels. He stepped up to us, holding a plate full of a dozen types of finger food.

"Finally!" he called. "Some faces I recognize! I didn't know you folks would be here."

Our host broke away from the woman to greet us. "Of course, they are my honored guests! Make yourselves at home. Det. Montgomery here is serving as tonight's crowd control. Not that I expect any trouble, no, but it is no secret that the surrounding woods play host to… less desirable activities. As the detective has clearly discovered, the dining hall has more than enough food," Skoller Keys said, pointing to our right. Then, pointing to our left, continued, "The ballroom is open for drinks and live entertainment. If you need anything, my servants are long-term employees who can answer any of your questions."

Challenge accepted. I thanked him with a forced smile and nod of a bow. Aeron was better with his bow at the hip, removing his hat and stepping his foot back for balance.

Keys smiled with appreciation. "Lord Fromm, if I am not mistaken?"

Oh, shoot. Aeron visibly flinched and stood a little straighter when coming out of his bow. "In Mystery, I am the common Private Investigator, Aeron Spade."

Keys waved his hand without consequence. "Common? Hardly! You are the Earl of Margen! Cousin of the King of Fairy!"

With his every word, Aeron shook his head harder and paled like a ghost while Det. Montgomery choked on his food. "The what?"

"The Earl of Margen!" Keys repeated, despite Aeron's pleading hands to stop.

"Please don't—"

"This young lad stands second in the succession to half of the Fairy Kingdom—would I be mistaken? Ms. Lanner, if you please. Flash a picture of our company." He waved over the reporter, who eagerly caught their frames. Aeron was the picture of terror while our host simply grinned. "Can you envision the tidings she may spread on the morrow? Our being together will surely give rise to countless whispers—rumors of alliances and confederacy. Have you taken our likeness?"

Ms. Lanner smiled like a hunter with the prize buck.

Keys stepped away. "I trust you will grant me a meeting in my study this evening?"

Aeron smiled gently through clenched teeth. "Later."

More guests walked in, and Keys excused himself to greet them.

Det. Montgomery continued to gape at Aeron. "Your cousin's a king?"

Still speaking through a ventriloquist's smile, Aeron muttered, "I'm going to kill that man."

Thankfully, my husband was better at reading social cues than Det. Montgomery as he placed a hand on the detective's shoulder and urged him back. "This isn't the best time right now. Maybe you should give him some space."

"Sure, your *highness*," he said, still guffawing at Aeron. "The whole time? Sure explains a few things though."

As soon as he left, shoulders relaxed, sighs released, and fake smiles flattened.

"Nine years," Aeron muttered. "I started at Spyglass University under the name of Spade when I was fourteen. Nine years of using this alias to separate myself from my birthright: up in flames. Even if I bribe the reporter to keep it quiet, Montgomery knows, and he can't keep a secret if someone else's life depends on it. How long until we can leave?"

Lapides, I was the wrong person to ask about social expectations, but I was the only one who saw the benefit of being there. "I'm sorry, Aeron. It's possible the only reason Keys allowed us to come was because he discovered your real identity. As soon as we find evidence of his criminal activities, we can leave."

Aeron moaned and slid a hand down his face until Micro nudged him. "Wanna start in the dining room? We can raid the buffet table while we're at it."

"Fine."

I nodded. "Nita and I will go to the ballroom. The faster we find something, the sooner we can leave."

We divided and conquered with determination, parting to opposite sides of the mansion.

The ballroom wasn't terribly large for a dancing hall, but large enoug h for any private entertainment. Blood-red curtains framed large windows. The wooden walls and ceiling were designed with intricate patterns. There was a grand piano and a standing microphone for live performers on one end, serenading a few sets of dancers with smooth blues and then a ragtime jig. On the far side, a few tables allowed listeners to snack and rest. I surveyed the occupants, recognizing the CEO of the Shigaqua Bank, A-listing actress Barbara Jensen, and actor John Olson. I didn't recognize the others, though based on their tailored suits and dresses, I assumed this was where the higher-ups hung out. Perfect for walking around and asking about connections and dealings with Keys.

I started toward two men nearby in a seemingly enthralling conversation about…stocks and automobiles. I doubted they'd know any of Keys' secrets, but it wouldn't hurt to try.

I didn't get the chance.

The lights cut, plunging the mansion into darkness.

CHAPTER 3

With the curtains closed, no light filtered into the ballroom from the power-outage.

"Shoot," Nita cursed. "Aeron."

Shoot was right. If this power-outage lasted longer than three seconds, Aeron would go into a panic attack. Childhood trauma of being eaten alive by a shadow did that to a person.

The butler's voice shouted from the main entrance, "Everyone, please stay calm. Our emergency power generator should turn on momentarily."

Unfortunately, "momentarily" was too vague of a timeline.

"I'll find Aeron," I said. "You check on the power source."

Without a word, Nita shuffled away in the dark. I only heard one step before she disappeared into the shadows.

Shadows. Right. How was I supposed to find Micro and Aeron in this darkness?

I fumbled my way back to the main hall, bumping into several people and walls. At least the main entry had a couple of windows to show some outside light. Not that there was much offered by the storm. Only enough to spot a vague shadow heading upstairs and a cluster of people grouped in the woods. Gangsters? Would they take advantage of our vulnerability to break inside?

Raised voices from behind me announced Sponsor's location—in the office? It sounded like he and the reporter were looking for the light switches. I continued across to the dining hall, calling for Micro and Aeron.

"Truth?" my husband called back. Thank the stars he was alright. I took his hand in mine for reassurance of his presence.

"Micro? Where's Aeron?"

"I don't know. We were filling our plates with food when the lights cut. I heard his plate drop, then he disappeared like a ghost. I've been calling his name, but can't find him."

"Shoot. Nita went to find the breaker." I squeezed his arm with gratitude and for the reassurance of his nearness.

We both began calling for Aeron as the lights flickered back on. The power had been out for maybe half a minute. Searching with our eyes, we still couldn't find my PI partner. At least that explained why he hadn't responded. I was about to explore another room when a curtain pulled back from the dining hall door to the terrace.

Aeron stepped inside, drenched and shivering from the cold rain. He stepped sideways, keeping his back to the wall and gripping a flashlight, one fallen ice cream cone away from a mental breakdown.

I ran to him and took his wrist to feel his pulse. Far too fast. "Deep breaths," I said. "It was only a power-outage."

"It's never just a power-outage," he muttered, quoting one of Horror's rules of survival. It was almost a fact in Mystery too.

As if to confirm his pessimism, a shrill scream echoed through the mansion.

Aeron and I shared a single look before we dashed up the stairs toward the screams. Despite his shaken appearance, as soon as the lights returned, so did Aeron's hero-mode. Others

198

followed, including Det. Montgomery, to the gathering crowd outside a room that appeared to be a gallery.

The many portraits and paintings on the wall distorted my perspective of how many people were in the room. Three stood on the floor, including Mayor Duncan, all staring at a body on the ground.

"What happened?" I asked.

"Our host is dead! Someone killed Skoller Keys!"

"What?" I asked. Sure enough, the body belonged to Skoller Keys. But there was no blood or signs of a struggle. "How was he killed?"

Det. Montgomery scoffed. "Not every death is a murder. There's no blood or wounds. It could'a been a heart attack."

I stared at him, incredulous. "That's impossible." Even if he was somehow as neutralized as my adoptive papa, Keys's stronger Fantasy line would be unnaturally healthy.

The detective shrugged. "Happens all the time."

"Not to—" Needing validation, I called out, "Aeron! Analyze the body."

"What?" he asked. "You're the one who usually gets up close and personal with the corpses. I just talk to their spirits."

I would have rolled my eyes if the situation wasn't so urgent. "Because out of everyone in this room, you're the most likely to recognize our host for who he is."

Aeron flinched. He probably thought that I referred to his connections as an earl to another rich family. I shushed Det. Montgomery when he asked for more information and waited for Aeron's analysis.

The young man crouched over the body and frowned in concentration. He flipped out his breast pocket handkerchief to avoid touching the body directly. He felt the vampire's neck for a pulse, then raised an eyelid to turn his flashlight on the dead man's pupils. He muttered a curse and opened the victim's mouth.

Det. Montgomery frowned. "What's he—"

"Curses!" Aeron fell back and scrambled to add distance between himself and Keys. "He's a vampire!"

I analyzed the crowd as they gasped and shied back. Was there anyone who reacted less than shocked, or maybe too shocked?

Det. Montgomery's frown deepened. "What do you mean he's a vampire? We ain't got any vamps in Noir. And how can you tell?"

Micro smirked. "Shigaqua has a different kind of vamp."

Aeron stood into guard position almost as well as Nita, who'd appeared behind him, likewise drenched from being outside. Aeron refused to take his eyes off the body. "I'm half Horror. My mom taught me all about recognizing and killing paranormal creatures. His eyes are tinted red, and he has retractable canines."

"Is he faking?" I asked.

Aeron shook his head. "I don't understand. His eyes are dead. Vampires don't exactly have souls or lights in their eyes, but his spirit has left him. He doesn't have a pulse, but that's no surprise. There's no stake in his heart, his head is still attached, and even if the sun was out, he doesn't have any burning scars. How else can a vampire die?"

"That's where I'm stumped too," I said. "But one thing's for sure; it definitely wasn't a heart attack." I turned to Nita. "What do you know about the power-outage? Was it forced?"

"Well, we're running on a generator now. The line was cut from the powerhouse, which is badly placed up by the park gate entrance. I passed two groups of questionable bystanders, but their lack of interest in the powerhouse makes me think they weren't involved in our outage."

Aeron visibly squirmed. "Meaning we're stuck here with dwindling power, surrounded by delinquents outside, and a killer among us?"

"A killer's among us?" someone nearby screeched.

A sharp gasp turned my attention to a snoop at the doorway. Ms. Lanner, the reporter, stared at us with gaping eyes and mouth. "We're all going to die."

"Incredible!" I said. "Are you a fortune teller?"

"What?" She jerked a little like I'd offended her. "No."

"Good," I said. "I was going to give you some tips on presentation, but as it is, you should leave the prophetic statements to professionals."

CHAPTER 4

"A eron killed our host!" an unknown middle-aged man shouted.

Still crouched like he half expected the corpse to jump up and attack, the young PI frowned at his accuser. "What?"

"People were calling for him in the dark like he'd gone missing," the man said. "Obviously, it was him."

Montgomery narrowed his eyes thoughtfully. "I did hear him mutter that he was going to kill Keys."

"No," a surprising voice argued. Nita. I blinked at her. She'd never argued for anyone's defense before—even for her own. She continued, "Aeron went outside during the power-outage. You can see he's still dripping, soaked from the rain."

"He could have gone around the house to hide his tracks," Montgomery said. "Besides, he recognized Keys as a vampire. Maybe he felt threatened by him?"

Aeron defended himself that time, saying, "I was taught to recognize supernatural creatures because I'm half-Horror. I assume that's why Truth had me analyze the body—wait, did you already know he was a vampire?"

Before I could explain my knowledge of the vampire, Montgomery pointed back at Aeron. "Being half-Horror only incriminates you further. It's their natural instinct to kill vampires, even if they're civilized."

"Was Skoller Keys civilized?" I asked. "Can we confirm that he wasn't drinking human blood?" Unfortunately, we'd never been able to prove his blood orders from the hospital. "My source says Keys was a Fantasy breed of vampire, meaning he had access to supernatural strengths, but at a greater cost—especially while living in magic-suppressing Noir. Was he a vegetarian vampire? Would that make him a humanitarian?" I snickered at the pun. "No, because vegetarians prefer vegetation over meat, so a humanitarian vampire would be an active vampire who prefers humans over other foods."

An array of confused and bewildered stares answered my philosophical ramble. At least they weren't accusing Aeron of murder anymore.

Unfortunately, the reporter had been writing notes and reflected on earlier comments. "Isn't the accused royalty? Even if he's trained with the skills, royalty rarely kills directly. They do public executions only for their own glory. Or they hire someone else to do it in secret."

Again, to my surprise, Nita defended, "That's not who Aeron is. He'd never kill anyone unless it was for self-defense. He isn't that kind of person."

"Maybe not," Montgomery said, stroking his chin, "but you might be. You're trained in martial arts and weaponry, and you work by sneaking around. Spade might have hired you to kill him."

"I sent Nita to examine the power failure," I said.

"And you—" Montgomery turned on me and Micro "—your friend was killed by someone connected to Keys. You also had a motive against him."

"What?" I asked, incredulous.

"Or," Montgomery—shoot him and his dumb mouth—kept theorizing, "maybe your husband did it."

"That's too far, even for you, Montgomery," I said. "Everyone heard Micro shouting for Aeron. Everyone in the dining hall is his witness."

Montgomery shrugged. "It could have all been part of the plan as your team worked together to kill him. You all had motives, means, and opportunity."

"So did a dozen other people in here!"

My shout was drowned in the accusations of those around us.

"Arrest Aeron!"

"Lock them up!"

"Murderers!"

"They killed our host!"

Nita went into an open offensive position while Aeron went closed and defensive against the growing mob. I shouted back our innocence as Montgomery folded his arms and smiled like a victor.

Micro palmed my shoulder with one hand while raising his other in a calming gesture. "Detective, how many times has Visionary Investigations helped the Shigaqua Police solve Cases?"

The mob quieted to hear the detective's mumble, but not enough.

"I'm sorry, could you speak up?" Micro asked, somehow calm. Then again, this wasn't his first time being accused of a crime he didn't commit.

"A few times."

"More than you can count or remember off hand?"

The detective glowered at my husband.

Micro gestured to me as if I was the grand prize on a game show. "How fortunate are we that Visionary Investigations is here to solve this murder?"

"Did you say Visionary Investigations?" Ms. Lanner asked. Oh, *lapides*. What did the reporter know about us, and how would she spin it? "Haven't I heard of you? Aren't you one of Shigaqua's most successful private investigation agencies?"

That earned a few surprised blinks from the crowd and from myself.

Micro grinned. "Yes! Yes, they are! Truth Locke Johnson, Nita Incog, and Aeron Spade—the Ace of Spades!"

"I don't trust that Aeron fella," the man called. He'd been the one discussing stocks with the car manufacturer earlier. "I don't care if he solved a buncha Cases. He could still be a murderer!"

I stepped forward. "We want to help solve this Case, but if you refuse us, we'll go willingly to the police station to give our statements."

Nita shook her head. "The path is almost flooded. Driving through those woods will be tricky as long as it's still raining."

Montgomery groaned. "I suppose it'll be easier to work the Case while everyone's trapped here."

"We can lock him in a room," one of the mob accusers said.

Aeron growled to the side. "Obviously, these duncical people have made their minds up about me and won't see reason until we shove the truth in their faces. How about this?" he shouted to the mob. "Lock me in a room for the next few hours. Just give me a pillow, blanket, and decent lighting, and I won't even attempt to pick the lock."

Montgomery tapped his chin as if his cleft had the on/off button to his brain. "You're volunteering to stay locked up?"

"Until I can prove my innocence," Aeron agreed. "A lot can happen in a few hours when we're stuck with a murderer in a vampire's mansion. But you can be assured that whatever tragedies happen, I'll have no part in them. I'll solve this Case in my sleep."

Montgomery hummed to himself. "Only if Ms. Incog agrees to being locked up in a separate room."

"Why Nita too?" I asked.

"Even if Spade's calling the shots, Incog's the most likely killer among you. Will she accept?"

"Lock them up!" a guest shouted.

"If they're such a great team, make them solve this Case alone!"

"I refuse to be consoled until those two are detained!"

Unfortunately, Montgomery's logic made sense. Nita caught my eye, waiting for instruction.

"Just say the word," she mouthed more than whispered, "and I'll incapacitate everybody in the mansion." *Lapides*, I believed she could do it. But that wouldn't solve our problem, only make it worse.

I nodded to the irritating detective. "Separate rooms. If something else happens, then they'll both have alibis."

Montgomery asked one of the servants, "Are there rooms that can be locked from the outside?"

"Like a dungeon!" the actor, John Olson, shouted.

His co-star, Barbara Jensen, added, "Lock them in the basement!"

"We can't let them escape!"

"Murderers!"

The servant wrung his hands nervously. "I only have keys to the upstairs guest rooms. We can put you two in those."

"Fair enough." Aeron complied and followed the servant with Nita. It wouldn't matter if Aeron was locked away. As long as he had the time to sleep and enter the spirit state, he could slip through walls and search the grounds for the killer.

Technically, Nita could pick her way through any lock and then sneak back in before anyone noticed, but what Montgomery didn't know couldn't incriminate us.

Reassuring the growing mob that all was under control, Montgomery urged the other guests to calm down and go to the billiards room or main hallway. He set another servant to guard the corpse and crime scene while he escorted my partners down to the other end of the hall.

The two guest bedrooms were directly above the dining room and occupied with a lip-locked couple in one room.

After clearing them out, Montgomery cleared his throat to address my partners. "You got any weapons on you?"

"A few," Nita admitted.

"I'll need those."

Without complaint, she unstrapped her Chopped Hi-Powers pistol and Remington 51. The detective's eyes widened as she continued to unload a set of throwing daggers and a pocket knife from the skin-tight folds of her dress. Montgomery studied her dress as if to find the pockets where she'd kept it all. I suspected she held back a few items as she usually carried five times more weapons in her everyday outfits.

Meanwhile, Aeron didn't bother to hide his stink eye to Montgomery while he handed over his Colt Detective Special. Again, I was fairly certain he kept wooden and silver stakes in his side pack, but it would be at gunpoint before Aeron relinquished those particular weapons while staying in a vampire's house.

He didn't even wait for us to shut the door before plopping onto the creaky double bed for an extended nap. Nita went into the room next door with a meticulous analysis.

As soon as Det. Montgomery was satisfied that their doors were locked, he turned away with both keys.

"Now," he said, "stay here. I have work to do to keep these rich snobs from doing anything stupid."

"Good luck," I said, sincerely. "Will you let me Read Keys' palm?"

The detective grunted and grabbed the servant with the guestroom keys. "Watch her to make sure she don't do nothing suspicious."

Apparently, that was his way of granting permission. I waited until Montgomery had shepherded the guests to the billiards room before returning to the gallery. The undead victim lay on the floor, just as we'd left him.

Shivers crawled up my arms as I considered taking the vampire's hand. I'd been nervous about Reading Mal Testa, but awful as he was, he was still human. I knelt beside the corpse, half expecting him to sit up and attack me for falling for his trap.

With a deep inhale then exhale, I reminded myself that Aeron had confirmed his ultimate death. Still, I reached for his hand as if reaching to pet a wild animal. I edged my hand into his and began a Reading.

I Read up to his breakfast before flinching back as if he'd bitten me.

Sidera et lapides! No—nope—nuh-uh! My mind screamed, "Abort! Abort!" as I roughly rubbed my hand against my dress to rid myself of his germs. I stood and retreated from the body.

"I can't Read him." I grimaced at Micro. "I mean, I can, but…it's revolting."

He wrapped a comforting arm around my shoulders. "Then we'll find another way to solve this Case."

I nodded grimly. That meant relying on mundane investigating skills. I could still do that, right?

With a thought, I turned to the servant. "You said you 'only' have the keys to the guestrooms. What other locked rooms are there?"

The servant shook his head. "Only Sir Keys and the kitchen staff are allow—"

"Your employer has been murdered," I said. "With the murderer still on-site, this whole mansion is a crime scene. If there are secret rooms where a killer can hide, we need to know about them." Also, I needed to verify my suspicions about the vampire's diet to confirm the requirements for his death.

The servant shook his head again. "You'd need to ask the kitchen staff. I know nothing."

The lights flickered from the overworked generator, and I hoped Aeron was too unconscious to be bothered by the questionable lighting. Assuming the kitchen was near the dining hall, Micro and I went downstairs. The dining room was built and decorated similarly to the ballroom, except long buffet tables lined one wall, covered with golden platters and delicate treats. Little tables with white cloths spotted the area, and a giant red rug covered the wooden flooring. There were a few people still munching on finger food, slightly confused from the screams and commotion from upstairs, but otherwise un-worried. I wanted to tell them the full truth and nothing but the truth, but Micro simply warned them to stay indoors and not to wander anywhere alone.

Micro and I found the kitchen behind a closed door. Unlike every other floor and wall in the mansion built of reddish wood, the kitchen was white stone and tile. The kitchen staff were busy rolling croissants, mixing a vegetable garnish, and washing dishes. They wore nametags proclaiming them as Terry, Doug, and Velma of On the Nose Catering. Shoot, they were hired help and probably wouldn't have the answers I needed.

"Excuse me," I shouted for their attention. "Your employer, Skoller Keys, is dead. To investigate his murder, we need access to every room in this house. I was told there's a room that only the kitchen staff have access to?"

The three chefs shared nervous looks. Terry with the croissants said, "We were only hired to cater this evening. We don't know anything about any locked rooms."

"But," Velma added like a church mouse, "we were strictly told not to go down those stairs." She pointed at a door. Interesting. I hadn't seen any other stairs leading to a basement.

Thanking them, I went directly to the door. A lantern hung on the wall, and we had it lit by the kitchen staff before heading down the stairs. The stairway was narrow and lined with red carpeting. The lantern wasn't bright enough to light the bottom.

"Maybe," I mused, "it's a good thing Aeron's not with us for this part. I'm pretty sure he hates stairs, basements, and dark areas."

"Maybe," Micro agreed.

Worrying about my teammates, I huffed. "I can't believe Montgomery had him and Nita locked up. None of us could have killed him, no matter how much we disliked him."

"Yeah," Micro said, "but Aeron's alibi is his incapacitating fear of the dark. It's not worth broadcasting his biggest weakness if only to satisfy Montgomery. There's no use arguing with stupidity."

Reaching the bottom, we found ourselves in a grim version of the second floor. The wood surrounding us was several shades darker, the air was significantly cooler, and there was a stark lack of decorative plants and portraits. The open area smelled damp and moldy.

Micro shivered. "You think the killer might be hiding down here?"

"No," I said. "I think Keys was a 'humanitarian' vampire."

He frowned. "We know he was ordering blood from the note sent to Romey's husband last year."

"Yes," I said, "but considering the number of missing people and the secrecy of this basement, I don't think the blood packets were his only food source."

Micro tensed and jerked the lantern from side to side. "You think he's keeping people down here? Is that why he hired a catering business for tonight? Because his usual chefs work with 'other' proteins? What if they're also vampires? What if he's grooming new vampires down here?"

"Unlikely," I said. "The magic-negations of Noir would make transformations nearly impossible even for a Horror or Romance vampire, but Keys was a Fantasy vampire, meaning he relied on magic. I don't think he's hiding other vampires so much as hiding his food source. Did you see the kitchen? It was the only white room. While the other reddish rooms can camouflage blood, the kitchen can be bleached, and I bet it's been bleached many times to remove blood stains. Also, the dining room rug was slightly curled. That means it's recently rolled out, probably to cover more blood stains, same as the red rug coming down these stairs."

"This door has a lock," Micro said, shining the light on a side door across the hall. "Should we break it open? Sometimes doors are locked to keep things in."

I analyzed up and down and across the hallway. "Something's off about this. This basement has the exact same floor plan as the upstairs, but there should be two doors here like those leading to the guestrooms with Aeron and Nita." I walked up to the blank wall, searching the edges for any crevices of false walls or hidden doors. Nothing. Putting my ear against the cold wall, I listened. Was that crying?

"Break the lock," I said.

CHAPTER 5

Micro and I searched the basement for a key or something strong enough to help us break the lock, feeling the tops of door frames, looking under clay pots, and peeking into the other basement rooms. They were all dusty, and the sparse furniture was covered with black cloths.

I grumbled, "I bet Nita could open that lock without a problem."

"Would you like me to?"

I jumped with a shriek. The woman who was supposed to be locked in a bedroom two floors above was standing behind me.

"Is that Nita?" Micro asked. "What are you doing here?"

"My job is to ensure your safety."

I groaned and slid my palm down my face. "Did anyone see you escape your confines?"

She scoffed with a little laugh. "No. I made sure of it. Well, do you need me to break a lock?"

"Yes," I said. "Then you need to go directly back to your room. If anyone sees you, they'll think you killed Keys."

"Because there's no use arguing with stupidity."

I blinked at her quotation of Micro's words. How long had she been following us?

Nita retrieved a gun from who knows where and smacked its handle against the lock. I shined my light on her weapon. It was an odd device, like an all-black spying scope but with a handle and trigger.

"What kind of gun is that?" I asked.

Nita shuffled uneasily, as if she was irritated that I'd noticed. "Well, it's a Welrod. It has a built-in suppressor."

I searched my memories, sure that I'd seen that gun sometime…somewhere…in a white room, bagged as a piece of "evidence."

"You had that with you when they found you on the lake," I said. "It's a rare model. I bagged it as evidence, hoping to use it to discover your identity."

Her uneasy shuffle this time spoke along the lines of guilt. "Which was why I stole it back…and why I hide it deeper than my others. I did my own research on it. It's a…well, it's a Thriller model that's old enough to function in Noir."

I tilted my head and blinked at her. More clues and more questions. I was becoming more and more convinced that Nita wasn't merely a bodyguard, soldier, or mercenary. She was something else, and I was almost scared to find out. But shoot my curiosity, I needed to know.

Micro scoffed. "It's a good thing Montgomery doesn't know you have that. He already thinks we're murderers."

"Keys wasn't shot," I said. "Which is part of the confusion. No wooden bullets or stakes to the heart, and no decapitation. How did he die?" Maybe we'd find some answers in the next room.

We pulled open the locked door. Inside, we flashed our lanterns over disorganized bookshelves covered with dust.

Footsteps on tile sounded above us, followed by a rushing of pipe water. We were directly beneath the kitchen. It was a terrible place to store books, with the risk of a leak or flooding.

"A library?" Micro asked. "Why would anyone put a lock on a library?"

I chuckled. "You have no idea how terrifying or powerful books can be, do you? But even if these books have forbidden magic, there's something more in here."

I went to the side where I would have expected a door based on the floor plan. The wall was solid with bookshelves, but there was less dust in front of one shelf. And were those scuff marks?

I grabbed at books and yanked them from the shelf, making a terrible mess of bending spines and folded pages.

Micro wrinkled his eyebrows. "Didn't you just say books can be terrifying and powerful? Knowing our luck, one of those books has a soul to curse anyone who abuses it."

"This shelf is a secret door," I said. "One of these books—"

One book caught and refused to be thrown, tipping instead with a heavy click. The shelf slid back and to the side.

I stepped in, sweeping my light across the dark room. *Please don't be more vampires. Please don't be more vampires.*

Instead, I found medical equipment for drawing blood, mattresses on the floor, and a tight line…of corpses. Names had been scratched into the wall above their heads. Ronald. Karen. Lisa. Gary. Susan… There were at least a dozen.

Whimpers from one corner led my light. Eight youths of varying ages huddled in the back. One of each blood type? They seemed relatively healthy despite their paleness from obvious vitamin-D deficiencies and recent blood loss. I recognized half of them from the missing people reports, including Mary Argall, the missing child we'd been hired to find.

"Thank the stars you're alive," I whispered, and ran over to them.

They screamed and ran to the other corner.

"Truth," Micro warned, "you're scaring them. They're traumatized. Mary," he called softly from the doorway. "Mary Argall."

Mary whimpered.

My husband crouched and held the shelf/door wide open. "Your mother sent us. She's worried about you."

"Mom?"

"Yes, you've been so strong, surviving all you suffered, but we can go home. Your mom is waiting for you."

She stood and timidly stepped forward, but glanced back at the others. Micro waved me back, and I reluctantly retreated through the doorway. People were confusing. It didn't matter how much I studied psychology or physical cues, I didn't understand people. Why weren't these kids thrilled to escape?

Micro continued to crouch at the edge of the doorway, speaking softly, "I understand if you're scared. Bring your friends along. There's strength in numbers. Yes, that's right, don't leave anybody behind."

At least Micro knew how to handle people. I stepped back and reconsidered the corpses. The freshest one was at least a few weeks old, preserved, yet moldy from the cold and humid basement. Most of the names were familiar from missing-people reports. Only Susan seemed fresh enough for a proper Reading, but I studied the bones of each one, noticing Karen had underdeveloped kneecaps and elbows. Nail-patella syndrome?

Retreating to Nita in the false library, I urged her again to return to her room.

"I'm glad you stayed in case there was something danger-ous, but I think we're good. We'll be in more trouble if you're caught outside of your locked room."

"There's still a murderer on the premises."

"I know. We'll deal with the murder after freeing these kids. I can't say I'm terribly eager to bring justice to whoever killed that kidnapping, blood-sucking villain, but these kids need a safe place to stay until we can take them home. Maybe I can convince Montgomery that you're the best option to pro-tect them, but you'll need to play the part in your room until then."

If she made any expressions of rebellion, it was too dark to tell. Her chin dipped with a nod, then she faded into the dark-ness of the basement.

It took some time for Micro to coax the kids out of the dungeon. As Micro attempted to explain the situation to the kids, I returned upstairs, poked my head out to the hallway and shouted, "Hey, Montgomery! You'll want to see what we found."

"Locke?" he shouted over the banister. "How did you—ah, shoot, of course you poked around. Just stay down there, okay? I'm pretty sure I got everyone upstairs and accounted for. It's all under control."

Even as he spoke, a curtain moved unnaturally in the ball-room. Montgomery turned away to shout at someone for something. I drew my Browning Hi-Power pistol and snuck across the main hallway toward the ballroom.

Going around the edges, I lost sight of the curtain momen-tarily. I hurried forward until the ballroom door was within sight again, watching all exits and entrances. But I couldn't see the edges of the room. Creeping forward, I increased my view little by little, hoping for more information.

A quick gasp and the tiniest of yelps reached my ears. No time to creep.

I swept around the column at the entrance, leveling my pistol at average body height.

A man dressed as a ninja stood behind a woman. Ms. Lanner.

His slice was so quick, so efficient, that the reporter's life was over before I could mentally question what was happening. There was something familiar in his stance and movements.

My breath hitched. "Who are you?"

The masked man jerked toward me, then something cut into my hand, forcing me to drop my gun. A throwing star? He aimed a suppressed pistol directly at my face. I knew that pistol. It was the same kind that Nita described as a Thriller model.

"You never saw me," he said in a muffled voice. "This woman was dead before you arrived. Now, scream."

As if I'd start screaming. I had questions! I needed answers!

Before I could ask any of them, he charged at me. I'd seen this speed before, this grace and fluidity. In fact, I'd seen better.

But Nita had never charged at me with murder in her eyes. The sight of this man—this killer—coming straight for me released a self-defensive instinct to scream.

I screeched in terror and dropped to grab my gun. By the time I recaptured my pistol and turned back toward my attacker, he was gone.

I was too stunned to follow, let alone catch him for more information.

Micro ran up behind me a second later. "Truth? Are you alright? What happened?"

I pointed at the open door where the man had fled. "There was a man here. I'll draw a picture, because I need Aeron's spirits to find him for questioning."

"A man? Oh—four!" Micro swore as he spotted the dead body and spreading blood. "He did this?"

"Yes," I said, "with enough grace and sufficiency to rival Nita. Micro, he might know her. Or maybe where she was trained to be a special operative. Right now, he's our best clue to discovering her past."

Micro's eyes bounced between me, the body, and the open door. "I'll call first responders. You work on that picture. The kids are in the dining room, devouring the appetizers."

I nodded. We'd get to the bottom of this. Though I wasn't sure if "this" referred to the vampire's murder or Nita's identity. Hopefully both.

CHAPTER 6

Det, Montgomery stared at us with obvious skepticism as I described the reporter's murder.

"Convenient, isn't it?" he asked, rubbing his chin. "You knew exactly where to find those missing kids, then came upstairs just in time to 'witness' the murder of Ms. Lanner—the woman with the means to spread Spade's royal identity across town."

"Yes, it was convenient—"

"Truth," Micro cut in. "He was speaking sarcastically."

"But it's still convenient," I said, "because Aeron and Nita are both locked up in guest rooms upstairs, so neither of them can be the killer. They have alibis." As long as no one saw Nita sneaking around to follow Micro and me down to the basement and back up.

"Meaning," Montgomery grumbled, "there's someone else going around killing people. But that don't mean I can convince everyone else that you're all innocent."

"Fine," I said. "Keep them locked up until word spreads that another murder occurred while they were locked away. The people will have a nice little panic with that. Have fun with crowd control. I have clues to verify."

I went up to the second floor to Nita's door and knocked. "Nita? Are you in there?"

"Where else would I be?" she returned from behind the door.

I smirked. "When you went for the power source, did you find anything that could help us identify the killer?"

Her voice returned quietly from within. "There weren't any trip-wires or timed explosives attached to the power. It's impossible for the same person who killed the power in the shed across the property to have also killed Skoller Keys in the mansion."

"Interesting," I said. "Then it was a two-man job. I can't say I'm surprised. The man who killed Ms. Lanner isn't the type who kills for his own reasons."

"There was another murder?"

Oh, good. She'd been in her room then. I detailed the second murder and my hopes of catching the unknown killer. Not only because of his possible connections to Nita's past, but also, "I expect he was hired by someone who helped him to kill the vampire."

"Meaning we either find his employer and convince them to give up his hired help, or we find the hired help and convince him to reveal his employer."

Yep. Since I'd seen the hired man's face, the second option seemed more likely, but how in the stars were we supposed to convince that son of a gun to give up his employer? Finding him and then pinning him down would be a trick on its own.

Det. Montgomery told us to stay put, but he couldn't expect us to solve the Case while standing still. Micro and I tiptoed back to the office. I needed a pen and paper to draw the attacker's face and assumed to find supplies in there.

Like all rooms except the kitchen, the office was decorated in dark mahogany and leather. A thick and intricate rug softened my footsteps as I made my way to the desk. No more tiptoeing. Nita would have been better at sneaking around, but I enjoyed the idea of taking point for this Case. With my upcoming retirement and the inevitable deadlines of Aeron's royal reinstatement and Nita's returned memories, I soaked in the moment for all it was worth.

A large desk featured orderly stacks of paper and rows of pens. I grabbed the closest pen and the blank top page to start my sketch. I already had an oval and crossbar for the eyes before thinking to check the other side of the paper. What was I drawing on? The page was a thick and fancy letter paper. I hoped it wasn't important.

Flipping it over, a casual glance would have called the typed page unremarkable, but then I started to read it. It was a letter from S. Duncan. *Lapides*, the Mayor of Shigaqua was Stanley Duncan. The beginning and end of the message was full of pleasant small talk, but it turned out the filling between the sandwich was meaty.

"While Shigaqua's nightlife can be vibrant and exciting, the consistent disappearance of beloved individuals is beginning to attract undesirable attention from both local law enforcement and, dare I say, Mr. Testa. Our public relations department has had its hands full, fielding questions, and the last thing I want is for the city to become associated with anything untoward or unseemly—particularly when it comes to the matters of...well, you know, Paranormals.

"Now, I understand that your needs are unique and that, as always, you have your own manner of obtaining your basic needs. However, I would ask that you consider scaling back somewhat the frequency of your nocturnal excursions, particularly in areas where such disappearances might raise an eyebrow or two. While I acknowledge your preferences for 'untainted' sources, a more selective approach toward the displaced, if you will, would likely serve best. It would be a shame if you continued and someone less understanding discovered your dietary needs.

"Should you ever need a discreet meeting place, the back room at the Pizzeria Tre is always available after hours. You know the one. No questions asked."

"Sidera et lapides," I cursed. The mayor knew about Skoller Keys's diet? My stomach twisted as I reviewed the mayor's request. Not only did Mayor Duncan know about the vampire's appetite, but he requested a focus on the vagrants. They were people too! I cringed as I remembered the mayor's campaign to "clean up the city" by solving Shigaqua's homeless population. I'd voted for him! Now, I wanted to puke.

I lifted the next page on the pile. A receipt for the electric bill paid in full and on time. Boring. Even if the single utility bill was quadruple the amount that Micro and I paid. The rest of the small stack was similar mundane utilities and upkeep.

Micro joined my side. "Are you looking for something?"

"Common sense."

"Oof, can't help you there," he teased.

"You have more than most people I meet. But this doesn't make sense. Why is this highly incriminating letter on top of this pile of boring bills during an open house party? It's like Keys wanted it to be found."

Micro shrugged. "You think someone planted it there?"

"Maybe," I said. "But who? Why?"

"Maybe they left something else too? Should we search?"

"Good idea."

We divided to conquer the room's secrets. I opened every drawer in the desk and ran my fingers along every seam, searching for hidden compartments. Micro wasn't quite as meticulous as he threw pillows and cushions from the seating, opened books toward the floor, and searched behind the wall paintings.

"There's a safe behind this painting," he said. It was a portrait of a woman in colonial clothing.

"I know we broke the lock to free the kids in the basement, but we aren't here to steal from Keys," I said. "There's no probable cause for us to break into that safe. Also, the incriminating letter was out in the open. If there's anything else for us to find—"

I paused as my fingers caught on a latch beneath the desk drawer. Why, hello there. Was it still breaking into something if the lock didn't require a combination or key, just a brain?

With a gentle push in the right spot, the false bottom of the drawer slid open. Inside was a packet of blood, a voice recorder, and a syringe with a strangely tan needle.

Micro was at my side the moment he heard the latch and sliding compartment. He stared at the items. "Okay, the blood makes sense for a vampire. Is that a sound recorder? Maybe he recorded some of his meetings? But what's with the syringe?"

"I don't know," I said. "Maybe he took blood injections?" Slipping out my handkerchief, I picked up the sound recorder. There could be more incriminating information on that. I pressed rewind, but the play button was jammed. "Shoot," I muttered. "We'll need to have this looked at."

"One Case at a time," Micro chuckled. "Work on that sketch of Ms. Lanner's killer, and then we can interview the mayor about his dealings with Keys."

Right, I still needed to accomplish the main reason we entered that room in the first place.

According to his research, Aeron needed two hours of sleep before entering the spirit state. The office clock chimed the second hour since the "party" began, but Aeron needed time to interact with the spirits, so I took my time with my sketch of the killer. Two hours was a long time to be locked in a house with a murderer or two, but at least it wasn't two hours with a vampire or two hours outdoors exposed to the drizzle and circling wolves (both literal and human). Shadows and a glint of metal caught my eye from beyond the office window. The house lights flickered as the generator struggled. Party attendees grew restless, asking for food, to use the bathroom, to go home…etc. They kept Det. Montgomery too busy to work on the Case. Was he secretly hoping we'd solve it for him? I wouldn't put it past him.

I finished my sketch of a twenties-ish male with a narrow face, thin and flat black eyebrows over dead fish eyes. I hadn't been able to catch their eye color, but I could describe his voice as a raspy tenor and a Thriller accent with its no-nonsense tones, no questioning inflections, and demanding volume. Unfortunately, the rest of his face had been covered with a summer scarf and skin-tight hood, but I hoped it would be enough.

I considered slipping it under the door to Aeron's guest bedroom, but I only had one copy. I held onto it, hoping Aeron or one of his spirits lingered around to catch the drift.

Showing my sketch to Det. Montgomery, I explained, "This is the man who killed Ms. Lanner."

He raised his brows at my drawing. "You got decent art skills, but that could be anybody."

"I don't think he was invited by Keys, but by an employer who helped orchestrate the vampire's murder. I'd like to show it to each of the attendees. Maybe one of them will recognize him."

"Sure, Locke. But I'd rather get your help with crowd control here. All these pompous partiers were hard enough to handle. Did you hafta bring the kids up before the Case was solved?"

I frowned at him. "You would have preferred that I kept the kids locked in the basement? Haven't they suffered enough? It's not like we can send them home in the dark or through those woods with gangs lying in wait."

"What if," Micro offered, "we let them watch each other. Let everyone group up in teams of three or four to search the house for this man."

Det. Montgomery scratched his chin. "That ain't a half bad idea."

"There's something else," I said, then showed him the letter on the other side.

"Shoot," the detective cursed. "You're saying we need to interrogate the mayor?"

"Yes. You don't accidentally kill a vampire, so whoever killed Keys must have known about his vampire secret. The mayor knew. That makes him a suspect."

The detective groaned and slid his hand down his face. "You also knew."

"Yes, I did," I admitted, "but I was under the impression that he was stealing blood from hospitals and not up to his full strength. I only had suspicions and came tonight to confirm his true diet. This letter implies that the mayor knew of Keys's diet for fresh blood."

Det. Montgomery read over the letter again. "You said you found this on top of the pile? What're the odds someone else could've read this and learned about Keys being a blood-sucker?"

I shook my head. "The wording is vague. Someone could just as easily assume that Keys was a werewolf from that letter. While a beheading and piercing to the heart could kill most paranormal monsters, Keys wasn't killed by either of those."

Det. Montgomery raised a brow. "We don't know what killed him."

"Exactly." Which brought us back to the original paradox of this Case. Not only did the killer know Keys was a vampire, but they killed him in a way to make it look like a heart attack. How?

As much as I detested the idea, I needed to Read the vampire.

CHAPTER 7

Det. Montgomery began to work around the room with the sketch of Ms. Lanner's killer and directed everyone to group up. The guests murmured and quickly found the handful of people they each trusted. I decided to procrastinate my interview with a vampire by interviewing Mayor Duncan.

The man was a portly fellow with good hair and a suit that rivaled Micro's simplicity. He fancied it up with a monocle hanging from his ear and a pocket watch chain drooping from a vest pocket. He squirmed a little when noticing my approach, then hid all nerves behind a straight back and a politician's smile. I'd seen that smile enough times on Aeron to know when it was fake.

"You should know," I said, "that your political career is as dead as the vampire. Not undead like he was, but dead-dead like he is now."

His expression twitched with humored confusion. "What are you talking about? Do I know you?"

"Probably not," I said, reaching for a handshake. The foolish mortal took my hand for introductions. With a solid pump,

I knew more than necessary. *Sidera*, that was a boring Reading. "But I know all about you."

He shrugged as if he wasn't surprised. He was the mayor after all.

"Truth Locke," I said, slipping my hand back and subtly wiping it against my dress. "Head Investigator at Visionary Investigations Agency. And you're Stanley Duncan, Mayor of Shigaqua, father of three children, the youngest is diagnosed with polio. You've been saving up to go to Procedural after your years of service, hoping to receive the treatment and cure for your child. You'd do anything to save your child, even if it means dealing with a vampire. I'm sorry, but the picture of the reporter's killer was drawn on the back of a condemning letter between you and our host. Everyone now knows that Keys was a vampire, and that letter confirms that you endorsed his appetite in a less savory direction."

His fake smile melted into surprise and then terror with each of my sentences. "How did you—"

"I told you, I know all about you. I know you did your best to appease your biggest sponsor, Keys, but you hated what he was and what he ate. You hated that he got away with kidnapping and murder just because he was rich and entitled. You hated him, but…you didn't kill him."

"No!" he defended. "I mean, yes, I hated him, but I wouldn't stoop to his level. He was a monster, but I wanted to remove him legally. I would have turned him over the moment I learned of his…condition, but Keys has connections and lawyers who can excuse him from anything."

"In the letter, you threaten to turn him over to Sponsor—or Mal Testa."

The mayor cleared his throat and wrung his hands. "I may have used some…phrasing to imply such a threat. I'm familiar with the tactic of hiring crooks to catch crooks, but I promise that I never acted on any such methods."

I nodded with a grim smile. "I believe you. Your days are spent with paperwork and meetings. Yes, you were in the room with the victim when he was killed, but you knew what he was. The moment we lost power, you expected him to attack you, so you stumbled away from him as best as you could."

"Yes," he said, blinking wide eyes at me. "I couldn't find the door, but it's exactly as you said. How did you know?"

"If I had time to explain, I would. As it is, I'm back to no suspects, meaning my work is far from over."

Lapides, it would have been too easy to catch the mayor red-handed like that. I ground my teeth as I considered Reading the vampire's palm again.

The door of Aeron's guest bedroom slammed against its frame as someone pounded on the other side.

"Hey!" Aeron shouted from within. "Somebody! I need to talk to Truth Locke and Nita Incog! I have important news that will help catch the killer! Hey! Is anyone out there? I need my teammates!"

I smiled as he claimed Nita and me as his equals and I arrived at the door. "What did you find, Aeron?" I asked through the door.

"Truth? My spirit friends saw Ms. Lanner's murder and followed the killer."

"Fantastic," I said, then called across the hallway to Det. Montgomery as he stood at the doorway of the gallery. "Hey! Are we good to free my teammates now? Spade might have solved the Case in his sleep."

"Took him long enough," Montgomery muttered as he unlocked the guest bedrooms. Nita and Aeron emerged, looking like they'd each enjoyed a nap while I spent the last few hours dealing with Montgomery, rescuing children, and witnessing the second murder.

"Did your spirits show you how to catch the man who killed Ms. Lanner?" I asked.

Nita stepped over to listen intently to his findings. She was never this interested when we found information about our victims or murderers. Then again, this was a man who might know about her past.

Aeron nodded. "They followed him, and I have a meeting with him in thirty minutes."

I raised my eyebrows at him. "How did you arrange that?"

"If I told you, I'd have to kill you." He shrugged.

Nita's impatience bled out through her expression. "If you don't tell me, I might kill you."

"I bet you could," Aeron laughed nervously. "Honestly, I don't remember, but Neil gave me this message when I woke up." He held up a small note with no more than a place and a time. Of course, it was across the property's woods in half an hour.

Eyeing his attire (a well-kept trench coat, silky suit vest, and a golden pocket watch), I said, "You might want to disguise yourself to blend in with the suspicious people in those woods and take backup."

"I'll go," Nita said, eager for the first time.

I suppressed my smirk and nodded. "We should all go. Of course, I'll stay farther away, and Nita can be positioned close enough to aid you if needed. What's your plan to approach him?"

Aeron scratched his head. "I haven't really figured that out yet. I have a hard time imagining him giving up his employer, partner, or any alliances to tell us who murdered Keys or how he became trained in the same arts as Nita."

"No," I agreed, "I bet he's been trained to stay silent even through torture. He's an assassin or mercenary of some sort. He's not likely to eat out of the palm of your hand." I snapped my fingers with an idea. "What if you try to hire him?"

Aeron frowned. "For what? Supposing he's taking offers, why would I need to hire a killer? Besides, as Montgomery has annoyingly pointed out, if I wanted anything so detestable, I could hire Nita for the job."

"A smart client wouldn't hire anyone they're connected to." I leaned forward with a mischievous smirk. "But every politician needs someone to do their dirty work."

"I'm not a—" His eyes widened with understanding. "You want me to reveal my lineage? I don't know whether he'll fall for it. My father's version of 'dirty work' is outwitting someone with words—which he's plenty capable of doing on his own. Then my mom," he paused to laugh, "she does her own 'dirty work.'"

"But you," I emphasized, "are not your parents. Can you do it or not?"

"I…"

"I'd do it," I said, "except he'd know that I can't afford him. Come on, it's for Nita."

He clenched his jaw and snuck a glance at Nita's subtle pleading before he relented. "Alright. I'll be on point and pretend to be an idiot who throws around his parentage to get himself into trouble."

CHAPTER 8

Aeron gave Nita his long dark overcoat to hide her dress, then took another ten minutes in the closet to find a suitable disguise while I grabbed a set of walkie-talkies from the servants, and a pair of binoculars for me. Aeron and Nita headed into the woods to scout the meeting spot that was close enough to the mansion that Micro and I could watch the exchange from a second-floor patio. Our point man emerged between the trees with his same fancy-pants suit, top hat, and cane sword. Nita was nowhere to be found.

My eyes bulged.

"Are you serious?" I asked through my walkie-talkie. "I told you to go in disguise. We have no idea what kind of animals or criminals might be lurking in the woods at this hour. It's a miracle that you haven't been robbed, mugged, and left for dead in a gutter in this park that's known for criminal activity."

He raised his hands in defense. "If I'm revealing my lineage and asking for expensive services, I need to dress the part. Besides, the fact that I can walk around this park without being robbed, mugged, or left for dead in a gutter speaks of my power and influence. I trust that Nita took care of any issues."

"He's right," Nita said from her own walkie-talkie. "I've steered away any intrusions for the meeting. This show of money and power is far more intimidating."

Alright, they had a point. "Fine," I said, "play it up. The more confident you are, the more he'll want to work for you. It won't matter who his employer is, or what they're paying him, he'll want to be on your side. Mercenaries and hitmen always need sponsors and funding. They care less about loyalty than about being on the winning team. Make him believe that's you."

"Right." He nodded and shook the tension out of his shoulders. "Just pretend to be my parents then."

I suppressed a laugh. He had no idea what his parents were like when I knew them, before they became direct heirs to a duchy, back when they were still timid and paranoid.

We wished each other good luck and then took positions. We were fifteen minutes early, but Nita said the mysterious man was likely to be early too, for scouting the position. Sure enough, as soon as Aeron dusted off a metal bench enough to plop himself down, Nita whispered from my walkie-talkie. "Movement from Aeron's ten o'clock."

Spying through my eyepiece, I saw nothing until a quick piece of metal flicked at Aeron from a shadowed area. Nita gasped and might have blown the whole operation if an invisible wall hadn't stopped the throwing star from hitting its target.

"Ah," Aeron said calmly as if one of his spirit friends hadn't just saved his life. "You're early. I also came early to keep you from setting any traps."

"Who are you?" the voice from the shadow rasped. Aeron's walkie-talkie barely picked up the sound. "How did you block my star? What do you know about the whispers in my ear telling me to come here? Make them stop."

"You should know," Aeron said to the shadow, "I've set my own precautions in case you try to kill me."

"Who are you?" the rasping voice almost shouted. "How did you discover and locate me?"

"Isn't that the million-dollar question? I have resources, and if you injure me with so much as a paper cut, those same resources will haunt you till the end of your miserable days. I'd say 'life,' but honestly, with those dissonant whispers, I don't imagine anyone lasting longer than a week. You cannot escape them, so you might as well chat with me."

"I can't," the shadow said. "Not with these voices in my head."

"Say please."

Micro coughed back a laugh beside me. I agreed. The kid was too good at this. We were lucky to have him on our side.

The shadow muttered, "Please."

"Give him a break, guys." Aeron rolled his eyes and wrist like he could hardly bother with the command.

With a relieved sigh, the shadow rasped, "Who. Are. You?"

"Aeron Fromm, the Haunted, Earl of Margen and Duke of the Dead. Go ahead, look me up. It's all true. Or, at least most of it," he finished with a dark chuckle. I shuddered at his fine imitation of his poltergeist. "Yes, I have a magical ability to visit the dead on a daily basis, even outside of Fantasy. Yes, I'm the heir to half of Fairy, Fantasy, and yes, I work in Noir as a private investigator. Not because I need the money—curses, no. I just enjoy their attempts to challenge me."

The shadow was silent for a good minute before it demanded, "What do you want?"

"Answers," Aeron said. "Who do you work for?"

The shadow scoffed. "As if I would tell you."

"You either tell me now, or I have my dead friends haunt you until you make contact. They'll float through your body, give you the chills, and always leave you with that prickly feeling that someone's watching you. I imagine that's a dangerous sensation to ignore in your field of work."

The shadow remained silent.

"What if," Aeron tried, "I wanted to hire you? As an earl, I could always use more security, or someone…discreet to take care of unpleasant tasks. Do you have something as flashy as a business card or file I could research? How am I to know if you're good enough for—"

"We're good enough," he snapped.

Aeron smiled at the emotional leak and waited.

"Arrowhead."

"That's your organization? How should I contact your services for hire?"

"You won't. We'll contact you after a solid background check."

"Hmm," Aeron mused. "Then you don't know who personally hired the hit on Ms. Lanner, the reporter?"

"No. My job isn't to ask questions. But I'm done here. With my mark disposed of, I have no reason to stay. So, will you leave me alone?"

"Wait," I hissed through my walkie-talkie and then whispered my request.

"One more question," Aeron said. "Which did you kill: the lights or the vampire?"

"Who said I killed either of them?"

"Did you forget my resources?"

The shadow grunted. "The lights. I completed my task without issue. It was my employer who failed in their part and required more work from me."

Interesting. Aeron nodded thoughtfully.

"If I don't hear from you within the week, I'll haunt you—I mean, find you again. You can bet your death on it. You may go. For now."

The shadow disappeared, and Aeron stood from the bench, brushing himself off. Nita emerged from the opposite shadows. I was about to call out to them when I spied Nita throwing her arms around Aeron's shoulders.

Whoa! A hug? She'd never initiated a hug with me in the almost-three years we'd known each other. I hunkered down with my binoculars and smashed my walkie-talkie to my ear.

"Arrowhead," she said. "That's who I worked for?"

"It's just a name," he said. "We don't know if you were affiliated." He set his hands around her waist as tender as a lover.

Shoot, that was a real problem.

I shouted into my walkie-talkie, "Sounds like you're a David Webb."

"A who?" Nita asked, breaking away from the embrace. I mentally congratulated myself for ruining their moment.

"He was a trained operative of sorts," Aeron explained. "You wouldn't be the first agent to lose all of their memories. Fortunately for you, they haven't hunted you down like they did with Webb."

"Why would they hunt me down?"

"I don't know," I said, "but maybe we'll find out. Good job, Aeron. Looks like we're finally getting somewhere with Nita's identity."

She grinned at him with the biggest smile I'd ever seen on her. Shoot. I wasn't supposed to see that smile. It was meant for Aeron and Aeron alone. He returned the smile with an added look that I only ever got from Micro. Shoot the son of a gun with stars and stones!

I'd failed as a mentor. I'd let them fall in love.

CHAPTER 9

I watched Nita and Aeron return to the mansion through my binoculars to make sure they didn't do anything else foolish. Thankfully, their lack of tomfoolery allowed my mind to pick apart the conversation with the Arrowhead agent.

He'd been the one to kill the lights, and he'd completed his "task." But then his employer failed "their part and required more work." So, the employer had killed the vampire but somehow failed… How? Keys was officially dead—not simply undead.

How had the employer failed? Was that why the Arrowhead agent killed Ms. Lanner? Had the reporter witnessed something to incriminate the killer?

I remembered seeing her drained face after the murder, hearing her false prophecy that we were all going to die. What had she seen or heard?

I shared my questions and theories with Micro but ended up pulling my hair for answers. I needed more information. I needed to stop delaying the inevitable and Read the victim's palm.

Micro and I passed Det. Montgomery on our way to the gallery. He frowned with annoyance.

"You haven't solved this thing yet?"

Micro bit back, "You could help out for a change."

"It's okay, Micro," I said, cutting off Montgomery's retort. "He's been helpful by keeping the other party members occupied. That allowed Aeron to sleep uninterrupted and will let me Read the victim's hand without others crowding around."

Montgomery raised his brows. "You ain't done your magic fortune telling on him already?"

Micro cringed at Montgomery's wording, then asked me, "You're really going to Read him? But don't you feel everything that person has done with their hands that day?"

"Yes." I grimaced. "I have a feeling it's not going to be pretty, but I can't see a way around it. I need to know how someone killed an active vampire without beheading or staking his heart."

The gallery was empty except for the victim's body on the floor. He was pale and still, but that was normal for a vampire. I would have suspected a body switch, except Aeron had confirmed his identity and curse. Aeron's trepidation of the monster crept into my own heart as I knelt beside the corpse, half expecting it to sit up like a zombie at any second.

Slipping my hand over Skoller Keys's hand made me feel dirty inside. As if simply touching the vampire spread his filth onto me. Grasping his hand was like reaching into a scorpion's den and then taking it by a single claw, knowing its other claw and poisonous tail were poised to attack at any moment.

Despite my queasiness, I held on and leaped into a Reading.

His river of life was less of a river and more of a trickling stream of blood. Traveling upstream was slow and filthy. There were very few break offs as the monster did whatever he wanted and needed to feed his urges. There was little else in his existence. His very long and gruesome existence. *Sidera*, he had to be a few centuries old for the length of his life stream. After what seemed like four hundred years, I reached a pivot where the stream widened into a river of murky water. Even before his bloody corruption, he hadn't been the most pleasant of men. Power hungry, conniving, and gluttonous. He'd been in his late forties during his transformation. *Lapides*, he'd been my age.

I continued up his life stream as he plotted his father's death to take over the company, married a woman purely for her wealth and status, and betrayed a friend to gain favor with law-men, seeing the decisions that slowly defined him. No wonder this monster had enemies.

Living a day in his undead life made me want to puke. I felt everything that he did as he caressed his own muscles while getting ready for the day. The man was disturbingly into himself. It only got worse when his hands lingered on the shoulders, waists, or cheeks of several servants as he interacted with them. I never felt utensils in his grasp. Only goblets and glasses. He didn't eat. He survived on liquids alone.

At one point, his right hand smacked with a powerful force against someone's cheek. There'd been no warning as his de-meanor had been calm before and after the strike. He'd drawn blood as it dribbled down his nails. Something wet, warm, and wiggling wiped off the blood. His tongue. I gagged.

He grasped a thick leather cushion before picking up pa-pers to read, respond, and file away. I figured he was sitting in his office, but none of the papers felt like the thick parchment letter from the mayor. I recognized the motions of opening the hidden compartment in his desk. He poured from his blood pouch and then raised a glass to drink before filling it again and returning the pouch to the compartment.

Eventually, he stood up from the leather chair. His hand grasped another hand and pumped with a shake. A greeting. Was this the beginning of the party? He continued with gallant gestures and grabbed a drink but didn't raise it to his mouth. He put on the act of a gracious host. A few more handshakes with clasped shoulders, passing drinks, and then a handshake that felt more…serious. They gripped tightly to one another and held at an angle that suggested proximity. Did I recognize those fingers with mal-formed nails?

It wasn't long after that I recognized a handshake with a formal grip of long, nimble fingers. Aeron. I was familiar enough with his hands that I could almost Read him through Skoller's hands. It helped that he held onto Aeron for an extra beat for the reporter's picture.

Skoller greeted a few others before his fingers slid up a wooden railing. That was him going upstairs. His hands waved through the air as if gesturing at the artwork. He twitched with mild surprise but didn't seem the least bit worried at the moment of the power failure. If anything, he seemed eager… hungry…like he wanted to use the chance to kill.

His hands jerked with surprise as something struck him. He quivered, tensing with fury, but the more he struggled for power, the weaker he became. His left hand reached for something at his chest while his right shoved against his attacker. I played it in slow motion as he spent the last of his strength to defend himself, surging with a supernatural force to throw off his attacker. I felt what he felt, the imprint he created within the attacker's manly chest of slightly overweight flesh.

Focusing on his left hand, he reached for the weapon. A tube with finger loops? He fell to the ground, his hand still weakly reaching for the weapon. Another hand that I recognized took hold of the weapon and plunged it deeper into the vampire's chest, ending my Reading.

I shivered as I pulled out.

"What did you see?" Micro asked beside me.

"He was living off of blood," I said. "He should have had his immortal powers and wouldn't be killed easily, but…he was stabbed with a poison."

"Poison?" Micro echoed. "What kind of poison could kill a vampire? And how was he stabbed? There wasn't any blood or wound."

"I have a few theories. Come on. Detective Montgomery!"

"What?" he called back.

"I need all the guests gathered in the gallery. All of them!"

"You solved the Case?"

"I think so. I just need to confirm one more thing," I said, hurrying down the stairs to the office. Opening the hidden desk compartment again, I retrieved the items. A quick examination proved one to be the smoking gun.

I knew the motive, means, and opportunity behind Keys' murder.

CHAPTER 10

All twenty-ish party attendees, plus the dozen staff members, and even the kidnapped kids gathered into the gallery, hugging the walls to stay away from the corpse in the middle. I would have preferred the kids to stay out of the Case, but we couldn't let any of them wander and become lost in this madhouse of murder.

Oddly, the kids were better behaved than the adults as the people in posh dresses and suits complained.

"Can we leave yet?"

"What's this all about? Did someone finally solve the Case?"

"If everyone is in here, does that mean the murderer is too?"

"Hopefully," Aeron scoffed. "That's kind of the point of big reveals. Truth? Care to clue us in?"

The setting was too perfect. I stepped forward and rubbed my hands together like an evil genius. "I'm sure you're all wondering why I've gathered you here today."

Micro palmed his face to hide his laugh. "Truth, now is not the time for impersonations."

"Fine," I mumbled and returned to business. "After some investigating, my team and I have deduced the events that led to the murder of Keys. If you all recall, our host stood in the main hallway to welcome everyone as they came in. We have some notable guests, such as Mayor Duncan, Mal Testa, and some A-list entertainers. We also have Detective Montgomery representing the Shigaqua Police Force and my team from Visionary Investigations. Ms. Lanner was among the first to arrive as a reporter for the Shigaqua Times. We are, however, missing a key influencer in tonight's schemes, because the person who killed Skoller Keys didn't act alone. In order to sabotage the power and murder the vampire, there needed to be two people involved. That second person," I said, "was a special operative from Thriller."

That drew a few gasps from around the room.

"Mayor Duncan?" I asked. "We passed around a letter addressed from you to the vampire. When had you sent that letter?"

He cleared his throat. "About two weeks ago. Obviously, he gave it little thought and continued abducting children to murder for their blood."

"Two weeks, you say? And he ignored it? Interesting. Why, then, would it be sitting on top of Keys' desk, out in the open?"

The mayor's face paled. "It was…where?"

"When Reading Keys' palm, I noted that he did some office work, but he never touched that letter with its thick parchment. Meaning someone else put it there to incriminate the mayor."

"But who?" the mayor asked.

"Who, indeed? It would have to be someone who knew about Keys' dietary preferences and who knew about the hidden compartment drawer in his desk." I held up the items from the compartment. "Where Mal Testa thought he could hide the murder weapon and the tool of his deceptive alibi."

Every face turned with horror to Mal Testa. The man was so accustomed to accusations, however, that he simply folded his arms and frowned at me.

"Those aren't mine."

Liar.

I held up the syringe with my handkerchief. "When I first found this, I thought it belonged to the victim. Considering the pack of blood beside it, I thought the syringe was another way that sick psycho ingested blood. However, there's only blood on the outside, and the needle is made of *wood*, like a hollow stake. Care to guess what's on the inside?"

No one spoke. Tough crowd, but I doubted they'd guess it, anyway. I handed the murder weapon over to Det. Montgomery with my handkerchief. "Smell it."

He did and wrinkled his nose. "It smells like garlic."

"The juice from minced garlic," I clarified.

That finally earned a response.

Aeron scoffed with a little laugh. "Fantastic. I doubt it would have worked on a vampire in Horror or even Paranormal, but the undead are weakened outside of their natural states. Keys had been drinking a lot to regain his powers, but such an intake would also increase his weaknesses."

I nodded. "I can confirm that he drank at least a pint with every meal. Meaning a stab to the heart with a wooden syringe and direct injection of garlic would kill him like a heart attack." Turning to the kidnapped youth, I asked, "How often did he feed from you?"

The oldest, a young woman of about seventeen years and named Barbara (if I remembered the reports correctly), spoke for the group. "About once a week. The servants referred to us as the 'cellar,' like we was fine bottles of wine for the creep to enjoy when he felt in the mood."

In a morbid way, it made sense. "He farmed your blood. It takes four to six weeks for the body to renew a pint of blood. With eight of you, that let him enjoy a pint or two of fresh blood every week between the packs stolen or bought from the hospital. Some of you were kidnapped months ago. Did any of you know a Karen Capone?"

My eyes flickered to Mal Testa to catch his reaction. Infinitesimal, but still there. His eyes narrowed, and his frown deepened. He recognized that name. As he should. Courtesy of Aeron's ghosts, I knew she was the youngest benefactor of Mal's empire. But she'd disappeared over a year ago. About the time that Mal hired Brody to start snooping around Keys' house.

Barbara nodded. "I heard about her. She was one of the first to be 'farmed,' as you put it. She was a talker, she was, always going on about how someone would find us and save us, as if she were important to somebody."

"But she died," I said, picking up the story. "About a year ago. There wasn't much to Read from her hands, but I did notice something interesting. She had nail-patella syndrome. A rare genetic disease that deforms nails and joints. Just like you, Mal Testa." I turned my condemnation back to Sponsor and his split nails. "I suspect you were furious with Keys for kidnapping and feeding off of Karen—your *daughter*. No one was supposed to know that she was your daughter, but you couldn't simply send a goon to kill a vampire. Keys tortured your child for months. This wasn't business. This was personal."

Mal Testa's frown boiled with anger. "That doesn't prove I killed him."

"No," I said, "but where do you claim to have been during the vampire's murder?"

"I was in the office downstairs."

"With Ms. Lanner, correct?"

His eyes narrowed.

"Here's what happened," I said. "You hired an agent from Thriller to sabotage the power. You also prepared a specific wooden syringe with minced garlic juice and a voice recorder of yourself asking about the lights. You invited Ms. Lanner into the office to verify your alibi and also to notice the mayor's letter that you planted on the desk. Then, your agent sabotaged the power, giving you about thirty seconds to go about the mansion unseen before the generator kicked on. Thirty seconds to flip on your recorder to act as your alibi, get upstairs, kill Keys, then return before anyone noticed.

"But someone did notice," I continued. "Ms. Lanner noticed something was wrong during the power-outage. Either your recording didn't respond correctly to her questions or you didn't return in time after killing Keys. My guess is the latter because you needed time to plunge the weapon deep into the vampire's chest in order to kill him, then retrieve it and hide it in the secret compartment. Whatever the reason, Ms. Lanner suspected you, and she needed to die, so you asked your hired man to do one more job.

"That again," I added, "was a mistake as I caught the Thriller man for hire in the act of murder. My sketch allowed Aeron's spirits to find him for an interrogation. He was true to his hire and didn't give you up, but he did say a few keywords that implied the truth of what happened."

"What truth?" Mr. Testa growled. "This is all theory and conjecture."

"It won't be when we play the sound recorder and hear your voice asking about the power-outage. Care to confess before the truth comes out?" I paused, enjoying the incremental signs of worry in Sponsor's body language. Again, I might not have noticed them without studying Nita's incremental expressions for the past two years. He didn't relent, so I did. "It seems jammed at the moment, but we have another way to determine the killer. Keys shoved his attacker. Vampires are known for their supernatural strength, so our attacker should have a bruising injury on his chest. Mal Testa, if you want to prove your innocence, you can reveal your chest."

"I shouldn't need to prove anything! This is—"

"Nita?"

With no further explanation needed, Nita rushed around Sponsor to grab his hands and pull them behind his back. The man shouted obscenities about unnecessary force and abuse, but I simply gestured to Det. Montgomery.

"Would you like the honor? A light touch should be enough."

Montgomery stepped up to Sponsor with a grin. "I always wanted to be the one to catch you." He lightly palmed Mr. Testa, who shouted and crouched with pain.

The detective grinned. "Mr. Sponsor, you're under arrest for the murder of Skoller Keys and Ms. Lanner."

I barely heard Det. Montgomery droning out the culprit's rights as the room burst into cheers. The mayor and major authorities of Shigaqua clapped and congratulated us. With Nita already holding Sponsor's hands behind his back, sliding cuffs around them was easy.

A knock on the front door sent everyone out to the second-floor railing that overlooked the main entrance room. The mayor went down to answer the door.

A policeman stood on the porch. "We received a distress signal from this location. Is everything all right?"

Mayor Duncan turned back to smile at me. "It is now."

❖

Wooden planks were set over the temporary moats to allow cars to come and leave the property. With police help, we made sure that the kidnapped kids were the first to go, headed to the hospital with officers to give their statements while receiving treatment. I had a larger cab arranged to drive Mary Argall with my team and me. It was our job, after all, to ensure her safe return home.

To my surprise, Nita was the one to entertain the young girl by pulling sleight of hand magic tricks on Aeron. Mary giggled despite her trauma as Nita smirked and Aeron spun around with confusion.

Micro wrapped his arm around my waist as I smiled at the sight of Sponsor being guided into a police rig. The man had the nerve to ask for my attention.

"Hey, wait a minute," Mr. Testa called through the open car door. I stood before him with my hands on my hips and half a mind to pay him no mind. "Your lost pup. What do you call her again?"

"Nita? What about her?"

"I might know who her master is. I have resources to confirm whether she's who I think she is. Give me a hand with my sentencing and I might have some answers for you."

Shoot. I'd been happy enough to consider Arrowhead as a major clue, but Sponsor (of all people) could confirm her identity? And what was that about a master? I knew she'd been through rigorous training, but I'd suspected a team of specialized trainers, not a single master.

I'd have to settle with the information I already had. Asking for information from Sponsor was like making a deal with the devil. He never gave anything for free.

I scoffed. "We caught you. I think that means our resources beat your resources. Which means I'll take my chances to say goodbye; we don't need your help. But thanks for the hint that her master might be linked to your network."

He sneered, but I simply grinned back as I slammed the car door on his face.

Following protocol, my team and I delivered Mary Argall to her mom at the police department and received more tears and thank yous than payment, but…that was enough for me. Besides, I was less worried about the fate of our agency with this last Case. Putting away Sponsor satisfied and encouraged me enough to make my own changes.

We returned to our agency building and went up to the Johnson penthouse to relax. Aeron collapsed on the sofa while Nita changed into simple pants and a shirt that let her sit comfortably in a meditative pose. I held onto the memory of them interacting with Mary, proud like a mama of the people they'd become.

Thinking of my own mama, I swallowed and stood before my partners.

"Aeron, Nita," I said, gathering my gumption. "I'm sorry. When I told you about my mama's lymphoma diagnosis, I didn't tell you the truth, the whole truth, and nothing but the truth. The full truth is that it's aggressive…and she's already in stage three."

Aeron sat up to show his respect for the seriousness of the matter. Micro joined my side and took my hand for support.

He explained, "We're going to visit Truth's parents for the weekends to help out."

"And," I added, "probably every weekend in the foreseeable future. I've been debating how much time to give to my parents until today. Everyone, I've decided this was my last Case. I'm retiring as a private investigator."

Nita's eyes widened slightly while Aeron frowned and asked, "What? What about the agency?"

"I'm retiring, not the agency. You two can still work the Cases together."

Only then did Nita's eyebrows constrict. "You want me to stay at the agency? You don't want me to stay with you?"

I scoffed. "Of course not. You'd be bored out of your mind with me. Besides, you don't need me anymore. You have Aeron to help you discover your identity. He's better at it, anyway. You react more with him, speak louder, and smile bigger with him. He'll help you learn your identity faster than I will."

She bowed her head. "I see."

Aeron's frown deepened. "You're not going to argue or tell her to stay?"

"No, Fromm," I said, making him wince from his real surname. If I only had so many more chances to tease him, I wanted to make use of them all. "That's not who she is. But when you find out, I'd better be the first one you tell."

Nita raised her eyes to meet mine with a little shimmer. "You'll be the first to know. Thanks for everything."

I reached my hands forward, and she accepted my unspoken invitation. She stepped into my arms and hugged me, burying her face into my shoulder.

Over her shoulder, Aeron's frown relaxed into somber acceptance. "It won't be the same without you."

"I don't expect it to be. The only constant in life is change, and I expect you two to make the best of what comes next."

"What comes next?" he asked.

I looked at Micro and smiled. "Just another bend in the stream of life."

The End

(for now)

ACKNOWLEDGEMENTS

Truth Locke is based on one of my oldest characters, created with The Sims 1: Makin' Magic (2003) when my completionist "main character" adopted a dog and turned it into a human. To make an incredibly long story short, there has always been a LOT more going on with Truth (especially when she inspired my favorite D&D character). I always wanted to tell her story, but went through several phases when considering "which parts" and "how."

Though I primarily watch fictional crime shows, writing a mystery-genre book was a bit of a challenge for me. Truth's story started as one Case, but more inspiration for villains and twists separated her full story into three.

I'd particularly like to thank "Murder, She Wrote," episode 22 of season 2, "If the Frame Fits," for the inspiration of "Death in the Family." I'd also like to thank the random book, "Soul Searching," that was placed under a fellow student's chair, igniting my brain with the pun "sole searching" and the basic plot for the first story. Inspiration for Undead Murder came from somewhere in Jim Butcher's Dresden Files series (between books 3 and 8, I think) when an undead creature seemingly died from natural causes.

I'd also like to thank my Creative Writing: Short Stories class in 2011 as my Final Paper was titled "Other Skills of an Herbalist," based on two characters: Truth and Michael. That short story was the first scene I wrote for this book and served as the base for chapter 9 of "Sole Searching."

It's been through a lot of changes since then. Those who helped it to become the book it is today include my amazing

Alpha readers; Jim Doran, Robyn Aimee, and Michael Smith. Jim has published a lot of short stories and recently published a mythical spy novel, DEED, so I really appreciated and valued his feedback. Robyn, thank you for being my cheerleader and romance-enthusiast friend. I still can't believe you based your main character off of me in *Yes, I'm an Author*. I man you.

Then to my Betas, thanks for picking out the final pieces that didn't make sense while also commenting on your favorite parts. This includes Colleen Dowda, Bettilee Hunt, NaDell Ransom, Bruce Tracy, Jazmin, and Marla Summers.

For the final edit, I get to thank Enchanted Quill Press for their proofread to put my pesky commas in place.

Michael… I had created Micro's character before I met you, but I changed his last name to reflect your own anonymity. Thank you for finding ALL of the loop holes and plot holes of my books to make sure they're solid before going to Betas. I love you forever.

Finally, I thank God. My beliefs in justice, in doing the right things for the right reasons (even—or especially—if they aren't popular), and hope for wrongs being righted (even if it's after the grave) come from the gospel and atonement of Jesus Christ.

ABOUT THE AUTHOR

C. Rae D'Arc has been involved in every stage of a book's life. As a writer, editor, retailer, reader, and reviewer, she has worked four part-time jobs at once. Thankfully, one of them actually paid her. She received her Bachelor's in English from Brigham Young University and now lives in the Tri-Cities of Washington with her husband and Aussie dog.

PS. To save you from hiccups, D'Arc only has one syllable.

Follow for more at:
www.craedarc.com
https://www.instagram.com/craedarc/
https://www.facebook.com/c.rae.darc/

"Why?" I wailed, holding Nita's dying body in my arms. "This isn't how it's supposed to end!"

"No," a cold voice said from behind me, clicking the pistol into position against Nita's skull. "But this is the ending for those who skip to the back of the book. This is your reward."

The bang burst my eardrums from standing too close, but I couldn't leave Nita alone in her final moment. If only I'd had the patience to read page by page, things might have ended differently.